A *New Orleans Revelers* NOVEL

THE ROOKIE
and THE ROCKSTAR

JIFFY KATE

Books by Jiffy Kate

Finding Focus Series (complete)
Finding Focus
Chasing Castles
Fighting Fire
Taming Trouble

Table 10 (complete)
Table 10 – Part 1
Table 10 – Part 2
Table 10 – Part 3

Turn of Fate (previously titled The Other One)

Watch and See

Blue Bayou
Come Again

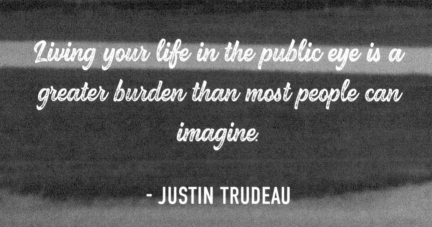

Living your life in the public eye is a greater burden than most people can imagine.

- JUSTIN TRUDEAU

CHAPTER 1

Bo

PRESSURE.

Typically, I love the feeling of being under pressure. I thrive on it, in fact. The tightness in my muscles and the tingling deep in my core, along with my heightened senses, help me stay focused. When my head is in the game—which let's face it, that's about ninety-nine percent of the time—I'm unstoppable. A force to be reckoned with. That's the reputation I've upheld since I started playing Little League baseball as a kid and it's what got me to where I am now, in Spring Training for the New Orleans Revelers.

The pressure I'm feeling tonight, though, is for a different reason. I knew it was coming, that it was part of the deal, part of being a professional baseball player, but that doesn't mean I have to like it.

"Just go and have fun. Shake some hands, sign some autographs, and you'll be fine. And don't forget to fucking smile once or twice."

That was the advice given to me from the team manager, Buddy Malone—*Skip*—last night when I tried to back out of the fancy-schmancy fundraiser I'm already late for. He informed me, under no circumstances, am I to miss this party—sorry, *gala*—because everyone wants to meet me, the big-shot rookie who will change the course of this team and, God willing, get us a championship ring.

See? Pressure.

The problem is, this added stress is useless to me right now. It's not going to add power to my swing or fire to my throw, like it would in a game. Instead, it's going to make me look nervous and jumpy and I'll probably end up being a dick to some big-wig. It's why I don't want to deal with this publicity bullshit—the only part of the deal that makes me want to run back to the minors.

I just want to play ball and win games, but I also want to make it to the major leagues.

Looking at my reflection in the mirror, I sigh. *It's now or never, Bo. No use hanging in the hotel bathroom all night like a fucking pussy. It's go time—make or break.*

As I step back and straighten my tux, I'm tempted, once again, to take Skip up on his threat to make me do suicides all day tomorrow when I get back to Florida. What stops me is the fact that it wouldn't be just my ass being punished, it would be the whole team's ass. He made sure everyone knew if I bailed tonight, we'd all pay for it. It's one thing for me to pay the price but I refuse to be the reason my teammates suffer...and subsequently hate me.

I may be an upcoming superstar but I'm no showboat.

Running my fingers between my shirt collar and neck, trying to create a little space to breathe, I shake the nerves out of my shoulders. This is my first publicity event for the New Orleans Revelers, and I know it's a test, so I can't blow it.

Before leaving the bathroom, I stop and do the one thing that I know will center me and calm my nerves, something that always makes me feel like I'm in control: I get in my batting stance.

Feet shoulder width apart, knees slightly bent, I hold one fist on top of the other like I'm holding my bat. I tap my imaginary bat across home plate one time in front of me, then again toward where the pitcher would be. I end my ritual with the sign of the cross over my heart before holding the bat up and over my right shoulder. Deep breath in, deep breath out, and...swing.

The bathroom attendant, who's now holding the door for me, stops me on my way out. "Hey, man, that was awesome. I've been watching you since you played for Eastern State. Can't wait to see what you do for the Revelers."

"Thanks," I reply, forcing my first smile. People who aren't privy to how all of this works assume it's a done deal—me making it to the big league—

but the fact of the matter is there are still two weeks left in Spring Training and I could be sent back down at any moment.

Taking another deep breath, I make my way down the long corridor to the ballroom and turn on what charm I can muster.

Everyone I meet seems to share the view of the bathroom attendant, most of them telling me how happy they are that I signed with the Revelers and how fun it will be to watch me play.

I sigh in relief as I see a few familiar faces, most of them seasoned players from the team and some of the staff. The owner of the Revelers, Pete Whitney, gives my shoulder a solid squeeze as he begins to introduce me to one old man in a tux after another. Each face fades into oblivion the second we move onto someone else, but I try to keep up the act of the superstar they expect me to be.

What started out as an ego boost quickly takes a turn for the worse. I had no idea what it felt like to be someone else's property on public display. I'm pretty sure I've been poked, prodded, pushed, and pulled more times than all the physicals I've endured in my life.

Over here, Mr. Bennett ...look this way, Bo...just ten more pictures and then you can sign these fifty fucking shirts...

And, don't get me started on the manhandling. Women I don't even know, but assume are here with their husbands or significant others, refuse to keep their hands off me. Many guys I know would be eating this shit up, loving the attention, but that's not who I am.

I know, I know. I sound like an asshole complaining about shit like this, but *this* isn't what I signed up for. Like I said, I just want to play ball, not be paraded around and whored out for everyone's amusement.

Glancing at my watch, I see it's close to ten o'clock, which means I'm almost home free. The first part of the gala and the only part I *had* to be here for was the dinner and socializing time. Once the entertainment of the night takes the stage, I'm hauling ass out of here and going straight to the hotel.

While everyone around me is wrapped up in their own conversations, I stand up, push my chair in, and turn to find the exit when I promptly run into Buddy Malone.

"Bo, my boy! You're not leaving already, are you?"

"I—uh, I was thinking about it, yes, sir. There's still a lot of Spring Training left to go." I want to add how bad I want one of those twenty-five spots on the roster, but he already knows that. "I was just planning on heading back to the hotel for a good night's sleep, unless you have something else you need me to do."

Am I a kiss ass? Sure. But this is my career riding on the line and there's nothing I wouldn't do to secure my future. I think I've made that clear by being here tonight.

He laughs and slaps the back of my shoulder. "No, son, you're free to leave. I just wish you knew how to relax," he says thoughtfully. "Don't get me wrong, I greatly appreciate your talent and dedication to the game but you're too young to be so serious all the time. This is the prime of your life. Enjoy it while you can."

Nodding my head, "Yes, sir. I'll do that," I reply with a tight-lipped smile, but it's an empty promise because I can guarantee his definition of *enjoying it* and mine are completely different. I know most professional athletes need to blow off steam and get their kicks outside of their sport, but that's not me. I relieve stress by hitting the batting cages. I zone out by spending time in the weight room. When I want to relax, I watch game film.

The house lights begin to dim and I use the opportunity to head for the door, stopping briefly to say goodbye to a few players and staff members I see on my way out, until I hear the opening notes of a familiar song. Turning back around, I see long legs in leather pants strut across the stage.

Lola Carradine.

I guess it wouldn't kill me to stay a little while longer.

CHAPTER 2

Charlotte

WHOEVER SAID IT'S EASIER TO SING IN FRONT OF A SMALL CROWD INSTEAD OF AN arena full of people was full of shit. Actually, I'm not sure that anyone ever said that, but if they did, I'd like the record to show they're full of shit.

Because as I stand here, staring out into this pond of people, the spotlight making me sweat under my leather pants, I inwardly cringe at their seeming disinterest.

When I'm performing for tens of thousands of people, it's honestly one of the few times I feel comfortable in my own skin. It's me and some of my closest friends in a dark room belting out our favorite songs. There's no judging, no negativity, just singing and dancing and *fun*.

This—standing in front of a few hundred people, feeling like I'm being judged on everything from my haircut to tonight's choice in combat boots—is not fun.

Don't get me wrong. I'm happy to be doing my part to help raise money for a worthy cause, even if I'm *technically* being forced to do so by my manager. But I'd much rather do it somewhere else, in a more authentic way. A ballroom full of rich, stuffy people who probably have never even downloaded one of my songs makes for a difficult crowd.

I'm trying, though, I really am.

"Looking good out there tonight," I call out from the mic, waiting for the transition to the next song. The other thing that sucks about tonight is that I'm not playing with my regular band—Flight of Feelings. All of them couldn't make it on such short notice, so Terry, my manager, hooked me up with this house band. They're not terrible, but we're definitely not winning any best performance awards.

Most people probably can't even tell, wouldn't notice the difference, but I do.

Music is my life.

It's in my blood.

It's what I wake up every morning to do and what I go to bed every night thinking about.

At least the crowd gives me a small pity *woo*.

My cheeks hurt from the smile I've plastered on for the last thirty minutes, but I can keep it up for just a while longer. I'm used to putting on a good face—smiling for the camera, appealing to the masses. It's what I do.

When I'm up here, I'm Lola Carradine, rockstar and all-around badass.

And tonight, I'm singing and dancing my heart out for this crowd, hoping they'll loosen up and open their pockets and pocketbooks for the local children's hospital, and all I'm getting in return are a few toe taps and shoulder sways. I mean, come on, this is New Orleans. I grew up not far from here; I know besides being generous and giving, they know how to party, so what the hell is up with this crowd?

Putting in a little extra kick when the current song comes to a crescendo, I at least get a few whistles. According to the sweat now trickling down my back, I'm putting on the performance of my life.

But that's every performance.

Go big or go home, right?

There's no sense doing anything half-assed.

Finally, it's time for my last song and I've saved the best for last.

It's a mash-up of the song that started my career and the one that reignited it and it's always a crowd-pleaser. Thank the holiest of holies, it's working here tonight.

The energy I've been waiting to get back in return for all I'm putting out is finally being given back to me. People are singing loudly, most of them now on their feet as opposed to occupying their seats.

It's as if everyone was waiting for the one and only song of mine they know and now that it's here, they can enjoy the show. A less confident person would let that sting, but I shrug it off, thankful they're at least finally showing some interest.

When the song ends, the crowd goes wild, demanding an encore.

I smile, my first genuine one of the night, wiping my forehead with the back of my hand and then using it as a shield against the lights.

"Thank you so much," I call out.

I wish I had something to give them, but I was given strict instructions—a five-song set, minimal crowd interaction. Get in, get out. Don't make a scene.

So, I give them one final wave, blowing a kiss as I exit stage left, heading straight for my dressing room.

Always leave them wanting more, right?

Normally, in my rider, I have provisions in my dressing room—bottled water, Swedish Fish, Doritos. Basic sustenance. But since this is for charity, I waived all of that bullshit. I didn't partake in the fancy dinner and I'm starving, so I quickly change out of my platform boots into more reasonable ones, grab my duffle bag and head out.

Once I get to the valet parking area, where Frank, my driver, dropped me off, I look around for the familiar car. There are several black, shiny sedans, but none of them with Frank behind the wheel.

Shit.

Terry and I didn't discuss an exit strategy this morning when we were going over the logistics of tonight. He probably wasn't anticipating me bolting out of the hotel as soon as my set was over and didn't feel the need to have a plan.

I take out my cell phone and quickly dial his number.

"Lola," Terry says, obvious satisfaction in his voice. "Great show."

"Hey, do you know where Frank went? I'm ready to leave."

"Where are you?" Terry asks. "I told Frank to meet you in front of the hotel."

"Why the front?" I ask, trying not to get pissy, but the front of the hotel means cameras and people. "That kinda ruins my plan for sneaking out unseen."

"That's because you're supposed to be *seen*. In fact, I have various people set up in the area specifically to see you. Bonus points if you've found someone hot to leave with you. A nice photo op would be the cherry on top of an already successful evening."

No, no, no, no.

"I'm done being your puppet for the evening," I say, sounding more like a petulant child than a twenty-nine-year-old adult, but I can't help it. I'm over it. "I'll find my own way home, thanks." I end the call, not waiting for his reply, before tossing my phone back into my bag and letting out a frustrated sigh.

It's really not a big deal to get myself a cab, that's not the problem. The problem is Terry and the way he's always orchestrating my life. I should probably fire him but he's been my manager for most of my career and the idea of letting someone new into my life is terrifying.

"You, uh, need a ride?"

Smirking, I roll my eyes, getting ready to ream out the douchebag who obviously thinks he's going to get lucky and so assuming, thinking I'd go anywhere with him. But before I can say anything, I practically swallow my tongue.

The guy offering is hot as hell—tall, classically handsome yet rugged enough to not come off as a pretty boy. And for fuck's sake, he can fill out a tux. Those broad shoulders become even more pronounced as he crosses his arms over his chest and turns toward an approaching car. When he clears his throat and begins to fidget, it makes me think his offer was an impulsive one and he's probably wishing he could take it back right about now.

"Uh," I begin, buying myself some time, because if he's really offering, I might take him up on it. Did I mention he's wearing that suit like he was poured into it? It's literally molded to his perfect body and now I'm imagining peeling him out of it.

If he's wearing a tux right now, it most likely means he was at the gala I just left, right?

So, he's probably a stand-up guy, right?

And I haven't ridden anyone in a while.

The fact that I'm trying to reason with myself about hooking up with some guy who just offered me a ride makes me question my self-worth and value. I might be a rockstar, but I don't typically do rockstar things, contrary to popular belief.

When he turns to fully face me, the first thing I notice is the slight blush on his cheeks and I'm immediately endeared to him. It's obvious he's caught off-guard by his offer. Maybe just as much as I am by the idea of accepting it. "I'm sorry for asking that," he says, shaking his head and fighting back a smile. "I'm sure you don't need a ride. I just saw you waiting and it seemed like you might not have one…" He drifts off and bites down on his full bottom lip, which makes all my girly bits tingle.

To be clear, I'm the embarrassing one; he's the super sweet and thoughtful gentleman. I'm the one with my mind in the fucking gutter.

"Oh, no, that's okay. I thought my driver would be here. I just need to make a call…" I pause and look up at him. Being nearly six feet tall, that's something I'm not used to. But this guy has me by about half a foot and now that I'm looking up at him, his baby blues are hitting me full force. He's really got everything going for him. "Thanks, though." I smile to show my genuine appreciation and he doesn't argue. He simply nods his head in understanding and continues waiting for his car to be delivered.

Now, I feel like an asshole for turning him down, but I can't get in a car with a complete stranger. I don't know what I was thinking. It's not safe for any woman to accept an offer like that, no matter how nice it is to receive.

And no matter how gorgeous the man offering is.

When the roar of a vehicle approaches, I notice out of the corner of my eye that he's hesitating. "You sure you don't need a ride?"

I glance back up and see Mr. Sexy Suit waiting beside the passenger door to his car and it's not what I expected.

A Toyota?

And not like a new, sporty type. A Corolla, maybe? And I'm talking early two thousands model. Not that I'm a car snob or anything, but *this* guy in *this* tux driving *this* car does not compute. I expected him to be in some fancy sports car or luxury SUV, not a mid-size sedan.

How does he even fit in that thing?

All I know is for the first time in a long time, I am genuinely intrigued by a guy. He's not someone Terry fixed me up with. He's not on the payroll. He's an unusually handsome guy asking a girl if she needs a ride home.

I should say no.

I should walk away.

But instead, against my better judgement, I decide to throw caution to the wind and be what everyone thinks I am: wild and reckless.

Hoping my bright smile covers the nerves I'm feeling, I step toward the car. "You know what? I do, in fact, need a ride," I say, sliding into the passenger seat and getting my first whiff. All man—spicy and clean. I watch as he expertly folds himself into the car, filling it, both figuratively and literally, with his body and manly scent.

He waits while I buckle up, keeping my bag in my lap because it irrationally makes me feel safe, as if it's the protective layer that will keep me alive if this seemingly nice man turns out to be an axe-wielding murderer. I'm distracted from my self-preserving thoughts when he asks, "Where to?"

Glancing over at me, I take a brief second to drink him in. He's younger than guys I normally date. His blue eyes are so pale they seem translucent. Before looking back to the road and pulling out of the drive, he gives me a warm smile. "I'm Bo, by the way."

My stomach uses that moment to remind me where I was headed before this serendipitous encounter. Laughing self-consciously, I place my hand on my stomach to silence the bear.

"Didn't eat at the party, huh?" He looks back at me and gives a sly grin. And once again, I'm mesmerized. There's this unspoken, understated confidence that rolls off him and it's single-handedly the sexiest thing in the world.

"No worries," he continues when I go mute. "I could still eat. They never feed you enough at those fancy shindigs, which is a damn shame considering how expensive the tickets are." He pauses to look over his shoulder before pulling out onto the one-way street. "Wanna grab a bite before I drop you off? I promise I'm not a serial killer."

He laughs and it's glorious.

"I would say trust me," he continues. "But that's what all the serial killers say, so I won't."

Now, I'm laughing and the small amount of tension that was lingering in the car dissipates.

I was not expecting him to be such a talker and a laid-back one, at that. This man has me captivated and there's no way I'm passing up an opportunity to spend more time with him.

"Yeah, let's eat." I return his smile and relax back into my seat, ready for whatever—dinner, drinks...more. Deep down, I'm just a girl looking for adventure.

What everyone else interprets as recklessness abandonment is really just that—my sense of adventure. It's what's fueled my entire career. When I was a kid, my mom took me to an audition for a commercial and the rush of adrenaline from walking into the unknown was addictive. It's what keeps me going back on that stage and writing songs. I love to feel my heart pound in my chest, proving I'm alive.

"I'm Charlotte," I say as the sights and sounds of New Orleans swirl around us. "Sorry I didn't introduce myself sooner, but I don't normally accept rides from strangers."

I want to add that I don't normally even talk to strangers—occupational hazard, I guess. Being a public figure, it's hard for me to know who I can trust, who's out for their own personal gain.

"I know who you are," Bo admits shyly. "But don't worry, I don't normally offer rides to strangers, so we're even."

CHAPTER 3

Bo

I'M NOT QUITE SURE HOW I WENT FROM WANTING TO GO STRAIGHT HOME AFTER THE gala to going out to eat with Lola Carradine.

I'm not even sure what made me talk to her. It's not like me, but I can't say I'm regretting my decision.

When I said I don't normally offer women rides, I wasn't lying. Even though I get approached by women before, after, and even *during* games, I never take them up on it and I don't initiate. Too many of them are just after what my future contract could give them.

During my first year in the minors, a teammate who was called up, found out a that a girl he'd been with two months earlier was pregnant. He claims he wrapped it up. Who knows whether he did or not, but she ended up taking him to the cleaners. Of course, he wanted to take care of his child, but it was more than that. She had him in and out of court, always causing drama. I don't want to take that kind of risk.

Tonight, standing in that ballroom, Lola Carradine captured me. The way she moved on stage and owned that entire fucking room full of stuffy suits was something I've never seen before. Everything from her gritty, soulful voice to her tousled dark hair is a complete fucking turn on.

Even though I was ready to bail, I couldn't move. I stood in the back of the room and watched her every move, feeling every note down to my bones. When her set was over and I finally made my way out to the underground valet and she walked up beside me, there was a current in the air. It felt electric, like I was being pulled to her.

That's when I stopped seeing Lola Carradine—the rock star—and Charlotte came on the scene.

Hearing her plea for privacy and escape to whomever she was talking to on her cell reminded me of myself and the next thing I knew, I was opening my car door for her and speeding down the road.

"Where are you taking me?" she asks, breaking the silence and my pulling me out of my thoughts. When I chance a glance over at her, the look on her face isn't scared or worried; it's more like…curious. Intrigued, maybe?

And her eyes, God, those eyes—dark, deep, and rimmed in black. I have to force myself to look back at the road and I'm struck with the reality that Lola Carradine is in my car.

Maybe I should've chosen a better place to eat?

I didn't really think too hard on it; I just started driving to my favorite place on autopilot. It's away from the Bourbon Street Crowd, a few blocks from the French Quarter. One of the guys from the team introduced me to it on my first trip down here last year. It's a bit out of my way but totally worth it.

"It's this crepes place I love. It's not technically a restaurant, I hope that's okay. I guess I should've asked what you wanted."

"Crepes sound perfect." The smile she flashes my way has my mouth going dry instantly and I have to clear my throat to ask a very important question. "What should I call you?" I decide to address the elephant in the car. I'm not going to pretend I don't know her. Everyone knows her. Well, unless you're over fifty or you've been living under a rock. Even then, I bet at some point, you've heard the name Lola Carradine.

"You introduced yourself as Charlotte," I continue, "but I know you as Lola. So, I was just wondering what name you prefer?"

She hides her smile by looking out the window, before finally answering. "You can call me either," she finally answers. "And, just for the record, I wasn't trying to trick you or anything. Charlotte is my real name. Lola is my stage name."

At the next stop light, I glance over to find her openly checking me out.

"You seem like someone I can trust with my real name," she says quietly, like she's trying to convince herself as much as me.

I decide to think about what she just said later because we've arrived at our destination and all I want to do right now is eat. I park my car and reach Charlotte's door as she steps out, offering my hand for help. Even though she doesn't really need it, she accepts it and holds onto it while I shut her door.

The feel of her hand in mine is oddly comfortable, especially for someone I just met. Knowing that I'm not *that* guy and this won't be ending with a fuck session, I drop her hand as casually as possible. I don't want to give her any mixed signals, but I also don't want to come off as some psycho.

"Wow, you weren't lying," Charlotte says with a sarcastic chuckle. "Definitely not a restaurant."

I shake my head and smile. "Nope. More like a taco truck," I offer, hoping she's okay with it. I don't know where rockstars usually eat and I'm trying to not overthink this entire situation or make any more of it than it is. Two random acquaintances, pushed together by fate, sharing a meal. "But they have the best crepes in town and they're open late, which makes it even better."

A few people order in front of us, none of them giving us even a second glance, which is a relief. It really didn't dawn on me that Charlotte might not come to places like this for lack of privacy until just now.

Walking up to the window, we look over the menu that's painted on the side of the trailer. I already know what I want, but I'm enjoying Charlotte's *oohs* and *aahs* as she peruses the menu.

"Gah, I can't decide," she says, biting at her thumb nail like she's choosing wall paint. I love her intensity and how serious she's taking this decision. "What are you getting?"

"The Chicken Florentine. It's one of my favorites."

The way she scrunches up her nose at my answer is so damn cute and in the warm glow of the lights hanging above us, I can make out a few freckles splattered across her nose and cheeks. Fucking adorable.

"I'm sorry," she scoffs. "But that sounds way too healthy. I'm sure it's delicious, though, no offense."

I laugh at her obvious distaste for healthy. "None taken," I tell her, thinking her disregard for healthy food is kind of a breath of fresh air. My body is a well-oiled machine and I have no desire to mess that up, but good for people who want to indulge, there is zero judgment here. "What are you trying to decide between?"

"Well, I know I'm getting one with Nutella but I can't decide if I want the Nutella and fruit or Nutella and bacon," she debates. "Oooh, maybe I can do both...oh, hell, they make crepes stuffed with eggs, bacon, and cheese? That settles it. I'm getting a breakfast crepe and a Nutella crepe for dessert." Her excitement over the crepes is doing something to me that I can't exactly put my finger on at the moment. However, my dick has a pretty good idea. To say his interest is peaked would be an understatement.

"You're a fan of breakfast foods, I take?" I ask, clearing my throat and inconspicuously adjusting myself.

"Shit, yeah. I could eat breakfast foods for every meal." This is said with a roll of her eyes and I'm, again, reminded of how similar our lives are. "How about you? Are you always so healthy?" I don't so much see her gaze on me, but feel it. "You don't have people telling you to lose weight, do you?"

"No," I say with a chuckle. "It's more for keeping my energy up, performing at the top of my game."

She's giving me a thoughtful expression, but before I can say more, it's our turn to order.

"We'll take a Nutella and Bacon," I say, glancing at Charlotte for confirmation and earning a wide smile in return, "a breakfast crepe, and a Chicken Florentine," I tell her. "Oh, and two bottles of water." Once again checking with Charlotte, she gives me a nod. After paying for our food, we step to the side to wait. The other cool thing about this place is that every crepe is made fresh right in front of you thanks to the windows in front of the griddle. I always get a kick at watching the magic happen and by the look of awe on Charlotte's face, she's enjoying it, too.

"Ever tasted Nutella?" Charlotte asks, as the guy behind the glass spreads what looks like chocolate onto the hot crepe.

"I don't think so," I admit.

"Well, hold onto your bowtie," Charlotte muses, her voice taking on that same seductive tone it has when she's on stage, "because you're getting a taste of Nutella and I predict it will blow your mind."

I swallow as my dick immediately hardens, getting stuck on the words *taste* and *blow*. I am a gentleman, my dick is not. Now is not the time to be getting a boner, for fuck's sake.

Thankfully, the cook calls out our order and when I step up to collect the food, a look of recognition crosses his face. "Bo Bennett, right?" he asks, pointing at me. "Is the team back from Spring Training already?"

I wasn't expecting that at all. I assumed if anyone would be recognized tonight it would be Charlotte, not me. She must notice my shock because she elbows me lightly in my side to get me to answer him. "Um, just for the weekend. We had a fundraiser to attend but we'll be back in Florida tomorrow."

"So, that's why you and your lady friend are all dressed up," he says with a wink. "Well, y'all be sure to take some extra napkins with ya so you don't get food on your fancy clothes. Have a good night!"

I give the cook a quick nod before following Charlotte to a nearby picnic table. She wastes no time sitting down and unwrapping her breakfast crepe, biting into it with a moan. I, in turn, focus on my own food so I don't stare at her like a fucking creeper.

Halfway through our meal, Charlotte sets down her crepe and takes drink of water. "Sorry I haven't been great company while stuffing my face...totally ladylike, I know." She twists her full lips and then bites down on the bottom one. Again, I can't peel my eyes away from her. Everything she does seems to be shooting signals to every cell in my body. "I didn't realize how hungry I was until I started eating," she says, her voice low.

"These crepes are amazing, though, right?" I ask, trying to keep my mind out of the gutter.

"God, yes. The best I've ever had," she declares as she unwraps the Nutella and bacon crepe, the smell of chocolate and hazelnut filling the air. "You have to share this one with me. There's no way I can finish it." Pausing, she looks up at me and when our eyes make contact, I feel like there's some unspoken conversation happening.

I'm into you.

I want to kiss those fucking delicious lips.

Where did you come from?

"There are still starving children in Africa," she says absentmindedly, her eyes still on mine. "Wasting food is a travesty."

She smirks, taking her first bite of what I'm sure is nothing short of amazing. "So, baseball player, huh?" she asks after a few moments.

"Yeah," I reply, still trying to make my brain work. "Do you, uh...do you like baseball?" The question sounds dumb, but I can't think of anything more intelligent to say right now. Charlotte Carradine has officially made me stupid. "It's totally fine if you don't."

Like earlier with the decision on what to order, she takes her time, really thinking about her answer. I love that she doesn't immediately reply, giving me what she thinks I want to hear, but instead going for total honesty. "Yeah, I guess," she answers with a shrug. "I don't really know a lot about it. The Revelers weren't around when I was younger. So, I'm more of a football kind of girl because that's what I was raised on." Her eyes meet mine and there's a glimmer of something there, something that makes me want to spend hours investigating it.

"Go, Saints," she eventually says, giving me a wicked grin.

"Who Dat," I reply, returning the gesture. I'm not sure mine comes off quite as lethal as Charlotte's though.

"So, are you new to the Revelers? You seemed surprised someone recognized you."

"This'll be my first year in the majors, *if* I can make it through Spring Training."

"So, no pressure then?" she asks with a wink.

"Absolutely none at all."

"Well, if you *were* under pressure," she continues, "what would you do to...relieve it?"

And there we go with everything that comes out of her mouth sounding like sex. I'm not certain it's intentional, but it still causes me to choke a little on my water and I have to clear my throat.

She continues, "I just mean, you don't eat junk food and you don't seem like a party-guy, so what do you do for fun, Bo Bennett?"

"I work out."

"No, I said for *fuuuuuun*." She exaggerates the word and I chuckle. I'm used to this kind of ribbing from my teammates and my family. It seems to be their mission in life to get me to loosen up.

"I like movies, books, video games...but I don't do much else because I like to stay focused on my career. I've wanted to go pro for as long as I can remember and I've worked damn hard to get here. I'm not gonna mess it up by changing my habits or work ethic." Once I stop talking, I worry I might've offended Charlotte. I know she wasn't trying to insult me but I felt the need to explain myself. I've only known her for a couple of hours but I want her to like me.

"I admire that," she says thoughtfully, her eyes roaming my face. For the first time tonight, I feel a little uncomfortable, like she's seeing deeper than my skin—the rookie, the athlete, the baseball player. "I think you're a good guy, Bo Bennett. So good, in fact, that you might not want to be seen with me. I kinda have a reputation for being a bad influence." I can't tell if she's still teasing or if she's being serious, but I'm very curious about what her idea of a bad influence is.

"Is that right?" I ask, dipping my chin, along with my voice, lowering it to a near whisper.

"Yeah," she says, her tone full of confidence as she darts her tongue out to lick a drop of Nutella from the crepe she's still working on.

We both sit in silence, the air crackling around us. When she misses a bit of the hazelnut, chocolate goodness, I lean in a little further until my lips are at the corner of her mouth, tasting the sweetness that is Charlotte Carradine.

The semi-startled, very uncharacteristic giggle that escapes Charlotte matches the jittery nerves that have settled in my stomach.

What the fuck did I just do?

"Uh, I'm sorry," I say, leaning away and giving her back her personal space. "I, uh..." I feel my face flush as my dick hardens for what feels like the millionth time since she slid into the passenger seat of my car. Fuck that. Since she stopped me from walking out the doors of that ballroom with her alluring voice.

She brings her fingers up to linger over the spot where my mouth was, lightly swiping away the last traces of the lingering sweetness. "Don't be."

"I should take you home," I tell her, realizing that if I don't, I might do something I'll regret, and I don't have time for regrets. There are still a couple weeks left of Spring Training and then I'll be in New Orleans for the season opener, *if* I make the team. The next month of my life is going to be a whirlwind and I need to be at my best—no distractions.

Her face falls a little, but she gives me a quick smile as she collects her trash.

I take it from her, depositing it into the bin up by the trailer, putting a nice tip into the jar before we walk back to my car.

"This was nice," she says as I open the door for her.

"Glad you liked it," I say with a chuckle, leaning against the open door, so I can see her face. Her beautiful, edgy, otherworldly face. She's nothing like anyone I've ever been on a date with and it's making all of this very hard.

Pun fucking intended.

"Not just the amazing crepes and the lack of cameras and people," she continues. "But hanging out with you. It was unexpected...you're unexpected...and that's my favorite thing. Everything in my life lately has felt so orchestrated, so thank you for being anything but."

"Charlotte," I begin, but she must see the look on my face or have a sixth sense for what I'm about to say, because she places her hand over mine to stop me.

Shaking her head once, she gives me a half smile. "Don't, okay? I know you probably have a lot on your plate right now, so you don't have to make any excuses. It was a nice evening. I enjoyed your company, but there are no other expectations."

On the drive to her place, other than her giving me directions, we're pretty quiet. And as I hop out of the car to walk her to the front door of her house, which by the way is a gorgeous two-story beauty, and nothing like I would've guessed from someone like her, she stops at a side door and motions toward it. "I use this entrance. There are usually paparazzi waiting somewhere near the gate to catch a glimpse of me coming home, waiting to spin it into some sordid tale."

There's a sadness that creeps in with that confession and it makes me angry. I don't like thinking that people out there are trying to make her into something she's obviously not.

"Don't be surprised if you show up in a tabloid tomorrow," she adds with an apologetic huff. "I really should've taken an Uber or called Fred.

Sorry if—"

It's my turn to stop her and I do with a quick kiss to the side of her mouth, the same spot I kissed the Nutella off of. "Don't be sorry."

"Thanks for...the ride and the crepes...and everything," she whispers, turning to punch in a code on a keypad that opens the door.

"My pleasure."

"Call me, maybe?" she asks, hesitantly. "When you're back in town, after the season gets going."

"I'd like that."

Holding her phone out to me, she turns her tone more businesslike. "Put your number in." I do as she asks and hand it back. "There," she says a few seconds later, stepping into her house and using the door as a shield. "I called you, so now you have mine and I have yours and if our paths cross again, Bo Bennett, well...I'll see you then."

"Yeah, I'll see you," I reply, walking backward toward my car—part of me, mainly my dick, screaming at me for walking away from this woman, but the other part of me telling me to run.

Because Charlotte Carradine could be a game changer.

CHAPTER 4

Charlotte

"CHARLOTTE."

I continue tapping my pen against the notebook on my lap, ignoring Casey.

"Char...Charlotte...Charlotte Renee Carradine!"

"What?" I ask, spinning my chair around to face her and throwing my notebook to the floor. "What do you want?"

"Why are you in such a bad freakin' mood?" she asks, giving me a look of complete annoyance. Blowing out a deep breath and rolling her eyes, she stands up and walks over to the espresso machine in the corner. "You've been in a funk for the last week. You either need to get laid or work out or do some flipping yoga...something, because I can't take any more of you ignoring me and Lord knows you haven't written more than a few lines of a song in the last week. Something's got to give."

She's right. I know she's right, but I don't have to like it.

Groaning, I lean my head back and stare at the ceiling.

"Who is it?" she asks as the espresso machine perks to life. "That guy the label sent over for studio time? Oh, or that guy Terry set you up with to *improve your image?*" she asks with a giggle.

"No one," I tell her, still keeping my eyes trained on the ceiling, because I've been trying to convince myself of it for the past seven days and failed miserably. I've tried telling myself that my chance encounter with Bo Bennett was nothing. It was a friendly meal and a free ride home.

And a hot as fuck kiss...on the side of my mouth. Who does that? I swear, I thought that was a precursor to some serious sheet time.

And I don't mean the music kind.

I mean, down and dirty sex with an almost stranger—no strings attached. He'd be gone the next morning. I'd be back to my creative self and songs would be written. Terry would be off my back. The label wouldn't be breathing down my neck. And all would be well in the world of Lola Carradine.

But no.

That is not what happened.

Bo Bennett turned out to be a surprise on every level.

First, I thought I had him pegged for a rich donor from the gala, but then they pulled his 2010 Toyota Corolla around and blew that assumption right out of the water. On our way to get something to eat, I was trying to guess who he was—waitstaff, hotel employee, the boyfriend of some rich chick—and once again was surprised when the dude that ran the crepe truck recognized him. An athlete, didn't see that one coming. I should've, given the event, but again with the Toyota.

I know he recognized me, but the way he was around me made me feel...real and seen. He looked at me like I was more than a song or a reputation. Our conversation was light and easy. And even though he's five years younger than me, I never once felt like we were on different levels. I've dated men twice his age and been less impressed with their maturity. When he leaned over and placed his lips at the corner of my mouth, I swear my heart skipped ten beats, waiting to see what would happen next, but then he pulled back and blushed.

He fucking blushed.

"Who?" Casey asks again, when I continue to stare at the ceiling, remembering every second spent with Bo Bennett.

"No one," I repeat, neither of us believing the lie.

"Maybe you should write a song about him?" she suggests, settling back into the cushy chair across from me with her frothy cup of coffee, legs crossed.

I huff out a laugh and shake my head, still refusing to make eye contact with her. She'd see right through me and I don't want to tell her about him. For now, I want to keep him to myself, if only in memory. Thinking about him makes me feel good. "It'd be a flop."

Actually, that's a lie too, because what girl wouldn't want to sing along to a song about a boy who smiles like he knows every secret and has skin that's been kissed by the sun.

I take that back, a man...someone who makes your skin tingle with a single look.

Bright white, super straight teeth.

That's always been a turn on for me.

Add that to a killer smile and a slight dimple in his right cheek and it's a deadly combination.

Not to mention what has to be a finely tuned body, but one I didn't get the pleasure of seeing. However, the way he filled out that tux, I know it's something to write home about...or write a fucking song about.

I've taken the liberty to look Bo up on the internet. I felt it was only fair, seeing as how my life is an open book and he probably knows every sordid detail about my past. His online image is as squeaky clean as his real-life persona. There's not even a drunken picture of him at a frat party in college. No women to be heard of. He played all four years at a midwestern college and was drafted by the Revelers, but he's spent the last two seasons playing for their minor league team in Des Moines, Iowa.

His luck seemed to change after he was called up at the end of last season, but was sent back to the minors before playoffs, which the Revelers lost, never making it to the World Series.

He's also five years younger than me.

So not my type.

All the more reason I need to forget about him, and his number burning a hole in my cell phone.

Picking my notebook back up off the floor, I begin to doodle—sometimes it helps open up the floodgates, allowing the words to flow—but all that appears on the page in front of me is his name.

What am I? Some lovesick teenager?

The next thing you know I'll be adding his last name to mine and planning our marriage and future children. Letting out a frustrated groan, I look across the room to Casey.

"Wanna talk about it?" she asks with a pleased expression. "I knew you'd come around."

"You can't say a word. Not to anyone. Not Mom or Dad. And especially not Terry."

She makes a motion of zipping her lips and tossing away an imaginary key. Taking a sip of her coffee, she wiggles down further into the oversized chair, like she's settling in for a bedtime story.

Annoyed at her and her carefree attitude—always the baby with zero expectations, cruising through life with no one watching her every move. Most people probably think she's envious of me, but really, I'm the envious one. I'm jealous of her freedom and that she can go anywhere she pleases without people gawking or imposing themselves into her daily life.

"Fine," I huff. "It's a guy."

"I knew it," Casey squeals. "Did you...you know?" My baby sister isn't a prude, per say, but she refuses to say fuck...or speak about sex without using code words for everything. We're polar opposites in so many ways.

"We didn't fuck," I tell her, knowing it'll earn me an eyeroll.

"Mom is right. You're so crude."

I laugh, looking her square in the eyes. "Just because I say fuck doesn't mean I'm not a lady."

"Oh, my God. Tell that to someone who hasn't lived with you for the last twenty-two years," she retorts, giving me a look so similar to our mother. When does that happen? When do we start looking, acting, and sounding like our parents?

The thought scares me.

Not that our parents are horrible or anything. I just don't want to be Tammy and Dean Carradine. I'm Charlotte. I'm a rocker. I love a good gin and tonic. I listen to loud music and this studio in my house is my church.

"So, if you didn't...you know, do the dirty, why is he messing with your head?" she asks thoughtfully, pausing to take another sip of her coffee. I think she likes staying here just for the freebies: espresso machine, home gym, all the Netflix she can handle, and grocery delivery. There aren't many things I splurge on with my earnings, but this house and the things in it, are essential to my well-being.

After a few seconds of me not answering, Casey jumps to her own conclusion and nearly knocks the chair over as she jumps to her feet. "Oh, my God. Did he turn you down?" she asks in mock disbelief. "Did a person of the male species not fall for Lola Carradine?" With her hand to her neck, like she's clutching the family pearls, she gawks at me, mouth hanging open, as she waits for my response.

I can't help the loud belly laugh that erupts. It's not that the idea of a man turning me down is absurd, although most men don't. I realize I'm not everyone's cup of tea. But it's her dramatics that have me rolling. Also, yes, I mean, kind of...Bo Bennett was attentive, but at the end of the night, he dropped me off and with one last soft, sweet kiss to the corner of my mouth, bid me farewell.

For fuck's sake, I sound like a Jane Austen novel.

"Is that what this is about?" Casey continues to push. "Did he dis you and now you've lost your mojo?"

"No, he didn't *dis* me," I scoff. "And who the fuck says *dis*?"

Casey stares at me with her hands on her hips, hovering over me. "I do."

"Well, 2004 called and they want it back."

She groans, plopping back down in her chair and picking her cup of coffee back up from the side table. "See, this is what I've been dealing with for the past week. So much shade."

"Okay, you can stop now."

"Look at you, turning twenty-nine and losing your cool status," she mocks with a raise of her eyebrows, lips positioned in a smirk behind the rim of the coffee mug. "Alert the presses, Lola Carradine is officially old."

My eyes narrow on her. I know what she's doing. I know she's prodding me, poking me—playing on my insecurities like only a little sister can do—until I lose my shit and tell her everything, but it's not happening. "Take it back."

"Which part? That you're not cool...or that you're old?" Her chipper little voice and high ponytail are really getting on my fucking nerves today.

"Out," I seethe, pointing to the door of the studio.

"What?" she asks, incredulously.

"Out. Now."

Her scowl tells me she's not happy, but she leaves anyway, slamming the door behind her. Once I'm convinced she's gone and not coming back for an encore, I reach over to the desk and grab my phone, opening it up to my missed call list and glaring at the number from a week ago.

I could just text him.

Once.

Just a friendly hello, asking how he's doing...maybe I could tell him I revisited the crepe truck and have taken it upon myself to try everything on the menu. I wouldn't tell him that I went back and ordered the Chicken Florentine and a Nutella, just to try to recreate our evening together.

No.

That would be weird. And desperate. And so fucking unlike me.

Maybe I could make up something to ask him?

Hey, Bo. My manager was wondering when the first game is...he's wanting to take some record label big wigs...

Blah. So stupid.

Again, who am I? And what has he done to me?

No, you know what. This is stupid. I'm Lola Carradine. I rock the stage. I own a crowd. I do what I want...say what I want...and I can send a fucking text to Bo Bennett.

Feeling irrationally empowered with that pep talk, I quickly punch on the number and select message.

Me: Hi, Bo. It's Lola. Just wanted to say I had a really great time last week. And the crepe truck was a great find. Thanks again.

Before I lose my nerve, I hit send and toss the phone back onto the desk like it's on fire.

There, done. No take backs.

CHAPTER 5

Bo

THIS WEEK HAS BEEN BRUTAL.

Not only has it been hotter than normal, but the coaches have been working our asses on and off the field. Every Spring Training starts out with about sixty players, but by the end of it, only twenty-five will make the opening day roster. Of course, it's everyone's goal to make it to the end.

It's what we've worked our whole lives for.

We eat, sleep, and breathe baseball.

Everyone dreads the tap on the shoulder—the signal that you're moving down.

Skip needs to see you.

I watched a few guys get the tap this week and every time they do, I feel a dead weight in the pit of my stomach. But instead of letting the anxiety of it all keep me from performing, I use it to push me—harder, faster, stronger.

"Good work out there today," Skip says, patting me on the back as we make our way down the steps and into the club house.

Wiping my forehead with a towel and untucking my shirt, I take a breath. "Thanks, Skip."

Another day down. Another day to live the life. But the countdown to twenty-five intensifies and I feel it, probably more so than the majority of the players left in this locker room because I'm one of the youngest, one of three guys who've never been on the twenty-five man roster. Other than my short stint on the bench at the end of last season, I've never been in the majors.

There's been plenty of talk, lots of predictions, about my future success, but all of that means nothing if I don't make the cut.

"We're all going to Shortie's tonight, Rookie," Ross Davies says, coming up behind me and placing his big, meaty palm on my shoulder. "Be there."

I shake my head. "No, no Shortie's for me tonight. There's a split schedule tomorrow and I'm playing first game." Meaning, I have to be at the field no later than nine o'clock, which in my book is eight-thirty. My dad always taught me that if you're required to be at practice at six, that's really five-forty-five, five-thirty if you're an overachiever, and I am definitely an overachiever. It's in my blood. I can't help it.

"Come on," he chides. "One beer...two max. I promise, it won't kill you. Actually, I think it'd help you loosen up, and everyone knows you could use some of that."

If it's not beers, it's women. They always think I need something.

Get drunk, you'll play better.

Get laid, you'll hit harder.

Get the stick out of your ass, you'll run faster.

"Rook, listen," Davies says, coming around to stand between me and my locker. "If you don't learn to have a little fun, this game will kill you." It's one of the most sincere statements he or any other player has said to me yet. Most of the time, I feel like I'm in a frat house again, being hazed by the upper class.

"I have fun," I tell him truthfully. "Lifting weights, running, batting... all fun."

He rolls his eyes and lets out a humorless laugh. "You need to get a fucking life, man. Do it before you wake up one day and baseball has left you in the dust." Sighing, he runs a hand over his recently buzzed head. All the returning players shaved their heads on the first day of Spring Training. Some look a little better than others. Davies can pull it off. "Listen, do you know what the average career of a pro player is?"

"Five-point-six years," I quote. I know all the statistics, everything about the game—the good, the bad, and the ugly.

"Right, so learn to love life outside of the game, because it won't be around forever."

I pull my shirt over my back and toss it into the gym bag on the floor. I need to do some laundry tonight before the hotel kicks me out for harboring toxic waste in my room. "I think the argument could also go my way," I tell him, kicking off my cleats and tossing those in the bag as well. "If I only have five point six years, I want to make the most of it. One of these days, I'll have all the time in the world to enjoy something besides baseball."

The thought actually makes my stomach turn. Life without baseball? What kind of life is that?

"Trust me when I say you'll enjoy the game a lot more if you have someone to share it with...and find some fucking balance," Davies warns, his finger poking my chest. "I'm looking out for you, Rookie. Been where you are and I promise, I know what I'm talking about."

With that, he kicks off the locker and walks around me, calling out once more over his shoulder as he leaves the room. "Shortie's, be there!"

Once I get to the hotel, I toss my bag on the floor and grab my phone off the nightstand, where I left it charging. It's been almost a week since I talked to my parents, and although they don't like to hover, they do like to know I'm alive and my dad always needs the scoop on how Spring Training is going.

He's a high school baseball coach and was once a minor league player for the Kansas City Bluebirds. He's also the reason I'm the player I am today.

My childhood was spent at the diamond and around players. I was never forced into the game, but growing up in the dugout, it seeped into my soul, took root there and never let go.

I expect to see a missed call or text from him, but instead of his name and message, I see hers.

Charlotte's.

It's the last thing I expected.

Sure, she's been in the back of my mind, only coming to the forefront when I let her, usually at night, when I'm trying to force myself to let the game go for a few hours. I think about her long brown hair that matches her warm brown eyes. Behind the dark liner she wears, there are flecks of gold and a smidge of green. I wanted to tell her about it, sitting in the glow of the hanging lights at the food truck. I wanted to tell her she's beautiful, but I didn't, because that would've complicated things and I don't have time for complicated.

I don't have time for Lola Carradine.

Charlotte: Hi Bo. It's Charlotte. Just wanted to say I had a really great time last week. And the crepe truck was a great find. Thanks again.

The message itself is benign enough. Part of me wants to reply back. I want to ask her if she's been back for more crepes. If so, what did she have? Nutella? My dick, who's been through a drought, is hoping for Nutella.

But I don't ask any of that. I can't, because one reply would be like a gateway drug. One hit. One time. And the next thing I know, I'll be needing rehab to get over Charlotte Carradine, because she feels addictive, like someone I'd probably never get enough of.

She's not in my plans, nor does she help me reach my goal.

Getting on the major league roster won't come any easier by texting her.

After a shower and dinner—chicken and vegetables I picked up from the local supermarket and warmed up in the microwave in my room—I collect my dirty clothes and some change off the dresser and head for the laundry.

The glamorous life of a baseball player: sweat, dirt, and body odor...and doing your own laundry.

What most people don't realize is that until you make it to the big leagues, most players don't make jack shit. Of course, it's better now than it used to be and I'm fortunate I have one of the higher salaries in the minors, but it's just enough to pay my bills and put a little in savings. I'm not destitute, but I also don't have housekeepers and chefs.

Although, even when I do make the big leagues and get a major league salary—because I will make the big leagues—I probably still won't have housekeepers and chefs. It's just not my style. It probably sounds cliché, but I'm not in it for the money.

I'm in it for the love of the game.

I'm in it for the rush of a good hit.

I'm in it for the feel of the ball hitting my glove.

I'm in it for the way my soul sings as the ball flies across the diamond, just in time to get a runner out at first.

Once I have my clothes dispersed between two machines with soap and money loaded, I hop up onto one of the washers. Pulling my phone back out, I go to make the call to my dad, letting him know I'm still here, but Charlotte's message is still open and staring me right in the face.

There's an unfamiliar pang in my chest that I try to shake, but I can't stop reading over her words.

Another thing that isn't my style is ignoring someone, and ignoring Charlotte feels like an asshole move. I doubt it's Lola Carradine's style to be the first to text a guy. Men chase her, not the other way around. So, the fact that she reached out to me feels kind of huge.

When my phone rings in my hand, I jump a little, but then sigh in relief.

Saved by the bell.

"Hey, Mom," I say, bringing the phone to my ear.

"Hi, honey. How's everything?" she asks, obviously doing more than just talking to me on the phone. That's my mom, the multi-tasker. Being a high school teacher, she's always worn many hats—wife, mom, teacher, bus driver, crowd controller, cheerleading sponsor, coach's wife. You name it, my mom has probably done it or knows how. She's one of the smartest, most capable people I know.

"It's going good," I tell her with a sigh, staring across at the blank wall as the washer below me kicks it into high gear. "I live to see another day."

"Where are you?" she asks.

"Laundry."

She laughs. "About that time, huh?"

"Yep, it was getting locker room level in my hotel room," I reply with a chuckle.

"Aw, well, I wish I was there to do it for you. I'm sure you're beat after all they put you through out there." She's being serious. If it wasn't for her job and the fact that it would be weird for her to pack up her life and follow her twenty-four-year-old son around the country, she'd do it. In a heartbeat.

"I can do my own laundry, Mom," I reply with a smile. "Thanks to you."

When she sighs, I know she's getting ready to get sappy on me, so I stop her.

"Hey, is Dad around? I wanted to run a few things by him. We have a game against Atlanta tomorrow and I'd like to pick his brain."

"Sure, honey. Just a sec." I hear her call out for my dad, but then she's quickly back. "You're eating well? Getting enough rest? Finding a way to relax a little?" she asks, sounding like Skip and Davies.

"Mom," I warn.

With a huff, she continues. "Don't 'mom' me. I worry about you and you're all the way down there in Florida and I probably won't see you for another month…"

"Unless they send me back to Des Moines," I add.

"None of that," she says, always seeing the glass half full. "You're gonna make it and you're gonna be great and your dad and I will be coming to New Orleans to see you play as soon as we can."

"Thanks, Mom."

After a good talk with my dad—getting one of his famous pep talks about finishing strong and that no matter what happens, this is still a step in the right direction—I hang up feeling good about tomorrow's opponent.

About the same time, the washer turns off and I hop down to move my clothes to the dryer.

I could leave the clothes and come back for them, but I don't really have anything pressing in my hotel room except the same four walls I've been looking at for the last month and a television playing the same movies I've already watched.

Swiping my thumb over the screen of my phone, I open it back up and go to my text messages, reading over Charlotte's one more time.

What could it hurt? A text message is as benign as it gets, right?

I start to type, but quickly delete the few letters, my heart beating faster in my chest with the mere idea of making contact with her.

"Quit being a pussy, Bennett," I mutter to myself, punching out a simple reply.

Bo: Hey Charlotte. I'm glad you're enjoying the crepes...and a little jealous. Have one for me.

I add a smiley face emoji, but quickly delete it and hit send before I punk out.

Later, when I'm back in my room, clothes put away and in bed, trying to force myself to sleep, my phone dings from the nightstand. Normally, I put it on *do not disturb* mode, knowing I need as much rest as possible to be at peak performance the next day, but once I'd text Charlotte and she didn't reply right away, I left it turned on.

Charlotte: Took you long enough to reply. :)

See, she can get by with the emoji shit and it's cute. If I would've done it, it would've seemed desperate or stupid or like I don't know how to talk to a woman without emojis.

Charlotte: If it was a bad idea for me to text, I'm sorry. We don't have to do this. I know you're busy.

The three little dots let me know she's still typing...or thinking...or wanting to say something else, so I hold back on replying just a few more seconds. But when they drop off the screen, I decide if I don't reply, this could be the end of our conversation and I don't want that. So, I take the bait.

Bo: Sorry, I was in the weight room most of the day and then came back to the hotel for a shower and food. And I had to do some damn laundry before I was turned in for harboring toxic waste.

Charlotte: LOL. Sounds like a busy day. How is ST anyway?

I smile at the screen and take a second to run a hand down my face, letting it soak in.

Lola Carradine—*the* Lola Carradine—is asking me about my day.

She was the star of a kid's television show back in the day—*Life with Charli*. It was actually a little before my time, but I still watched reruns. Then, about ten years ago, she fell off the face of the planet. I remember being in the grocery store with my mom and she was reading an article about her, commenting on how she didn't know how a pretty girl like her got mixed up with drugs.

The other night, when I couldn't sleep, I googled her. It felt like an invasion of her privacy with all the details of her life being so readily available.

Drug rehab.

Boyfriends.

A change in career for Charlotte Carradine.

Lola Carradine was seen leaving Chateau Marmont with a band member, Cruise Salvatore.

Are Lola and Cruise dating?

And then there was a grainy photo of someone who looks like Lola leaning over a table, snorting a line of what looks like coke.

Page after page of gossip mixed with facts.

When I closed out the search tab, I felt sick, not just because of what I'd read, but because I didn't want to learn about her like that. In the two years I've been in the minors, watching major leaguers I know go through shit with the media. I've realized that the tabloids can spin a story from nothing.

Bottom line, Charlotte—*Lola*—Carradine is someone people love to talk about.

And now she's texting *me*.

Bo: ST is great.

That's such a weak answer and doesn't even come close to scratching the surface on what this past month has been like.

Bo: Actually, it's the most grueling thing I've been through so far and stressful as fuck but I'm hanging in there.

Charlotte: Tell me about it...like what do you do all day? I thought people who were there were already on the team?

Bo: We practice a lot...lots of drills, batting practice, fielding balls, working out in the weight room, running our asses off. But we also play games, kind of like scrimmages. It gives coaches and managers a chance to see the talent in action.

There were about sixty guys here a month ago and now we're down to about thirty. A week left to go. I'm hoping to make it on the twenty-five man roster. We've got four more games this week...if I make it through them, I'll be in.

Charlotte: And if you don't?

Bo: Back to Des Moines

Charlotte: That'd suck

Bo: Tell me about it

After a few minutes of no response, I almost put my phone back on the nightstand and force myself to try to sleep, but instead I ask her a question I've been wondering since our impromptu date.

Bo: Why are you in New Orleans?

Charlotte: I live here. Duh

Chuckling to myself, I appreciate her quick wit and smart ass response. She's so real...and normal...easy to talk to.

Bo: Are you from here?

Charlotte: Originally, then my parents moved our family to Los Angeles. When I was looking for a place of my own, I found this house and bought it.

Bo: Interesting choice. Being Lola Carradine, I'd think you'd need to be in L.A. or New York or somewhere like that.

Charlotte: *eye roll* Those are the last places I need to be. Trust me.

I want to ask why. I want to know everything. Instead, I tell her goodnight.

Charlotte: Goodnight, Bo Bennett.

A few seconds later…

Charlotte: Knock em dead tomorrow.

CHAPTER 6

Charlotte

TODAY IS GOING TO BE A GREAT DAY, I CAN FEEL IT. I DIDN'T SLEEP MUCH LAST NIGHT but I was still up before the birds, already bursting with energy. So much so that, after my first cup of coffee, I decided to cook breakfast.

My favorite 80's music channel is blaring and when I'm not flipping bacon or scrambling eggs, my spatula becomes my mic, helping my impromptu kitchen concert be the best it can be.

Until Casey walks in.

Stomps in, is more like it.

"What is going on here?" My sister is wrapped up in her robe with a rat's nest for a bun on the top of her head and she's missing her left sock. "Who are you and what have you done to Charlotte?"

I roll my eyes at her. "It's me and nothing is wrong. I'm simply making breakfast. You don't have to eat it," I say, throwing the challenge out. We Carradines never pass up breakfast foods. I'm pretty sure it's even written on our family crest.

I watch as she eyes the bacon, eggs, and toast plated on the kitchen island, in addition to the cut-up fruit and coffee already prepared in the French press, just waiting to be poured. "You do know it's not even seven in the morning, right? Did you pull an all-nighter or something and you're hopped up on caffeine still?"

Laughing, I shake my head and try to decide how much to tell her. I don't want to say too much about Bo because it's so new and, really, what's there to tell? We've shared one night out and a few texts. That's no big deal.

Then, why does it feel like one?

"I wrote a new song last night." The truth is, I completed one song and started three others and I'm dying to get in the studio. This is the real reason I'm up so early. I'm inspired and can't sit still and it feels amazing.

"That's great! Are you gonna tell me about your inspiration or are you still keeping it a secret?" Casey chews on a piece of bacon, not giving me any eye contact. I've obviously hurt her feelings by not giving any details about Bo, so I decide to share just a bit, hoping it's enough to satisfy her. For now, anyway.

"I was up late texting the guy I hung out with after the gala the other night."

"And?" Clearly, she's unimpressed.

It's times like this where our age difference is glaringly obvious. People her age don't think twice about texting; it's simply how they communicate. If I would've said I FaceTimed him or sent him a Snap, she'd be all up in my business. What she's failing to realize is that I rarely communicate with guys via technology at all. I'll do an occasional phone call or email but I'm normally more of a face-to-face kind of girl. The fact that I texted an actual conversation and not just one word responses is huge for me.

"And, nothing." I shrug to play it off. "It was fun and different and exciting, so I stayed up to write about it."

"Exciting, huh? Did y'all, like, do the cyber nasty? Because, that would be something to write a song about." She waggles her eyebrows at me as she sips her coffee.

"Ew, no, Casey. What the fuck? We just talked, you know, to get to know each other better."

"Wow, that sounds stimulating. Just kidding. It really doesn't, but if you're happy, I'm happy."

I flip her off behind her back as she rinses her dishes and puts them in the dishwasher. She's my sister and I love her, but, damn, if she isn't annoying as fuck.

"Seriously, though, Charlotte, enjoy taking your time with this guy. You never know, it might actually be worth it this time."

As she walks toward the stairs, she yells over her shoulder, "I'll be running some errands later and I'll bring home some celebratory grub!"

"What are we celebrating?" I ask, confused.

"You finishing these new songs and being one step closer to your new hit album!"

Her words and thoughtfulness give me an extra jolt of excitement and I smile to myself.

Maybe Casey isn't so annoying after all.

I end up spending a good four hours in the studio and, even though I desperately need a break, I feel like a new person. It's been a while since I've felt this creative and allowed my true vision for a song to be put down on paper and then recorded. I have a reputation in the music business—a few of them, if I'm being completely honest—for writing and performing strong, female-driven songs but what I've accomplished today is, by far, my most honest work. It's fearless and powerful while remaining catchy and fun.

Except for one song.

Eyes of a Stranger is a ballad and written through a mirror's reflection. Mine, to be exact. In a way, it's a love letter to myself but the lyrics, at times, are harsh and deeply personal. It's still a work in progress and I'm not sure it'll ever make the cut, but it feels cathartic to shed some light on some of my demons.

After I shower and eat a late lunch, I decide to tackle some of the business items on my to-do list. Up first is calling my manager, Terry, and giving him an update on my studio work. Normally, I dread calling him but not today. I'm excited to tell him about the progress I've made. Hopefully this means I'm back on track and able to make the late summer release we had planned.

The first few minutes of our talk goes well. Terry is very happy to hear about the new songs and seems really interested in what I've created today. But, then, things go south.

"You've been invited to a movie premiere next week in L.A.," he says matter-of-factly. "I already have a designer set up for you. They'll meet you at the hotel. You'll be attending with Cody DiMarco, one of the stars of the film. It's just what you need."

What I need? How in the hell does he think he knows what I *need*? I hate when he makes plans for me without ever asking or taking into consideration what's best for me.

Also, I don't need my manager setting me up on dates, especially ones I have no interest in.

"I'm assuming your silence means you're not happy with this news," he continues. "Let me remind you, we're still trying to rebuild your career and—how shall I put it—*revamp* your public persona. Mr. DiMarco has managed to keep his image perfectly clean over the years and being seen with him would greatly improve yours."

Cody DiMarco jumped onto the music scene with his teenaged boy band years ago and has had a fairly successful transition into the movie business, kind of the reverse of my own career. Terry is right in that Cody's reputation is great and the public love him but what he doesn't seem aware of is that Cody pays a shit-ton of money to keep his image the way it is.

"Terry, the only reason Cody has the rep he does is because he keeps his dealer on staff. Literally. He also keeps his little harem of barely legal women well-paid and stoned. So, no, I will not play your little game and go to the premiere with this douchebag or any other douchebag you try to set me up with."

"Lola, doing charity events can only get you so far. Pictures last forever, you know—once on the internet, always on the internet—which means you still have a lot of work to do to get back in the public's good graces. I'll give you some time to think about it. Call me back tomorrow with a different attitude and a better answer."

He hangs up and it takes every ounce of strength in me not to throw my phone against the wall and smash it to bits.

This. This is what I hate about my career. Playing games, being fake, and selling my soul all to sell more albums and concert tickets.

Yes, I made a mistake a few months ago. In fact, I've made quite a few over the span of my career but, so what? Everyone messes up at some point in their life. The difference is all my mistakes make the covers of every trashy tabloid and every gossip website. I've apologized multiple times and I've done everything Terry and my PR team have made me do, but it never seems to be good enough.

But, no more. I refuse to leave *my* career and *my* life in the hands of anyone else but *me* and fuck anyone who tries to stand in my way.

I'm about to head back into the studio when Casey walks through the front door. She takes one look at my face and demeanor and her shoulders sag in defeat.

"So, you already know, huh?" she asks.

"Know what? What are you talking about?"

She tosses the paper bag she'd been carrying onto the coffee table before sitting in the chair across from me. "I found these at the newsstand. I bought every copy they had, I swear, but I don't know if it'll do any good."

Dread runs through my veins like ice water. I don't want to look at what's inside. I'm ninety-nine percent sure I already know what I'll find but being the glutton for punishment I am makes me reach in anyway and pull out a stack of magazines.

Right there on the front cover is a picture I've seen many times over the last few months and it's not pretty. This time, though, there's more than one picture and the two new ones are even worse than their predecessor.

The picture that started this new bullshit in my life is a grainy, somewhat out of focus image of someone who looks a lot like me leaning over a table and snorting a line of cocaine. Newsflash: it's really me snorting coke. Just like it's really me in the "new" clearer picture showing the same thing but from a different angle. It's also really me in the third picture shown kissing a woman who is sitting on my lap.

For the record, I've never denied being in those pictures or doing the things they show me doing, even kissing Kylie. We were high and drunk, and I get frisky, regardless of sexual orientation. My management and PR teams tried to cause doubt to the validity of the first photo, but I knew it was a lost cause and released a statement admitting my guilt along with a heartfelt apology, much to the dismay of Terry and my family.

In the letter, I spoke briefly about being at a party and succumbing to peer pressure. I vowed to seek help, although, I'm not an addict. It was recreational, I swear. I also donated a large sum of money to various addiction-related charities before hanging my head in shame and hiding out in my home here in New Orleans. I thought it was all going away but, apparently, I was wrong.

"Are you okay?" Casey asks, concern evident on her face.

"No, but I will be. I'm going to go up to my room, if that's okay. Thanks for getting these, I really appreciate it."

Once I'm alone and snuggled under the blankets on my bed, I allow myself a few minutes to wallow. All of the positive energy I was relishing in just moments ago is gone and I feel like a deflated balloon...empty and just sad.

I'm simply at a loss as to what I can or should do to make this go away. I've owned up to my mistakes but people don't seem to care about that. They only want drama and to focus on my imperfections because it keeps them from dealing with their own. I'm a fighter and my gut is telling me to keep fighting but I don't have it in me right now.

Maybe I should call Terry and agree to go on the stupid date with Cody.

I wonder if these new pictures are why he set the date up in the first place and if so, that means he knew about them and didn't warn me. *What an asshole.*

My sadness slowly morphs into anger the more I think about it and I wish I had someone to vent to, besides Casey. Of course she would listen, but I feel like she's too close to the situation to be objective.

Besides, I don't like to wrap her up in the ugliness of the business. She never asked for any of this. I've always tried to protect her as much as possible.

Lying here, staring at my ceiling, the only face I can see is Bo's. But I try to shake it...him. No way. There's no way I can talk to Bo about this. He'd go running for the hills, I'm sure, and I wouldn't blame him one bit. I even tried to warn him while we were at the crepe truck. I told him he doesn't want to be caught with the likes of me. If he knew about this, he'd believe it and then what?

He'd start ignoring my text messages?

I'd never see him again?

No, I definitely can't share this with him, not right now anyway, but I would love to hear his voice again. That would definitely make me feel better. But I can't just call out of the blue, right? What if he's busy with his team? I'd worry about him seeing the magazine, but I know he's at Spring Training and the only thing on his mind is making it to the majors. I doubt he's reading gossip rags. God, I hope none of his teammates show him.

I decide to settle for a text message and ask if he'd be up to a phone call later. My phone starts buzzing as soon as I pick it up, scaring me and almost making me drop it. Shocked is an understatement to how I feel when I see Bo's number flashing on my screen.

He's calling *me.*

Is he psychic?

I quickly hit the "accept" button and say hello, not caring if I sound desperate or nervous.

"Hey, Charlotte. Is this a bad time? Is it okay that I called?"

He's so sweet, I swear. Not even trying to fight back my grin, since he can't see me, I reply. "Hey! Yeah, I'm glad you called, actually. I was just thinking about calling you...too."

Smacking my head, I roll my eyes at my stupidity. For being able to stand in front of thousands of people and bleed on a stage, sometimes I can be a real dork. But when I hear him blow out a gust of air like my answer relieves him, I can't help but smiling a little wider.

"Yeah?" he asks, like he's not sure if he can believe me. "That's cool. How was your day?"

Is it weird that I like that he's not completely full of himself. Being an athlete, I would think he'd walk around like he's God's gift to women, but Bo Bennett is nothing like that. Actually, I'm beginning to wonder if he even knows just how fucking sexy he is.

Like, GQ material.

"Well," I begin, wondering how honest to get with this being our first phone call, "It started off strong then, kinda crashed and burned...but it's much better now...thanks to you."

Oh, my God. What is this guy doing to me? I have no chill. None.

"Anything you want to talk about?" he asks—attentive, sincere.

I consider it, consider telling him about Terry and the constantly resurfacing photos of me doing a line of coke...the publicity dates...everything, but I decide not to. I just want to put it all out of my mind for now. "Nah," I finally say, clearing my throat and licking my suddenly parched lips. "Tell me about your day. Have they decided on the final team roster yet?"

"They did," he hedges, sounding kind of hopeful, but leaving me hanging.

"And…" I throw my blanket off and sit up, genuinely anxious to hear if he made the team or not. I've watched videos of some of his big games on YouTube and he's nothing short of amazing, like fucking badass. The Revelers would be stupid to not have him as their starting third baseman this season.

"You're now officially speaking with the New Orleans' Revelers third baseman!"

"That's amazing...Not a surprise though," I add, smirking and biting down on my lip as an image of him comes to mind. I watched this video the other day of him catching a ball and firing it across the field. *So fucking hot.* "Congratulations! I'm so happy for you, Bo."

"Thanks. I couldn't wait to tell you. I was wondering if you'd like to go to the home opener in a couple weeks. I can get you a ticket." His voice quickly changes from ecstatic to shy and I find myself swooning just a bit.

Okay, a lot.

"I would love to see you play. Of course, I'll be there. I bet your parents are over the moon. What did they say when you told them?"

"Oh, shit. I haven't called them yet. I got the official word, got in my car, and called you. I should probably let you go, so I can tell them," he says with a nervous laugh.

I can't help but laugh before agreeing that he should definitely call them now. I even promise to keep it our secret that he called me first. Before hanging up, he asks if we can talk again later tonight and I immediately say yes.

CHAPTER 7

Bo

"HEY, ROOK," DAVIES SAYS, WALKING INTO THE LOCKER ROOM WITH A TOWEL AROUND his waist. "Get laid last night?"

I huff a laugh and shake my head, not giving him a verbal response because I know I'm going to get harassed regardless, might as well keep my mouth shut and let him say whatever he's going to say.

"Rook." Davies steps beside me and folds his arms, forcing me to look his way. "What did I say about first game jitters?"

"Don't have to worry about me," I tell him with a shrug. It's true, I've never been one to let first games get to me like some players do. I don't force myself to puke up my nerves. I don't say ten Hail Marys. I don't need a shot, a hit, or a woman. The work I put in every day is the only insurance I need.

Sure, it's the major leagues, but I've been here before. Granted, my ass never left the bench, but sitting in the dugout for a few games last season gave me the chance to see what it would feel like and I think I worked through some of the mental game.

"You know what happens to rookies who strike out every at bat, right?" he asks with a cocky smirk.

I nod, not giving him any leeway. "Not worried," I quip. And I'm not. I'm also not trying to jinx myself or anything, but I've never struck out in my first game on a new team.

In my first high school at bat, I knocked it out of the park.

They called it beginner's luck, until I hit sixteen more that season. Not only a school record and state record, but also a national record.

In my first college at bat, I hit a double and by the end of the game, I hit for the cycle.

In my first minor league game, I hit a grand slam.

"You'd look mighty pretty in that sombrero," Davies ribs, pointing to the golden hat hanging on the wall in the middle of the lockers. He laughs, nudging me with his arm. When I don't reply, he adds, "You know I'm just messing with you."

"I know," I tell him, focusing my attention on my new locker. It's still setting in that I'm here—in the New Orleans Revelers club house—and I have a starting position.

Skip set the batting order and he has me batting fourth, in the clean-up spot.

Pressure?

Sure.

Nerves?

Of course.

But I'm here for it. It's what I live for.

The pre-game dinner for the Revelers is not your typical pre-game dinner. Most ball clubs have their standard PB&Js before a game or maybe subs from a local deli. The 1894 Baltimore Orioles accredited their pennant win to gravy. I'm hoping the shrimp po' boys everyone is now inhaling is our team's gravy.

"Po' boys before the game," Davies says to Mack Granger, our catcher, as they cheers their sandwiches. "Beignets and beers after."

Ew.

I mean, I love a good beignet, although I haven't indulged in many as of late. But beignets and beer...that sounds like a hard pass for me.

"Rook," Mack shouts over the clubhouse chatter. "Beignets and beers!"

It sounds like a battle cry as everyone chimes in with him and I shake my head and smile, but I'm not one to mess with tradition or superstitions. We all have them, especially baseball players. Being the new guy, I know I have to adapt. I want to. I want to be a part of the team and for them to learn to trust me and accept me, know that I'll have their back on and off the field. It's one of the non-sport related things I really love about the game.

These half-dressed fools, cheersing sandwiches and chanting about beignets and beer are more like brothers than teammates. We spend so many hours and days together, seeing each other more than our own families, if you don't learn to love each other, you won't make it.

"Beignets and beer," I call back, half-eaten po' boy in the air, earning me some slaps of camaraderie on my back and guys walking by and rubbing my head.

Apparently, that's another tradition of theirs: rubbing the rookie's head for good luck.

As we're all finishing up getting dressed, gearing up to head out to the field for pre-game warm-up, I start to feel the nerves. My parents are going to be out there tonight, which isn't unusual. When I played the minors, in Des Moines, they were at most of my home games. It was only a three hour drive and one they promised they loved making. Even now, with it being a plane ride away, I'm sure they'll make whatever games they can.

My dad said he and Mom were planning a few weekend getaways around my away games.

When I'd called them about starting tonight, I could feel the pride seeping through the phone. My mom cried, of course, and I wouldn't be surprised if my dad did too. He's a softie. Even though he's a tough coach and keeps the boys in line, being more of a father figure off the field, they know he loves them. He works hard getting his players noticed, finding them scholarships, and working overtime to help improve swings.

Knowing they're out there brings me a lot of confidence.

Knowing Charlotte is out there brings me a lot of...I don't know, a different kind of nerves...excitement...anticipation.

When I called her, on auto-pilot, like it was the most natural thing in the world, I almost hung up before she answered. I don't know what I was thinking. I guess I wasn't. I was just going with how I felt, and I was feeling like I needed Charlotte to know I made the team.

In the last week or so of Spring Training, making the team and being based in New Orleans took on a new meaning. Being here means I have a chance to see her again. I know I said I don't want distractions and I mean that, but texting her at night actually helped me take my mind off the game and focus better during the day.

I'll never tell Davies he's right. He already has a big fucking head what with the cameras always flashing his way and making that damned Body Issue by *Sports Illustrated*. Apparently, he's a big deal with the ladies, but unfortunately for all of them, he's taken.

Happily married since his rookie year.

"You ready, Rook?"

Speaking of the devil.

I turn to see Davies and Mack both staring me down, like they're looking for cracks in my armor.

"Ready as I'll ever be."

They both nod, standing shoulder to shoulder, eyes trained on me. Mack is also known as Brick...like brick wall...because he's huge and because, as a catcher, nothing gets past him.

"Feeling sick?" Mack asks, his gaze scanning my face and then he reaches out and touches the back of his hand to my forehead, like he's my fucking mom.

"Nope," I tell him, meeting his stare and giving him a cocky smile, as much as I can muster. "Cool as a cucumber."

"Got the game shits?" Davies asks, cocking an eyebrow.

"Game shits?" I repeat, chuckling. "Never heard of 'em."

They look at each other and begin talking amongst themselves, like I'm not still standing right in front of them.

"Ate the po' boy, hasn't puked, no game shits," Mack ticks off on his fingers.

"Good color, no cold sweats," Davies adds. "Oh, and did not get fucking laid last night." That last line earns me a sideways glance of disapproval. "Fucking never listens to my advice."

"You know what this means?" Mack asks, an arm coming up to rest on Davies' shoulder. When they both turn their heads in unison on me, I start wondering if this is rehearsed. Most baseball players have a lot of time on their hands, maybe they've been working this one up all day while the rest of us have been watching game film and going over stats.

"He must be…" Davies starts.

"Walks like a duck, talks like a duck…"

They nod, thoughtfully still eyeing me and quite frankly making me fidget.

"A cyborg," Mack finishes, Davies nodding his agreement.

"Maybe some iRobot shit?" Davies asks, looking back at Mack. "Like no feelings or emotions."

"What's that called?" Mack asks as I roll my eyes and continue pulling out my batting gloves, getting ready for the field. I don't have time for these jackasses and they obviously think they're way funnier than they actually are.

"Oh, wait, I know this one," Davies says. "I took psych in college, actually thought about being a psychologist one day," he adds, considering his options, like he fucking needs them. "A sociopath."

His voice is grave and serious.

"Should we be concerned, Rook?" he teases. "Did the team docs give you a good psych eval?"

He and Mack walk away, laughing at themselves...me...their own ridiculousness, who the fuck knows.

"Golden sombrero," Davies calls out over his shoulder, pointing to it on the wall. "Don't make us dust it off, Rook." The sincere smile he gives me over his shoulder lets me know this is all for show. It's what they do— harass the newbie. I can take it. Actually, it dispersed some of those nerves I was feeling a few seconds before they walked up.

I was kind of inside my head for a few. Now, I feel present, ready to get out there and make my presence known.

Right before I walk out of the locker room, the last one out, I take a quick second to really center myself, looking around and letting it all sink in one last time before I walk out there. There's still a couple hours between me and the plate, but it's my last moment of solitude. Everything from here on out will be in front of tens of thousands of fans who came to watch their home team hopefully get this season off to a good start, set the tone for what's to come.

Feet shoulder width apart, knees slightly bent, I hold one fist on top of the other like I'm holding my bat. I tap my imaginary bat across home plate one time in front of me, then again toward where the pitcher would be. I end my ritual with the sign of the cross over my heart before holding the bat up and over my right shoulder. Deep breath in, deep breath out, and...swing.

Touching the fleur-de-lis that's painted on the wall beside the door leading to the dugout, I close my eyes and take a deep breath, letting the sights and sounds wash over me.

Dirt.

Sweat.

Hot dogs and beer mixed with fresh air.

This could be any field, on any level.

My dad has always reminded me that it's just a game—one game.

The only game that matters is the one you're getting ready to play.

When I get out to the field and we start our warm-ups, I take a chance to look for my parents. Spotting them, right away, I give a tip of my head. My dad has his pre-game face on, steady and focused, like he could somehow will this game to a victory. My mom is smiling from ear to ear and gives me a slight hand raise, not a full-on wave. She's nervous, I know she is. She's always been one to internalize more of the game than my dad or I put together.

Mom takes baseball seriously.

She might be a coach's wife and a player's mom, but she lives and breathes it as much as we do.

The two seats to their left are empty, but I try to not notice, not think about whether or not Charlotte will take me up on the seats. She said she would. I left them for her at Will Call.

The ball is in her court...or maybe field would be a better analogy.

It's probably better that I don't see her now anyway, I need all my focus on this field.

The rest of the pre-game duties are a blur.

Warm-ups.

A little batting.

Fielding some balls.

Back to the locker room while the visiting team takes the field.

Then everyone is back out for the National Anthem and for the first time in my life, I take the field with the Revelers as a starting member of the team. Taking off my hat as they call out my name and number, I wave it at the crowd, earning an even louder cheer.

It's everything.

Everything I've worked for.

I've earned the spot, now I have to keep it.

On my first at bat, there's only Davies on base. He grounded a ball down the line and made it to second. I block out the fans, block out the opposing players, and take the plate.

Squaring my feet and then my shoulders, I ease into my stance. Knees slightly bent, I place one fist on top of the other, like I've done thousands of times in my life.

One game.

This is only one game.

I chant that to keep my nerves at bay, to keep the voices in my head from screaming, "don't fuck this up!" Those voices are always there, but I don't let them win.

I tap my bat across home plate, then again toward the pitcher, staring him down for the first time.

Doing the sign of the cross, I send up a silent prayer before holding the bat up and over my right shoulder. Deep breath in, deep breath out, and... swing.

My first attempt doesn't make contact, but the motion felt good. He threw me a fast ball and had I made contact, it would've been out of the park, straight down the middle.

Setting it up again, I go through the ritual. Only, instead of the pitcher, I point my bat a little to his left, only noticeable to me, but if this was pool, I'd be calling my pocket.

Deep breath in, deep breath out, and...

The solid crack of the bat making contact with the ball lets me know it was a good hit, I felt it all the way into my bones as it radiated through my body. The reverberation like a siren song.

I don't flip the bat.

I don't even wait to see where it went.

I just run.

Because my dad taught me to never get cocky.

"Regardless of how far that ball flies, you've gotta make it around the bases. Just run, son. Tuck your chin and haul ass."

His words stick with me as I clear first and head for second, the roar of the crowd behind me.

As I turn to the corner, I see the third base coach signaling for me to run, so I do, with everything in me and slide.

It was a triple, the ball landing short of the right field wall.

Davies made it home and I earned my first RBI.

Mack left me on base, but we're on the board and that's all that matters.

After the game, a win, I indulged in the beignets and beers. If nothing else, I'm a team player, and after a win like we got today, my first at bat as a major leaguer, I wanted to celebrate. It didn't matter that the combination sounded revolting. It was actually not half bad, and being a part of the team, knowing I'd contributed to the outcome of the game, was the best feeling.

When I eventually make my way out of the club house and to the spot I'd told my parents to meet me, I wonder if Charlotte will be there. I mentioned it to her also, but I don't even know if she made it to the game, so I don't know if she'll be here.

And what if she is?

What do I tell my parents?

Is it weird that I'm more nervous about that potential interaction than my first major league baseball game?

Rounding the corner, I see my mom first. Her beaming smile tells me everything I need to know.

"You were outstanding," she says when I get close enough for a hug. It's been a few months since I've seen her and I missed her—missed these hugs.

"Thanks," I tell her, giving my dad a smile over her shoulder.

"Real proud of you, Son," he says, slapping my shoulder and pulling me into his side. "Great game today."

"Thanks, Dad," I tell him, suddenly catching a glimpse of dark hair covered by a purple ball cap with the gold R on the front.

She came.

"You'll never believe who we sat next to at the game," my mom gushes. "I mean, I know celebrities come to these things...but right next to us... in the same row," she continues, her eyes growing. "Lola. Carradine." Squealing, she slaps my shoulder playfully. "Can you believe it? I told your dad that it must be my lucky day. My son plays his first major league baseball game and I get the lucky seat right next to Lola Carradine. I mean, I know she's had that drug trouble and all, but I still really love her...her music. Remember when she was on *Take the Stage*?" She talks so fast and excitedly I don't get a chance to interject, but I see Charlotte behind them and her face pales when she realizes my mother obviously knows who she is. I start to call out to her, but then she quickly takes the hand of the girl next to her, who seems disappointed as she's yanked away from the scene.

Maybe she doesn't want to talk to me in front of my parents?

Maybe this is too much, too soon?

I wouldn't disagree with that. I mean, I haven't had a girl meet my parents since I was in high school. Both of my college girlfriends were casual and short-lived. Thrusting Charlotte into the spotlight with my parents wasn't my smartest idea to date. But I meant well. I wanted them all here today.

As my mom continues to talk animatedly about the game, bouncing from Lola Carradine to the catch I made in the seventh inning, I watch as Charlotte disappears down the corridor.

CHAPTER 8

Charlotte

"WHO WAS THAT?" CASEY ASKS WHEN WE TURN A CORNER. "WHERE ARE WE GOING? Wasn't that the guy who made that awesome play in the 7th inning? We should get his autograph."

I huff, breathing heavy like I've run sprints and not a few yards down a corridor. Meeting the parents was not on my agenda today or ever. I don't do parents...and I definitely don't do parents when I've only known the guy for less than a month. I should've guessed they were Bo's parents the way his mom was nervously sitting on the edge of her seat and his dad never sat in his. That should've been my clue, but I was so busy watching Bo that I never let my mind go there. He never mentioned his parents coming to the game.

"Casey, I'm going to need you to shut up."

Her brows furrow as she yanks her hand away from me. "Are you on drugs?" she asks, squinting as she gets closer, her eyes scanning my face. "Is there something you're not telling me?"

"No!" I exclaim, looking over my shoulder and then back to her. "You know I said someone gave me the tickets for the game?"

She nods leerily. "Yeah," she drawls. "People give you stuff all the time."

"Well, the guy who made the great play," I hedge. "Bo Benn—"

His name falls from my lips and my eyes go wide as I hear him call my name from behind me. Turning, I shove Casey behind me, like out of sight, out of mind.

What is wrong with me?

"Hey, Bo." I smile, trying to even out my voice, using years of practice to perfect a few sentences. "Hey, I saw you were busy with..." I gesture where he came from and he finishes for me.

"My parents." He exhales, running a hand down his face and I get stuck on the way the muscles in his forearms tense. "Sorry, I should've warned you they'd be sitting beside you. I've been so focused on making the roster and this game that I wasn't thinking clearly."

No, he wasn't.

But also, of course he wasn't.

"It's fine, really," I assure him, because it is. I'm just being a freak who suddenly can't handle a normal situation. "I just didn't want to interrupt. But I did want to say thank you for the tickets."

About that time, I feel Casey push me out of her way as she steps around me. "Hey, I'm Casey," she says, offering him her hand to shake. "The little sister. You must be her muse."

My eyes go wide as Bo flashes me a lopsided grin.

Panty-melting grin.

Oh, God.

"You know, I know you're busy...and we've really got to get going," I start, trying to cut the sudden thickness in the air between us. Casey fully enjoying herself to my side as she folds her arms over her chest and sighs. "We have a thing…" I continue. "Right, Case?"

Casey shakes her head. "What thing, Char?"

"You know," I tell her with a deathly stare. "With the...people."

Words.

I use them.

She gives me an evil smile, but thankfully, changes her expression to one of fake realization. So fucking fake. "Oh, that's right...the thing and people," she says with an even faker laugh, throwing her hands up in the air. "I mean, when you're Lola Carradine, there's always things and people, *amiright?*"

God, I'm gonna kill her.

Surely Mom isn't too old to make another one just like her.

"Well," Bo says, glancing between the two of us with the oddest expression on his face—knowing endearment—like he's fully aware of the scam, but he's going to let me get by with it...

Because why?

Because he likes me?

"There's another home game tomorrow," he says, taking a few backward steps, putting space between us that I immediately regret, because damn it, he smelled good—fresh and clean with a hint of that hard-earned sweat still lingering.

However, the way he's walking backwards gives me a nice glance at his muscled chest and torso beneath the tight, white t-shirt he's wearing...and long fucking legs.

He must be, what...six-foot-three...four.

"I could leave some tickets for you again at Will Call."

The offer startles me. I don't know why, but I balk. "No," I say firmly. "I have to work in the studio tomorrow." It's not a lie, but it's also not the truth. I have to work in the studio, but there's no time frame. I own the fucking studio. If I want to put the hours in from midnight until six in the morning, I can. If I want to work from dusk until dawn, I can. If I want to take a few hours out of my day to watch a baseball game, then I'm going to fucking do it.

"Okay, well, text me later?" he asks.

"Sure," I tell him, because even though I don't want to commit to coming to see another game tomorrow doesn't mean I don't want to talk to him. I do.

I want to talk to him.

I want to kiss him.

I want to do all sorts of dirty things to him.

But one thing Lola Carradine—or her counterpart Charlotte—doesn't do is relationships.

"God," I whisper, once Bo is out of sight. "Why did I turn that down?"

"Because," Casey whispers in return, "You don't want to seem too desperate."

I roll my eyes. "What are you now, the relationship guru?" I ask as we start to walk toward the exit.

"No," Casey says, intertwining her arm with mine, "But he really likes you."

"No," I argue, pulling my baseball cap down low and slipping my sunglasses on. It's multi-purpose. It keeps me from being noticed, not that it happens all the time, at least not here, but also because the sun is fucking bright and it's already hot here in New Orleans.

"Yes. He does. You obviously didn't see the way he looked at you," she muses as we cross the parking lot. No valet or drivers for the Carradine girls. We came here just like regular folk—parked our own car, walked a country mile, ate ballpark food, drank in the sun. It was a good day.

Seeing Bo take the field made my heart do this funny trick, something I haven't felt in a long time. I tried to ignore it, but every time he made an appearance, same damn thing.

And standing face to face with him, even though I was trying to play it off, it was even worse...or better, depending on how you look at it.

"We need food and wine," Casey says, reaching the car and slipping in the driver's seat. "And then we're going home and Googling all the pics of Bo Bennett...shirtless."

"Oh, my God. You're such a closet whore."

After pigging out on some Creole chicken from Verti Marte, the rest of our evening became a montage of Bo Bennett.

Casey turned into a sleuth, trying to dig up dirt, even though I told her there was none to be had.

"I don't get it," she finally says, tossing her phone to the side.

"What?" I ask, fully reclined on the couch as I try to let my food digest. For small girls, we can pack it away. The coffee table looks like our very own buffet...except all the containers are now mostly empty.

"There's no way this guy doesn't have some skeletons in the closet.

I mean, a guy like him...and all those girls who love athletes. There are Instagram accounts dedicated to guys in baseball pants. He has to, at the very least, have some hook-ups that have made it to the internet. You don't play his level of ball and walk away squeaky clean."

"There's nothing, Case. I already told you."

She sighs, leaning her head back on the couch as we both zone out, probably also both thinking of Bo Bennett. And honestly, that pisses me off a little. I don't want my sister thinking about Bo Bennett. Actually, I don't want anyone thinking about Bo Bennett.

Except me.

"He's a good person," I say, tamping down the irrational jealousy. "Probably too good of a person for me."

Casey sits up abruptly and shoves me. Hard.

"What the fuck, Casey?"

"Well, what the heck, Charlotte?" she challenges. "What did I tell you about talking down about yourself?"

"What did I tell you about turning into Mom?" I volley back.

Her eyes narrow. "What's so bad about Mom?"

I chuckle, loving how she can defuse a situation in a split second. There's no one like Casey. Of course, she's my little sister and I'm probably biased, but she *is* a good person. And she is like our mother, but in the best ways. I always mean it as a compliment even though I use it to get her riled up.

"You're a good person, too," Casey says quietly, settling back on the couch beside me, like she can hear my inner thoughts. "And I think a guy like Bo could use a girl like you. You'll spice up his life...give him a little adventure." She raises her eyebrows suggestively and laughs.

"Closet whore," I mumble.

After we tidy up the living room and say our goodnights, Casey heads for bed and I head for the studio. Bo still hasn't texted, but that's okay. If I was him, I probably wouldn't either. I'm sure he knows I was blowing him off.

Well, not *blowing him* off, I muse...but that would be fun.

Again, like he's psychic, my phone buzzes in my back pocket and I take it out to see his name on the screen.

Bo: Hey Charlotte

Charlotte: Hey Bo

I smile to myself as I open the door to the studio and walk inside. Our text messages are probably juvenile, but I don't care. They're the most carefree, fun thing I've experienced in a long time. Plus, I kind of missed my childhood. I didn't go to a regular school, was tutored on set for most of my middle school and junior high. I never had normal relationships. My first date was when I was fifteen and the guy was my eighteen-year-old co-star. He picked me up in a BMW and took me to The Ivy. There was nothing normal about it.

Bo: Thanks for coming to my game today.

Charlotte: Thanks for the tickets. We had fun.

Bo: Your little sister seems nice.

Charlotte: Is that code for annoying?

Bo: LOL

Bo: I never had siblings, so it's cool. I'm glad you brought her.

Charlotte: I could say something seriously mean but she's not so bad.

There's a long pause and I wonder if that's the end of tonight's conversation, feeling a little disappointed if it is. Our nightly routine of texting mixed with a couple phone calls here and there is what has brought me out of my writing slump. Casey wasn't lying when she said he's my muse. Although, I wouldn't have admitted that to him.

Thanks for that, Case.

Bo: Sorry again for springing my parents on you like that without a warning. I was going to introduce you and then realized what a mistake that was...

A mistake?

My stomach drops and I suddenly feel a little crushed inside that Bo would be embarrassed to introduce me to his parents. I know, I know. I didn't want to meet them in the first place. But there's a difference between me wanting to meet them and him wanting me to meet them.

Bo: That came out wrong. I would've loved for you to meet them and my mom would've flipped over you. But it was a mistake to not give you a heads up. Next time, full-on introductions, but be prepared to sign autographs and relive your days on Take the Stage.

I laugh and cringe a little. My time on the talent show was equally the best and worst thing that ever happened to me. I mean, it restarted my life, giving me a new career—the one I'd always dreamed of. But it was also a period in time when I was trying to figure myself out. Let's just say there were many variations of Charlotte Carradine—and later, Lola—on the stage of *Take the Stage*. Not to mention, the behind the scenes shots they referred to as *The Daily Stage* was a freaking Barbara Walters special. The producers' goal every day was tears. They didn't care how they got them—piss you off, scare the shit out of you, show you pictures of your dead dog—as long as they got them.

It was all about the views.

Never mind the souls you're crushing in the process.

But that's Hollywood...that's show business...that's living life in the public eye.

The thought actually makes my stomach turn. Not for the first time do I wonder if Bo realizes the life he's stepping into. It doesn't matter if you're an actress, musician, athlete, the second you sign that big contract and start performing for the public, they feel like they own you.

Charlotte: I'm sorry I bailed like that. I'm just not good at stuff like that.

I hesitated a little with how to word that, not wanting to be too presumptuous. We're not in a relationship, right? This is just friends... talking.

Bo: Neither am I.

Smiling at the phone, at his honesty, I reply—going out of my comfort zone because Bo feels worth it.

Charlotte: Well, I guess we can be bad at it together.

CHAPTER 9

Bo

I'M ON MY FIRST CHARTERED FLIGHT TO MY FIRST MAJOR LEAGUE AWAY GAME. IT'S definitely not like the minors. Playing in Des Moines, we traveled primarily by bus.

I'll admit, it's nice. The leg room alone is worth writing home about. Also, the food, or the fact that we were served actual food and not pretzels and peanuts, is also a nice perk.

The chatter was a little loud when we were first getting in the air, all the players joking around and yelling at each other about the Fortnite game they're playing and the Mario Kart competition they had last night at Mack's house. He's one of the few players who isn't married and has an actual house. Players are always gathering there to play video games and poker. But now that we're a couple hours into the flight, everyone is pretty much passed out.

I've got my eyes closed, but I'm not asleep, just faking it so I can catch a few moments of peace and quiet. Away games for rookies are a little more taxing than they are for the vets. I carried five bags from the stadium to the bus and again from the bus to the ticket counter.

I'm also wearing a ridiculous suit that was hanging on my locker when I got to the locker room this morning. Hot purple pants with big yellow flowers and bright yellow suit jacket.

At least it's team colors.

When I was back in the minors, I remember a guy who'd got called up for a season telling us that they made him dress like Marilyn Monroe on his first away game.

Some guys get pissed and call it hazing. I call it a rite of passage.. If they didn't give me a hard time and make me carry their fucking bags, I'd think they didn't like me or didn't have any faith that I'd be around for long. The fact I'm now sitting here in a suit that could be used as a beacon on a ship makes me feel like part of the team.

When my phone vibrates in my pocket, I pull it out, expecting some kind of encouraging message from my mom or some player stats from my dad, but it's neither.

Charlotte: Hey Bo.

I smile at her familiar greeting and quickly message her back.

Bo: Hey Charlotte.

Charlotte: Are you in the air?

Bo: Yep, headed for Sacramento.

Charlotte: Looks like I'll be in Cali this week too.

My heart immediately speeds up at the thought of her being close, reachable. We shared a quick dinner after our last home game the other night, dipping into a local place she goes to occasionally. It was just as nice as the first dinner we shared. The conversation flowed easy. She's funny and witty and interesting. I could listen to her talk for hours. The lilt of her voice paired with its huskiness is intoxicating.

I don't drink.

Or do drugs.

But I decided the other night that I'd happily do Charlotte.

And I mean that in every sense of the word, which is scary as shit.

I went into this thing not wanting a distraction, but I quickly realized that distraction or not, I couldn't get enough of Charlotte. She's so different than what I thought she'd be. Something changed after that first game. Seeing her with her little sister humanized her, endeared her to me. I've always seen her for more than what she is on the stage, but that day, I saw Charlotte, the sister...just a person making her way through this world like anybody else.

My parents have always taught me that it's not what a person does for a living that makes them important or valued, it's who they are as a person that counts.

Being a professional baseball player doesn't mean shit. I hit fucking balls and catch them. It's not rocket science or a cure for cancer. The thing that makes me like Charlotte so much is that I can tell she feels the same about herself. She's just doing what she loves, but she doesn't think that just because she's a rockstar and playing on the radio in people's cars and homes and every club around the country, that she's any better than anybody else.

She's real.

And she's beautiful.

And, yeah...

Bo: Sacramento?

I laugh, doubting she's going to Sacramento, but it'd be nice. I'd like to see her.

Charlotte: Ha! I wish. But no. LA.

Sitting up a little straighter in my seat, my stomach gives a twist. Charlotte confided in me the other night that she's not a fan of L.A. It's where a lot of her band members live and they're not the best influences. Being in New Orleans gives her a break from the music scene, helping her find her balance and make good choices for her life. The idea of her being there and potentially in harm's way doesn't sit well with me.

Bo: Concert?

She didn't mention one when we talked last, but I know her manager springs things on her at the last minute.

Terry.

I already don't like that guy. I knew I didn't like him from the first night I met Charlotte when he tried to force her in front of the cameras, knowing she just wanted to lay low and head home. He seems like a bully to me and I've never liked bullies.

Charlotte: I wish.

For a second, I think I'm going to have to pry it from her, but then the three little dots appear, letting me know she's typing.

Charlotte: UGH. It's this stupid movie premier. Terry is making me go and I have to walk the carpet with Cody DiMarco.

She adds an eye roll emoji and continues typing.

Charlotte: I didn't want to go, but he says it's good publicity. Not sure if you know about the whole photo of me doing a line?

She pauses and so do I. I actually do know a little, but I'd been waiting on her to bring it up and tell me about it herself, instead of jumping to conclusions or passing a judgement where it's not mine to pass.

Charlotte: That's seriously cringe worthy to type. But I did it. I owned up to it, made my apology, but that's never good enough. That's why I've been doing benefit concerts and stupid publicity dates. I'm not complaining about the benefits. I don't mind doing anything for charity, but I'm over all the publicity bullshit.

Another pause.

Charlotte: Sorry for dumping all this on you. I really just wanted to text you so if you saw a photo pop up of me with some guy you wouldn't think it's...

Charlotte: IDK. Gah, I don't even know what this is between us, but just know I'd rather be with you anywhere than with Cody fucking DiMarco on the red carpet. That's all I wanted to say.

Letting out a deep sigh, I run a hand down my face.

Bo: Thanks for telling me.

I almost leave it at that, but I can't leave her hanging.

Bo: I'd rather you be with me, but I hope you have fun at the movie premier.

Charlotte: Hope your games go well this week.

Bo: Thanks.

I do leave it at that, because honestly, I don't know what else to say and I don't know if I can do this. Am I ready for all of this? I know being with Charlotte won't be easy or private. Eventually, it'll be the two of us showing up in grainy photos. Do I want that?

"Who are you talking to?" Mack asks, leaning over the back of the seat in front of me.

I quickly click the screen off and put it back in my pocket. "No one."

Lie.

Charlotte is so someone, but I don't want to get into that with Mack Granger. I've seen what the gossip rags write about him. I've heard the stories. He's a womanizer.

"A girl?" he asks, of course not giving up that easily.

"No," I tell him, leaning back into my seat and closing my eyes, but then I feel the plane begin to descend and the flight attendant walks by, telling us we're approaching Sacramento. Unlike a commercial flight, she doesn't ask us to put up our trays and laptops. She just smiles, like really smiles, flashing her bright white teeth. "I'm gonna have to ask you to take your seat in a few minutes."

"Sure thing, darlin'," Mack replies, letting his Texas drawl really come out. Once she moves on to the row of seats behind us, he turns his attention back to me. "So, who's the chick?"

My silence does nothing to shut him up.

"Someone I know?" he asks, his tone turning thoughtful. "That hot thing that works in the office? Red head?"

"No," I reply, leaning back again and closing my eyes.

"Well, I know you haven't been anywhere to meet anyone. The guys tell on you, you know. Field, gym, eat in, to bed early...you're about as boring as they come, Rook." The levity in his words tells me he's just giving me a hard time, but he's also still not giving up. "So, is it someone from back home? Old girlfriend? Oh, I know...some chick you were bangin' in Des Moines?"

"Mack."

"You can call me Brick," he says and it almost makes me open my eyes. Almost. But I decide to play it off, like he didn't just give me permission to call him by the nickname that only the other vets usually get the privilege of using.

"Someone I met at the gala," I tell him.

"Ahh." Excitement ebbs into his tone. "Nice, man. I knew I should've gone. She from New Orleans? Local?"

Cracking my eyes, I see him looking at me like a dog who thinks you have bacon.

"Local."

"She hot?"

I groan, realizing there's no getting around this, so I sit up, adjust myself in the seat and level him with a stare. "If I tell you, can you keep quiet?"

With his brows furrowed, he cocks his head in disbelief. "Of course, man."

After a few seconds, most of them spent mentally kicking myself in the balls for even thinking about telling Mack Granger about Charlotte Carradine, I finally spill it. "Ever heard of Lola...Carradine?" I ask, dropping it to a whisper.

Mack's eyes grow two times their normal size. "You mean that rocker chick?"

I nod.

"Long brown hair, long fucking legs? That Lola Carradine?" he asks, seeking clarification.

I nod.

Then he whistles and looks off to the side. "Are you fucking with me?"

A huff of a laugh escapes me and I realize that in this situation the truth probably sounds more like an elaborate fabrication, something to get him off my trail.

"You're serious." It's not a question this time, it's a statement.

I nod.

"Fuck," he drawls. "You ain't playin' around, are you Rook?"

Laughing again, I shake my head, saying any of this out loud sounds crazy. I haven't told anyone so telling Mack kind of makes it real. "I don't know what the fuck I'm doing," I admit.

"I'm going to need you to take your seat and buckle up," the flight attendant says on her way back up the aisle. Instead of turning around in the seat and doing like she asks, Mack gives her a smile and walks around to plop his ass down beside me, then buckling his seat belt.

"So," he says, once the flight attendant has moved on to the next row. "You're fucking Lola Carradine."

I immediately shush him, looking around to see who might have overheard him, but everyone else seems to be doing their own thing. "What the fuck, man?"

"No one cares," Mack says with a roll of his eyes. "Dude, you've gotta get past this goody-two-shoes thing you've got going...it's not good for your image."

"What?" I ask with another laugh.

"You and your nose-to-the-grindstone, eye-on-the-road-ahead thing. We all get it—you work hard, you're not a slacker. That's cool. But most of the guys think you've got a stick up your ass and you need to lose that... ASAP. It's not a good look, Rook." He huffs a sigh, like it's taxing for him to give me this talk, but someone has to do it. "Everyone is on edge their rookie season. No one wants to make a mistake. But let me clue you in on a little secret...mistakes make you human. People relate to that. So, don't feel like you can't let loose every once in a while."

"Duly noted," I tell him, relaxing back against the seat and fighting back a small smile.

"So, are you fucking Lola Carradine? Because, if you are, that's some major cool points and you're kinda lacking in that area, so—"

"I'm not fucking her," I say, cutting him off. "Just talking to her."

"But you want to fuck her," Mack says, like it's a given.

Of course.

I'd be lying if I said the thought didn't cross my mind, like every day and every night and any time in between when I allow myself to think about her. Not just fucking, but being with her...kissing her, in particularly, but that'd probably sound like a pussy answer, so I keep it to myself.

"I don't know what I want," I admit. "I like her...a lot. She's...amazing, and not just because she's Lola Carradine. I'm more attracted to Charlotte, that's her real name, and I like talking to her."

"So, what's the problem?"

"She's Lola Carradine," I answer. "And I doubt whatever we end up doing will be uncomplicated and I don't have time for complicated. I'm here to play ball."

"Fuck that, man," Mack says, groaning. "Listen, you could play great ball in your sleep. So, forget that. You're gonna kick ass on the field regardless, but I promise, if you find a way to release that extra tension in your shoulders...ease the stress...you're gonna be fucking MVP." He says this so matter-of-factly.

"You sound like Davies."

"We talk," Mack admits and then sighs. "Listen, we joke around a lot, it's what we do. The season gets long and we spend a lot of time shooting the shit and keeping ourselves entertained when we don't have games to win. But bottom line is we love this game...we love playing for the Revelers... we love New Orleans. The whole organization is great, so we want to see it succeed. We also like you and we think you'll have a great career, but Davies and I both see parts of ourselves in you and we just want to help you not make mistakes we've made. So, when we give you advice, it comes from a good place."

Not gonna lie, I kind of choke up. I've had guys over the years give me bits and pieces of advice here and there, but most of that has come from my dad and other coaches. I've always come into a team where I'm the one everyone is looking up to, but it's not like that at this level. Guys like Mack and Davies have literally been there and done that. I look up to them. So, for him to care enough to tell me this shit means a lot.

"Thanks, man," is all I manage to say.

"What's got you second guessing Ms. Carradine?" Mack asks, switching gears and lightening the conversation back up. "Besides being a distraction?"

"She's going to be in L.A. this week for a red carpet...with some actor."

Mack hums. "Yeah, that wouldn't fly for me either. If a chick is with me, she's with me."

"Well, that's the thing, Charlotte isn't really with me. We just talk and we've been out to dinner a couple times. That's it."

"But you want to be with her," Mack adds.

We sit the rest of the flight in silence and I let the conversation marinate, soaking into me. I want to be with Charlotte. The question is: can I handle Lola?

Once the plane stops on the airstrip, the team files out, bags in hand and boards a charter bus waiting to take us to the hotel. The other nice thing about playing in the majors, no shared rooms.

The ride to the hotel is quiet. Surprisingly, Mack keeps his word and doesn't mention Lola...or Charlotte. Davies has been quiet the entire trip, seemingly deep in thought. The two guys I share an apartment with, Jorge and Luis, are occupying the seat in front of me. Both guys have been on the team a couple seasons. We all get along well, but they're on a different time schedule than me. I hit the gym early for an extra workout, while they stay up late playing video games. But it's cool...they're cool, much better than the roommates I had in Des Moines. There it was like we had a revolving door, women coming in and out at all hours.

I'm not one to judge.

To each their own.

But that's just never been me.

Sure, I've had a few hook-ups, but I've mostly just avoided it. Sex means a little more to me than most guys. I'm not a fuck 'em and leave 'em kind of guy. Call me a pussy or whatever, but for me, it's more than just a release. And I've had girlfriends over the years, two fairly long term relationships in college. But with each one, they would pressure me for more of a commitment, especially the girl I was dating during my senior year. When talk started picking up about the draft and what round I'd go in, she started asking about my plans and whether or not they included her.

"In five years, where do you see us?" she'd asked.

And when I really forced myself to think about it, I saw myself playing baseball, but that was about it. I didn't see myself with her, not even a year down the road.

My mom told me when I meet the right girl, I'll find a place for her.

I've been telling myself that won't happen until my first love— baseball—is gone. I've never felt like I have room for two loves.

I'm a one-woman guy, loyal to the bone.

Game one in Sacramento gives us our first road win of the season, but it had nothing to do with me. I grounded out in my first at bat and was thrown out at first. My second at bat was a strike-out, leaving Chan and Martinez stranded on second and third. In the eighth inning, I finally got a good hit, but it was caught at the wall. And then, I let a ball roll right past me in the ninth inning.

But we won, no fucking thanks to me, and at the end of the day, a W is all that matters.

"Don't get down on yourself, Rook," Davies groans, passing me as we walk to the elevators. "Tomorrow's a new day."

"Yeah," I mutter, keeping my head down.

I just want another shower, a hot one, and a bed. It's been a long day and I'm spent. Last night, I slept like crap, mostly thinking about Charlotte and wanting to text her but trying not to be *that guy*. A guy I didn't even know I was capable of being a month ago, especially with a girl who's not even mine.

"Tomorrow, Rook," Mack says, giving me a slap on the back.

"Wanna head to the bar with us?" Luis asks as we walk down the hall to our rooms.

"Nah, I'm gonna turn in early, hit the gym early," I tell him. "Work off some of this tension."

Dipping into my room, I shut the door before I have to listen to any of their smartass comments about getting my dick wet. I'm not saying they're wrong. At this point, I'm thinking they might be spot on, even though I hate admitting it. And I'm a little pissed at myself for allowing my feelings for Charlotte to get this far.

I didn't see her coming.

Didn't realize she'd be someone I couldn't forget.

Wasn't aware that she'd force herself into my head.

When I ditch my clothes I changed into at the field and turn on the shower, the hot water is a welcome reprieve, taking my mind off the shit game I played and the girl who's taking up residence in my thoughts. But the longer I stand there, Charlotte seeps back in...nice and warm, just like always. Warm, brown eyes. Warm smile. Warm hands.

Last week, we were eating at this hole in the wall place, a table in the back, everyone ignoring us like we were nobodies, and Charlotte was laughing. Her head was tossed back, mouth open, eyes closed—totally in the moment. And then her hand came down and rested on my arm, before she continued with her story about a fan who threw their pants up on stage.

She thought maybe they were an extra pair...or they had something else on over them. But when she looked out into the crowd, there was this guy, standing in his briefs. The best part is they weren't boxers or even boxer briefs, they were bright, white Fruit of the Looms.

I was laughing with her, but on the inside, all I could focus on was the feel of her hand on my arm. It felt good...right. I wanted more—more touching, more of her...more of her touching me.

The memory has me sliding my hand down my chest to my cock, which is now standing at attention, also remembering how good it felt. For about the dozenth time since I met her, I jack off to a vision of Charlotte. It's not a full release, but it takes the edge off.

After I'm dried off and sprawled across my bed, zoning out to a random movie on the television, I grab my phone to see if I've missed any text messages or calls. But just like when I first got back to the room, nothing.

Part of me wants to pull up Safari and type in Charlotte's name, just to see if anything pops up.

But that feels intrusive.

If she wanted me to know something about her life, she'd tell me.

When my phone dings, my heart skips a beat, thinking maybe Charlotte has ESP and is texting me, but instead it's Mack.

Mack: Rook?

Bo: Yeah?

Mack: You heard from your girl?

I roll my eyes, wishing I'd never confided in him.

Bo: No.

Bo: And she's not my girl.

Mack: Have you seen this?

A few seconds later a picture comes through of Charlotte, smiling at the camera, wearing a fucking gorgeous red dress, slit up to her waist. Her hair is up, exposing her exquisite neck.

The thing that really gets my blood boiling is the guy with his lips on the neck I've daydreamed about tasting. His hands are also claiming her waist, pulling her to him.

They look like lovers.

They look happy.

She looks happy.

Yeah, this is what I can't do.

I'm a confident guy, not particularly jealous, but I can't do this.

My phone buzzes again, but I don't answer. I have nothing to say to Mack, so I turn it to silent and place it face down on the nightstand. We have another game tomorrow. That's what I'm going to focus on. The one thing I can control is me...I can get to sleep, be at the gym early tomorrow for cardio, be prepared for tomorrow...That's me. That's who I am.

But even when I tell myself I'm not going to give Charlotte or the guy she's with in the photo another thought, it's a lie. I can't get it out of my head. I'll have to thank Mack for that tomorrow.

Ignorance is fucking bliss.

Doesn't he know that?

I'm also worried about her. I know what she told me about Cody DiMarco—about the drugs and the crowd he runs with and the people she left L.A. to get away from. For her sake, I hope she doesn't let him drag her down. She's too good for that.

Some unknown time later, I'm asleep when I hear a banging on my door. Assuming it's one of the guys and praying this isn't some kind of rookie initiation where they have me streaking through the hotel, I climb out of bed and walk to the door.

Swinging it open, I about swallow my tongue.

Long legs in fishnet pantyhose.

A corset barely containing large tits.

Straight black hair.

And nothing else.

"Hey, Bo," she croons, lashes batting.

"Uh…"

"Boys said you could use a little TLC." She licks her bright-red lips as she lets her eyes roam. "Looks like I'm in for a treat. You're quite the… package."

Oh, fuck no.

Huh uh.

Nope.

"There's been some mistake," I tell her, going to shut the door, but she stops me with her foot that I now notice is in a stiletto…a mile high. The kind of shoes you see and wonder how anyone walks in them without breaking their neck.

"No mistake, baby…no regrets," she says, her hand coming up and resting on my chest.

As politely as possible, I remove it and gently push her back into the hallway.

"I don't think so," I reply. "Did they pay you…do you get paid?" I'm not sure how this works, but I'm guessing she's not standing at my hotel room door for free. "I can pay you, but then you've gotta leave."

Her seductive act drops and she huffs, placing her hands on her hips.

"They told me you'd be a hard sell."

"Yeah, listen," I turn to the bar where I'd put my wallet earlier and take out what cash I have. "Take this," I tell her, placing the bills in her palm. "Consider it a tip…or whatever."

She looks at the money and smirks. "You don't have to," she says, handing it back, but I refuse it. "Look, the guys paid me. So, don't worry about it."

"No, take it. I'm sure you had better things you could've been…doing," I say hesitantly.

Her eyebrow hitches and she takes another look, ogling my chest…six pack…and then lingering a little too long at my dick. A few more seconds of that and I'll need my money back, because she'll be the one owing me. This ain't a free show.

"No," she says on a sigh. "I'd do you for free."

An instant blush hits my cheeks and I dip my head so she doesn't see.

Taking a card from her cleavage, she hands it to me. "If you change your mind…"

I smile, holding the card up. "Thanks."

She waves and walks away, and I watch her until she disappears around a corner, waiting for one of those sons of bitches to stick their head out. I can guess who was behind it, but I'd love to know for sure. However, every door remains shut, so I close my door and go back to bed.

CHAPTER 10

Charlotte

THIS IS EXACTLY WHAT I WAS AFRAID OF, EXACTLY WHY I DIDN'T WANT TO AGREE TO this stupid farce of a date.

The premiere was fine. It was a typical red carpet event with mics being thrust in my face, while camera flashes burned my retinas. I was a bit confused as to why anyone wanted to talk to me at all because, technically, I was just a spectator. It wasn't my event; I had nothing to do with the movie. I haven't put out a new album in over two years. And yet, it seemed like the reporters were frothing at the bit to talk to me, more interested in me than Cody DiMarco.

But that's Hollywood—whatever sells.

Maybe Terry was right and this was a positive move for *cleaning up* my reputation.

Sometimes, I really hate it when he's right.

Regardless, tonight didn't go as I'd hoped. What I'd hoped for was going to the premier, taking a few interviews, being seen, and then disappearing back to my hotel room where I'd scrub my face clean, crawl in bed, order room service, and text Bo.

It's one thing to show up and answer a few quick questions, give a couple of soundbites...I'm totally fine with that. What I don't like—no, what I *hate* is having to put up with bullshit like Cody DiMarco putting his mouth and teeth on me *without any warning* and pretending to enjoy it. His little whispers about playing nice for the camera made me want to kick him in his balls.

But there were lots of cameras.

And they were all trained on us.

Him, the star of the movie.

Me, his date and current hot gossip topic.

Since we left the premier a few hours ago, I've been whisked to three parties, had drinks thrust in my hand and drank them because I needed something to get me through this night. But now, here I am, hiding in a bathroom in a club I don't even know the name of, wishing I had magical powers so I could disappear.

My head is spinning thanks to the last drink I just guzzled before finding my way in here. The music from the club is a muffled roar. The bathroom only has two stalls so occasionally someone is yelling at me to get out, but I don't.

I'm not leaving.

Because on the other side of that door, down a long dark hallway, there's a VIP table where Cody DiMarco is sitting with other well-known celebrities and they're doing lines of coke. I'm not an addict, but I know what it's like to experience the rush of a high.

It's nice.

For a while.

But then, you come down, and all the bullshit you were trying to escape is still there and now, not only do you have the normal day-to-day bullshit to deal with, but you have grainy photos leaked of you across the internet. Everyone is talking about how you're *spiraling*.

Will Lola Carradine be the next untimely death? Is she still an addict? Did her drug rehab from ten fucking years ago not work?

Well, jokes on them, because I was never at a drug rehab. I've never been to any kind of rehab. I can say no to any substance, when I want to.

That's never been my problem.

But tonight, already feeling the pressure caving in around me, I want to say yes, just to escape...just for a moment.

Once the bathroom empties out, I fumble around with my tiny black clutch and pull out my phone. Staring at the blank screen for a minute, I contemplate what I want to do.

What I really want to do is call Bo.

I think just hearing his voice would put me at ease, help me think clearer. But it's late, like really late. Powering my phone up, I note that the screen reads one thirty-two.

Bo Bennett is a good guy. He's a machine. He wakes up early and goes to bed early. In the short time I've known him, one thing I've noticed is he's consistent. Some might say he's boring, but I say he's dedicated. He knows what he wants and he's willing to do anything to get it.

A part of me wants to be on the receiving end of that kind of devotion. A very large part of me. I've never been truly in love before, but I can see myself falling for someone like Bo.

The other part of me, the unselfish part, wants to tell Bo Bennett to run for the hills. I want to yell at him to run as far and fast as he can, because I know what I am to him. I see it in the way he wars with himself when he's with me. I'm a distraction. I wasn't in his plans.

He doesn't pick up random women and take them home.

He's not a one-night stand kind of guy.

He's good.

And strong.

And steady.

And so fucking sexy...and the crazy thing is I don't even think he knows it.

Which only makes him more sexy.

And I want him.

All of him.

All to myself.

But I'm Lola Carradine and I don't get that luxury.

Swallowing down the lump in my throat, I lean against the bathroom stall for support and swipe my thumb across the screen, heading for the last text message Bo and I shared—me telling him about tonight. In a way, I was warning him...trying to give him a heads up. Trying to protect him, just in case he's feeling what I'm feeling. Because I know if I was in his position and saw a photo of him with a random chick, I'd feel hurt.

I know I shouldn't do what I'm about to do, but the vodka I've been drinking all night tells me otherwise.

One ring and my heart leaps.

Two rings and I close my eyes, trying to quiet the thrum in my chest.

Three rings and I know I should hang up.

But I hang on, just in case he has a voicemail box that's set up. Maybe I can at least hear his voice...leave him a message. I lose track of the rings until a sleepy "Hello?" breaks through the line. Breathing heavy, I stare at the peeling black paint on the wall across from me. "Charlotte?" Bo asks a few seconds later, a rustling sound in the background. "Are you okay?"

"Hey, Bo."

"You okay?" he asks again and it sends warmth through my body. Nobody besides Casey and my mom and dad ever ask me if I'm okay, and even they forget to do that from time to time. I think they all assume I've been in this business so long that it comes easy to me, but it doesn't.

And sometimes it just feels fucking good for someone to ask if you're okay.

"I'm stuck in a bathroom," I tell him, not wanting to completely unload on him. "Well, not literally." Laughing to myself, I tilt my head up and turn my attention to the ceiling. "But if I leave, they'll want me to do a line...and I don't want to, but I've had too much to drink to make good decisions, which is also why I called you...sorry I called you."

"It's okay...so, you're okay? You're, I mean..." Bo starts and stops and then lets out a deep breath. It makes me wish I could see him, be close enough to feel his breath on my skin. "Do you need help?"

"No." I blink back rogue tears that spring up from nowhere. "I just needed to hear your voice."

We sit in silence for a few seconds.

"Am I too much for you?" I ask. "I'm too much...I'm...I'm a distraction. And you're too good for me," I admit, feeling the truth of my words down to my toes that are still cramped in these fucking stilettos. The only thing about what I'm wearing tonight that feels like me is the leather jacket, and I had to fight for it. "You're too good for me, Bo Bennett, and if I was a better person, I'd lose your number and not mess up your life...but I like you...a lot."

"I saw a picture of you." His words sound pained. "I didn't go looking for it. One of my teammates sent it to me...I told him about you...and he sent it to me." There's a pause and I wait to see what he's going to say next, my heart beating furiously, hoping this isn't where Bo Bennett and I end— in a shabby bathroom of a club. This isn't me. It's not him. We fit better in New Orleans, tucked into a hidden booth in an unknown restaurant.

That's home.

That's Bo.

"You looked beautiful," he says. His voice is barely above a whisper. "But I hated seeing his lips on you."

My breathing stops, stuck in my chest.

"It wasn't what it looked like," I assure. "It was Cody being the asshole that he is and playing it up for the cameras. Trust me that the behind the scenes was the polar opposite of whatever the paps tried to make it out to be."

"I believe you, but I wanted it to be me," he confesses. "I want to be the one kissing you."

"You do?" I ask, my hand going to my chest, holding in the warmth that's settled there.

"Yeah."

I can picture·the light blush that creeps up on his chest when he steps out of his comfort zone, like the night he kissed the side of my mouth.

"And I'm gonna take you out on a date...a real one." His voice dips down to a low, gravelly rumble and it shoots straight to my core, causing my stomach to tense.

"You wanna take me on a date?" I ask, just wanting to hear him say it again.

"Yes," he says, pausing. "I'm gonna take you on a date...I have a day off when we get back. Will you be back in town?"

"Flying back early in the morning," I tell him. That wasn't the original plan. Terry had more publicity shit scheduled for me, but I just made an executive decision. I need to be back in New Orleans.

"I'll be back late tomorrow night."

"Text me?" I ask, needing that open line of communication with him.

"Yes."

I sigh, kicking off the wall and straightening out my dress. "I've gotta go so I can schedule an Uber and get the hell out of here."

"Text me when you're back to your hotel room?" he asks.

I smile.

"You sure?" I ask, knowing it's late and seriously past his bedtime. "I know you get up early and you have an early game tomorrow."

"Never too late for you," he insists, his voice taking on the consistency of honey, dripping through the phone and making me wish I could teleport myself to Sacramento.

"Okay."

CHAPTER 11

Bo

"I DON'T EVEN DRINK RED BULL AND YOU THINK I'M GONNA PUT MY DICK IN SOME random chick?" I ask Mack incredulously.

He just tosses his head back and laughs as do the other guys sitting around us—Davies, Jorge, Phil, Luis. I have a feeling they're all in on it, but I'm not mad.

It's not my money down the drain.

Well, it was my fifty bucks, but I felt like I owed it to her for her trouble.

"You shoulda seen your face," Luis laughs. "It was priceless."

"How the fuck would you know?" I ask, remembering the incident with vivid clarity. There wasn't anyone else in that hallways besides my scantily clad new acquaintance...Sparkles, I think was the name on her business card. I thought about leaving it in the room for the next person, but quickly decided against it. That wouldn't be something I'd want traced back to me, so I flushed the evidence down the toilet before I left.

"Peephole, dude," Luis confesses. "I had a fucking front-row seat."

I groan, leaning my head back onto the seat of the bus. At this time of night, everyone on this bus should be dead on their feet, but we're not.

The adrenaline rush from our first sweep has us all on a high we probably won't come down from for a while. Our chartered flight puts us back in New Orleans before midnight. Since we have an off day tomorrow, most of the guys will probably head out to a bar or Mack's house, but all I can think about is Charlotte.

Ever since our phone call last night, which feels like a week ago instead of a day ago, I've needed to see her. When she told me what the photo of her and DiMarco portrayed was not as it seemed, I've felt this insane need to put my eyes on her—the real Charlotte—and see for myself that she's okay...she's there...and he's not.

I sound crazy.

I do.

Even in my own head, I sound crazy.

And I don't even want to know what that says about me.

A month ago, I didn't want a distraction.

Now, I want her.

Tipping my head up, I glance at all the guys sitting around me and I let my mind wander. They all make it work. They all have relationships—girlfriends, wives, one-night-stands. If they can do it and continue to play at the level they all do, then why not me?

For the first time in my life, I want to try.

I want to try to balance.

Maybe it's finally making it to the majors that's freeing up this place inside me.

Or maybe it's Charlotte.

"You coming over?" Mack asks when we get to the field. "Late night poker?"

"Nah, man," I tell him, appreciative for the invite, but needing something—someone—a little more tonight than being part of the team. "I'm going to call it..." I start for the lie, but end with the truth. "I'm gonna call Charlotte."

A slow, wide, knowing smile grows on Mack's face.

"That's my boy," he says, clapping his hand on my shoulder. "Go get your girl."

Thankfully, the rest of the bus was caught up in their own conversations, paying us no attention. I'm okay with Mack knowing about Charlotte, but not the whole damn team. They're all up in my business enough as it is. If they had an inkling there was a girl, they'd have a field day with it.

Once we get to the field, I wave my goodbyes, Luis and Jorge letting me know they're going to Mack's. Even though we're roommates, we don't see each other much more than my other teammates. Maybe it'll be different once we settle into the season, but the first couple weeks of being in New Orleans has been a whirlwind.

Climbing into my car, I start it up and pull out my phone.

After midnight.

My manners tells me it's too late to call anyone, let alone a girl I'm interested in.

Booty calls.

Those are the only calls usually made at this time of night, and even though I want what that implies, I want other things more—conversation with Charlotte, her laughs, her warm eyes on me. I'd also settle for hearing her voice, and knowing her, she's still up, so I hit her name and wait.

"Hello?" Charlotte says, sounding surprised…pleasantly surprised.

"Hey."

"Hey," she replies, and I can hear the smile in her voice.

It's not lost on me that we no longer feel the need to announce ourselves. The first couple times Charlotte and I spoke on the phone, our beginning lines were "hey, it's Bo" or "hey, it's Charlotte." But now, it feels familiar… good.

"Hope it's not too late," I tell her, still sitting in my car in the parking lot as the rest of my team files out, leaving me the last man standing.

"Nope," she sighs. "Just finished up rewriting the verse to a new song." She sounds a little sleepy but content. "I was just getting ready to text you and see if you'd made it back."

"Just got to my car."

"Headed home?" she asks, and if I'm not mistaken there's a hint of hope there.

"Uh," I start, but suddenly feel a rush of heat. I'm not a forward guy, but I'm also not someone who shies away from something he wants. It's just the thing I usually want doesn't walk on two luscious legs and have a body that won't stop. It's not a living, breathing person that I can't get out of my head. "I was thinking about maybe stopping by for a minute?"

I leave it as a question, wanting to clarify that I'm not expecting anything, except to see her, but wait to see what her response is instead.

"You wanna come over to my house?" she asks, a hint of teasing creeping into her normally seductive tone.

"If it's a bad idea—"

"Bo," she stops me mid-sentence. "It's a great idea."

"See you in about ten minutes?"

"See you then."

Excitement, that's what I hear in Charlotte's voice right before the line goes dead and my heart takes up residence in my throat.

When I pull up into Charlotte's long drive, I stop at the gate and before I can even roll my window down to push the button, it opens for me. The house is lit up and looks gorgeous, even at night. Everything is white— the house, the pillars, the big-ass stone wall surrounding the property. It makes it feel like it's cut off from the outside world. Driving up to the spot Charlotte guided me to the first night I drove her home, I park my car and smirk. It's quite the contrast—my old Toyota and her impressive abode.

A jolt of nerves hit me when I see the door of the house open and get my first glimpse of Charlotte.

Gorgeous.

So fucking gorgeous.

Unlike the first night I met her, her hair is wavy and piled on top of her head and she's not wearing any make-up. The baggy sweats mixed with her relaxed smile tells me I'm getting the purest version of Charlotte Carradine, and I fucking love it.

She's beautiful.

"Bo Bennett," she says, her smile growing. "I heard you made quite the winning play tonight."

The smile I'm wearing is unavoidable, between her and her comment, I can't help it. "You heard about that?" I ask, running a nervous hand through my hair.

"I might've googled you." She shrugs and gives me a wicked smile, opening the door wide for me to step inside.

"Wow," I say, getting my first glimpse of her kitchen. "This is nice...and it smells amazing in here. Are you cooking?"

Closing the door and resetting the alarm, she walks over to the large island. "I'm heating up some leftovers, thought you might be hungry."

"Starving, actually," I admit. "I almost stopped for something on my way over but everything that's open this time of night in New Orleans is usually overrun by people partying on Bourbon Street. And I'm not much for fast food."

"Good thing I have some food I picked up at Verti Marte."

"Creole Chicken?" I ask, my mouth immediately watering at the thought. Charlotte and I ended up there one night last week after a late game.

"Yep," she says with a pleased smile. "Wasn't expecting you, but it's like the universe just knew." Her eyes drift to mine and they seem to sparkle in the bright white kitchen. "Want a quick tour?"

I glance around for a second before answering. "Sure."

I'm starving and the food in the kitchen smells amazing, but I want to see her place. If Charlotte is going to let me in, I'm not going to turn her down.

"Casey's already in bed," she says as she passes by me and walks toward a great room that's filled with overstuffed furniture and a large television mounted on one wall. There are personal effects, mostly sheets of music in frames along one wall and a large canvas on the other. But it's the piano in the corner that really catches my eye. It looks expensive and I have the feeling it's not just for decoration.

"Do you play?" I ask, pointing to the sleek black instrument.

She nods and twists her pouty lips, hiding her obvious insecurity. Who would've ever dreamed she even has any? "I do, but I'm not great...I'm no Elton John or anything, not even good enough to play on stage, but I love it. Sometimes when I'm stuck on a song, it helps to sit down there and just feel out the melody on the keys. It's completely different than picking it out on my guitar."

"Wow," I tell her, seriously in awe. "I can't play anything. I mean, I've never tried, but I've always been impressed by people who can."

"You should try," she encourages. "A lot of athletes are good with their hands...and timing," she drifts off and if I'm not mistaken, I catch my first glimpse of Charlotte Carradine blushing. And it makes my stomach tighten and my hands ball into fists at my side to keep from reaching out and touching her. "They usually make, uh, good musicians."

After she shows me around the rest of the common areas of the house, the one I'm most impressed with is her studio. It's state-of-the-art and from the second we walked inside, it's like I can feel the creativity buzzing in the room. There are boards of lights and knobs connected to large monitors, a huge window in one wall that leads into a side room. In there are a couple microphones and some weird foam panels. Charlotte explains that they're for acoustics, which I'll have to take her word for.

The studio is her version of a baseball diamond.

She knows every inch of it like the back of her hand.

In there, she's in her element, at the top of her game...living her best life. I can see it in her expression, the way her eyes light up and she talks animatedly about it. Seeing her like that makes me like her even more. I love her passion.

As we finally settle in on one of her oversized couches, Creole Chicken in hand, she clicks on the television. "Hulu or Netflix?" she asks, going to a menu on the screen.

"Uh, I don't get a chance to watch much television, so whatever you want."

"Netflix it is then," she says. "So...what are you in the mood for? Action? Comedy? ...Romance?"

I give her a half-smile, wanting to tell her that I'd watch anything, as long as she's sitting beside me on this couch, but instead, I shrug. "You choose."

"Are you a Julia Roberts fan?" she asks, pointing the remote control toward the television as she scrolls through menus, punching buttons faster than my roommates when they're playing Call of Duty.

"I'm not sure I'd say I'm a fan," I answer, noncommittally. "But I thought she was great in *Pretty Woman*. Call me old school, but I think movies made in the eighties and nineties are better than most of the movies made today. And yes, I realize I wasn't even alive in the eighties, sue me."

"*Notting Hill?*" she asks, cocking her head in my direction.

"Excuse me?" I reply, unsure of the question.

"*Notting Hill*," she repeats. "Probably Julia's best work to-date—she's a movie star and her co-star, Hugh Grant, is a bookstore owner in *Notting Hill*," she explains. "It's hilarious and heartfelt...everything a movie should be."

Her passion for this movie sells me without even seeing one scene.

"Notting Hill it is," I tell her, unable to stop my smile growing as she beams at me.

After she makes the selection, she trades one remote control for another, dimming the lights. "Good choice," she says, like it was all my idea all along, as she gets comfortable in her spot—legs crossed with her bowl propped on a pillow. With her hair in a messy ponytail-bun thingy on the top of her head and her face fresh of any makeup, Charlotte looks ten years younger than her actual age. If someone didn't know her, which is kind of hard these days—between her childhood acting and current music gig—they'd maybe guess that she's pushing twenty.

She'd definitely get carded at a bar.

Once again, it's on the tip of my tongue to tell her how beautiful I think she is and maybe it's the dim lights or the comfortable atmosphere, but before I can stop myself, I mumble, "You're so pretty."

Her big brown eyes slide slowly over to mine and if the room was better lit, I think I'd see that blush from earlier creeping back. "You're not so bad yourself," she whispers.

We watch *Notting Hill*, which I admit is a great movie, and eat our Creole Chicken. Well, Charlotte eats hers like a lady and I do my best to not inhale mine like a starving child from a third-world country.

I ate today, both before and after the game, but I also expelled a lot of calories and nothing tasted quite as good as the bowl of food I just finished.

I was meant to be in New Orleans.

Everything about this city agrees with me—the warm temps, the rich culture, delicious food...and the beautiful creature by my side. Charlotte has somehow inched her way over and is now tucked under my arm that's resting on the back of the couch.

Peering down at her, I watch her as she gets lost in the movie. Every once in a while her tongue darts out to wet her lips and I have to think of every baseball stat I know to keep my dick from making its presence known.

I'm a gentleman, my mom and dad raised me to be one.

But I'm also just a man.

A man who hasn't been with a woman in almost a year.

And I'm trying my fucking hardest to keep myself in check.

But when the credits begin to roll on the screen and Charlotte rests her hand on my thigh, her fingers moving slightly, I'm a goner. When my breath gets caught in my chest, she turns her gaze from the television to me.

"Sorry," she says quietly, looking down at her hand, and I swear to God, her eyes get caught on the bulge in my pants. It's like she physically stroked me and I'm back to baseball stats, closing my eyes to breathe. But that's a lost cause, because with each deep inhale I'm coating my insides with the scent of her...sweet, spicy, musky...delicious.

Soft lips graze the edge of my mouth and I jerk, my eyes flying open to meet Charlotte's, which are now less than an inch from my face. "I've wanted to do that since you licked the Nutella off my mouth at the crepe truck."

It's a quiet, honest confession that goes all through me.

The feel of her lips is still on the small spot at the edge of my mouth and I want more.

Reaching up, I wrap a loose strand of her hair around my finger, stroking her cheek with the pad of my thumb. So soft. "What else have you wanted to do?" I ask.

She pauses for a second, searching my face, and then leans in, placing her lips directly over mine. At first, it's a chaste kiss...our lips hover over each other's, making occasional contact. Then, I can't stand it anymore, the need to taste her overwhelms me and I go for it, swiping my tongue along her lips.

When she groans and gives me access to her mouth, I feel adrenaline push through my veins.

It's like I just hit a pop fly and I'm running for my life around the bases.

Charlotte's hands come up to grip the front of my t-shirt, balling it into her fists, and the next thing I know she's straddling my lap, grinding herself against me. It takes every ounce of restraint to not flip her onto her back and have my way with her, but instead, I grip her ass and let her use me for her pleasure.

With her hands now roaming through my hair, our kiss increases in intensity and Charlotte's soft little moans continue. When I squeeze harder on her ass, kneading the voluptuous mounds, she breaks away from our kiss, leaning her forehead into mine. "Oh, my God," she breathes, her hips still making slow movements against my dick that's trapped inside my jeans, begging for release.

"We should…" I start, trying to find the right words, because as much as I want this…want her…I also want to do this right.

"Slow down," Charlotte finishes for me, breathless. "I know."

We share the same air, our noses and foreheads touching as we try to come down from the momentary high.

"I want to take you on a date," I tell her, pulling her closer to me. "And I want a lot of other things, but I really want to take my time with you."

I feel her smile against my cheek. "I like that."

"I like you," I admit, my hands making lazy trips up and down her back.

"Stay the night?" she asks. "Just to sleep."

"We'll see," I tell her, already knowing the answer to that when she turns around and presses her back to my chest, using me as a pillow.

Draping my arm around her, we use the television to distract us from what we really want to be doing. At some point during the night, I wake up to a warm body covering mine. I'm wedged further down into the couch, and Charlotte has flipped over, her leg tossed over mine.

It's the most intimate thing I've ever experienced. I've never just slept in the same bed as a woman, and even though we're still on the couch, it's close enough. Brushing her hair off her forehead, I place a kiss there, wrapping my arms around her to make sure she doesn't fall off and I go back to sleep.

CHAPTER 12

Charlotte

WAKING UP ON THE COUCH ISN'T UNUSUAL FOR ME. SOMETIMES, AFTER A LATE night—or early morning rather—in the studio, I'll come in here and flip on Netflix to help me get my mind off of songs and lyrics.

But last night was different.

This morning feels different.

Bo was here. I can still smell his spicy, clean manly goodness. It's all over the pillow beneath me...and me. That was probably the best night's sleep I've had in ages.

When I hear Casey laughing in the kitchen, I jump up from the couch and walk quietly in that direction, pulling up short when I see my little sister perched on the island. She's full-on belly laughing, but that's not what stops me in my tracks. That honor belongs to the man—yeah, man—standing in my kitchen wearing the white t-shirt and faded blue jeans he showed up in my house in last night.

He's barefoot.

His hair is tousled from sleep.

And he's wielding a spatula, using it like a baseball bat to re-enact something for my sister.

With the stack of pancakes on the plate beside the stove, paired with the growing heap of bacon and the large glass of green...something...I'd expect my kitchen to be in complete disarray. But everything is nice and tidy. The dishes soaking in the sink.

"Morning, sleepyhead," Casey says in a knowing tone, shooting me a conspiratorial smirk. "Did you know we had a boy sleepover last night?" She points to Bo, faking shock and awe.

Bo laughs, giving me a wide, sparkling white smile, not looking the least bit embarrassed or out of place. "Good morning, sunshine."

I smile back at them and give a small wave.

"You should totally take a selfie," Casey teases. "Woke up like dis."

I roll my eyes and fluff my hair, which I'm sure looks like a wreck. It was already messy before Bo came over. And then we...well, I guess we made out? Dry humped? I haven't done that since I was a teenager. Giving a light chuckle at the thought, I ease my way into the kitchen, wondering what this new-found territory means for us.

When Bo leans over and places a soft kiss on my cheek, whispering, "Beautiful," I melt.

Apparently, we're doing this.

Whatever this is.

I'm here for it.

"Bacon, huh?" I ask, returning the kiss with a hug, needing to feel him close to me and breathe him in one more time. "I took you more for an egg white omelet kind of guy."

"How very stereotypical of you," he teases when we break the hug and he goes back to his task at hand. "But truthful, which is why I have this."

The green thing I noticed in the glass beside the stove is now in Bo's hand. I cringe. "What's that?"

"Well, the only vegetables you had in your fridge or freezer was frozen spinach, which worked out quite nicely. So, it's coconut milk, banana, frozen spinach, and a spoonful of peanut butter."

Casey jumps off the counter and walks over to place an empty glass in the sink. "It's actually really freakin' good."

"As for the bacon," Bo continues, "I haven't had the pleasure of indulging in real bacon since the last time I was at home. Normally, it's turkey bacon for me. Gotta watch my girlish figure."

With his back to us, Casey and I exchange a wide-eye understanding that there is nothing girly about Bo Bennett. I also squint my eyes at her, as if silently telling her to not even go there. I share everything with my sister, but not men...and definitely not Bo. It's not lost on me that he's actually closer to her age than mine, but that's irrelevant, because he's mine.

There's a five year difference between us, but age has never been a big deal for me. Usually, the guys I date are older. I tend to go for someone who's more mature, but Bo's nothing like other guys I've dated, regardless of their age.

He's mature and committed. He's honest and chivalrous, which according to my mom is a lost trait. But it's not lost on Bo. Last night, I was ready to go all the way. I wanted him in my bed. I wanted to feel him... everywhere. And I could tell he did too, but there was also this barrier, something that let me know we wouldn't get there, not last night.

And I'm okay with that.

Contrary to popular belief, I'm not the typical musician who's sleeping with bandmates and groupies. At twenty-nine, I've had three serious relationships. And I'm not saying I'm virginal, I've done the one-night stand thing in the past, but that's not me, not at this point in my life.

I'm smarter, wiser, and less tolerant of people's bullshit.

"Breakfast is served," Bo states, handing me a plate of bacon and pancakes.

"Smells amazing," I tell him, walking over to the breakfast nook and taking a seat. Casey and Bo sit on either side of me and we fall into comfortable conversation, playing an old Carradine Family Favorite, Fave Five. It's a game we used to play any time we sat down at the dinner table. My mom said we didn't spend enough time as a family, so what little time we had—which was usually dinner—we had to use wisely.

"Favorite band," Casey says.

"Is that a loaded question?" Bo asks, side-eyeing me.

"Nope, give us your knee-jerk response," Casey says before taking another bite of pancakes.

"Queen."

Casey snorts, "How about this decade?"

"Lola and Flight of Feelings," he muses, smiling down at his plate.

When Casey catches my eye above his head, she quirks her eyebrow at me, silently asking, "*did you hear that?*" I'll admit, it's impressive, not many people realize my band even has a name, so kudos to him for doing his homework. I'd like to reward him for that answer.

"Favorite Ninja Turtle," Bo shoots back, eating a piece of bacon like it's fucking gold...savoring each bite, and making me wish I was the fucking bacon.

Get a grip, Charlotte.

Without thinking, and totally oblivious to my inner, dirty thoughts, Casey replies, "Donatello because he wears purple."

"Raphael," I add, trying to get my head out of the gutter. "He's pretty badass."

Bo nods his head in agreement, a thoughtful expression on his face like we're discussing politics or world hunger. "I'm more of a Leonardo guy myself. He's wise, calm, and a brutal trainer."

"You've put way too much thought into that one," Casey teases.

"Favorite ice cream," I say, making it an easy one.

Casey shakes her head, "that's like asking me to pick my favorite child."

"Of which you don't have," I deadpan.

"But if I did."

The table goes quiet for a second and then Casey rebounds with a response. "Fine, if you're making me choose, Cherry Garcia."

"Rocky Road," Bo says. "Hands down. When I go off the rails...I do it in a blaze of glory."

"All or nothing," I tell him, licking syrup off the tip of my finger, knowing exactly what I'm doing and getting the exact response I was going for.

Bo swallows hard, his eyes focused on my mouth. "Balls to the wall," he murmurs absentmindedly.

"Okay, no balls talk at the table," Casey chides. As she stands up, her chair scrapes the tile and breaks the momentary trance Bo was in. I watch as he shakes his head and then clears his throat.

"I have to go home and shower, then put in a couple hours at the gym, but then I'll be back to pick you up...say seven o'clock?" he asks, changing the subject as he starts to clear the table.

"Sounds great," I reply, taking the plates from his hand. "You cooked. I'll clean."

"No, I'll wash up the dishes," Bo argues, trying to take the plates back from me, but I don't let him.

"I'm going to shower," Casey calls out, exiting the kitchen and tossing a wave over her shoulder. "See you later, Bo."

"Later," Bo calls back.

"No one ever cooks for me," I tell him, standing on my toes, loving that I have to do that with him if I want to look him in the eyes. "So, I'll clean up." Placing a soft, slow kiss on his lips, I win the tug-of-war.

"Well, you did feed me dinner and breakfast," Bo counters, our mouths still in touching distance, his breath smelling of sweet syrup and yummy bacon. *I could have him for seconds.*

I let out a content sigh against him, smiling lazily. "I'll think of a way you can repay me."

After Bo leaves, I walk dreamily through the house, loving the way his presence lingers even after he's gone and also pinching myself to make sure the last twenty-four hours were real. After the whole Cody DiMarco incident, I wasn't sure if Bo would stick around, figuring I was too much for his structured life. So, the fact that he called me last night and took the chance on me is giving me all the feelings.

And he's taking me on a date.

A real, honest-to-goodness date.

I can't remember the last time I went on one.

Casey helps me get ready, picking out my outfit, claiming if she left me to my own devices I'd walk out of the house looking like a rocker chic.

Duh.

But the ensemble she helped me piece together is a nice change. It's a little Charlotte and a little Lola. The yellow sundress is feminine, helping me feel girly and pretty. While the combat boots are badass and help me keep my edge. My trusty leather jacket pulls the outfit together and when I look at myself in the mirror, I feel like I'm ready for anything.

With my dark hair in curls and my makeup much lighter than what I'd wear for a concert or public appearance, I feel...softer, but in a good way.

Bo pulls up in the drive at six fifty-eight. I don't even make it to the backdoor before there's a light tap. When I open it, I'm left with the same feeling from this morning...stopped in my tracks, but in a completely different way.

He's wearing a black button-down shirt with the sleeves rolled up to his elbows, putting on display those strong forearms I'm so attracted to. In place of his standard faded jeans are a pair of dark washed denim and where he's normally wearing sneakers are some stylish black boots.

I swallow.

Hard.

And then give him a once over one more time, for good measure.

"I don't know," Bo murmurs, coming close enough to touch a strand of my hair, catching it around his finger like he did last night, making my stomach flip and coil. "Maybe it's a bad idea to take you out..."

I pause and lick my lips, tasting the sweet lip gloss I applied just a few minutes ago.

"You're too gorgeous for words," he continues. "I kinda want to keep you all to myself."

Oh, sweet Jesus.

"But I promised you a date and I never go back on my promises."

Those words ring true. I believe him. I believe that he's always true to his word.

Bo holds my hand as we walk to the car and when we get there, just like every other time we've ventured out together, he opens my door and waits for me to get inside. As we approach the main road, he turns left.

"Where are we going?" I ask, realizing he never said where he was taking me on a date, just that he was taking me on one.

"This little restaurant one of the guys from the team told me about," Bo says, eyes on the road, one hand on the wheel, while his other is still holding mine. It makes me think he needs to touch me as badly as I need to touch him. "Do you like Thai?"

"I love it."

The smile he shoots my way is pleased, reassured.

He's such an enigma.

One would think, since he's an athlete—a finely tuned one, at that— he'd be confident, possibly even cocky. On top of his abilities, he's extremely attractive. Typically, when a man of his caliber reaches his mid-twenties, he's self-assured, and often, self-absorbed. Years of people and women telling him how wonderful he is completely goes to his head.

But not Bo.

When we turn into the small parking lot of the restaurant, he parks and hops out to open my door.

Again, the fact that we're here, at a no-name restaurant, not some fancy place that offers valet, speaks volumes about who Bo is as a person.

And that's someone I'd like to know...and someone I'd like to know me. The real me. The Charlotte that only my family gets to know. I haven't felt this in a long time, maybe ever.

Once we're seated inside the restaurant, without fanfare or anyone recognizing either of us, we both decide quickly on what we'll have and hand the menus back to the waiter. He's the first person that's acted like he might possibly know us. The way his eyes scan each of our faces, like he's either memorizing them or trying to convince himself one, or both, of us is who he thinks we are is a tale-tale sign.

Over the years, I've learned to pick up on all the warning signs. However, in a place like this—in my hometown, with Bo—I'm not worried.

It's not like living in L.A. When I was there, I felt like a prisoner in my home. Every time I stepped a foot out the door to even check the mail, there was a camera. I had prescriptions for anxiety, insomnia, acid reflux... you name it.

The month after I bought my house and moved back to New Orleans, all my previous symptoms disappeared. It was one of the signs that let me know I was doing the right thing, making the right move for my life.

It was the first of many.

I'm still struggling with reclaiming my life, but I'm better at standing up for myself today than I've ever been. And unlike most celebrities, I'm not afraid of turning thirty. I feel like I'm just hitting my stride.

"You sure this is okay?" Bo asks, pulling me out of my thoughts.

I shake my head to clear it, taking a sip of my water. "Sorry, I was just…" I wave my hand around my head and laugh. "Just thinking about how different it is here."

"New Orleans?" he asks.

"Yeah, back in L.A..I can't go anywhere without feeling like people are watching me. When I'm home, it's like even if people are watching me, I don't feel like it's a threat."

Bo's brows pull together. "But in L.A. you felt threatened?"

"Sometimes." I shrug. "Like this one time, I was just stopping for coffee, nothing going on...it'd been months since my last album...like a random Tuesday. I walk in, order the coffee, and turn around to half a dozen cameras aimed in my direction. Once that happened, people started stopping to gawk, creating a mob outside the coffee shop. I just remember feeling trapped and I didn't want to make it worse by staying, so I hauled ass. A few of the paparazzi chased me to my car." I swallow, remembering the way my blood was pumping by the time I got inside my car and locked the doors. "It was scary."

I feel Bo's hand on top of mine and he squeezes reassuringly. "I'd never let anything like that happen."

"I know," I tell him, offering a smile. "And I don't think anything like that would ever happen here anyway."

He pulls his hand away and I immediately miss his touch. When he clears his throat, I know there's a question coming, something that's on his mind.

"So, tell me about the other night," he says, leaving it more of a request.

Taking a deep breath, I let it out, kind of wishing our food would show up and I could be saved by the Pad Thai I ordered.

"Other than it being a fucking recipe for disaster?" I ask, letting out a humorless laugh. "I felt set up. Terry knows I don't want to be around people like Cody DiMarco, but it's like he doesn't care."

"Why don't you fire him? Find someone else," Bo says with conviction. "I'm sure there are people out there who would fall over themselves to get the chance to work with you."

The blush on my cheeks is almost instantaneous. For some reason, a compliment from Bo Bennett makes me a little self-conscious.

"Well, I don't know about that," I say, humming my indifference. "But Terry's been my manager since I started on *Life with Charli*." He's been with me through everything. I want to tell Bo that, but I don't think we're ready to go down that road...yet. "I can't imagine starting over with someone else."

Bo lets out a deep breath, leaning back in his chair and distracting me with his sexy forearms when he crosses them over his chest. "Some of the guys have been talking about financial managers and PAs and that I need to start thinking about stuff like that, but I'd rather not, you know?"

I nod. I do know. The second you let someone else start running any part of your life, it's downhill from there. "But the sad part is that for you to do your job, you'll probably need someone else to take care of the mundane, day-to-day tasks," I tell him honestly. "It sucks."

He cracks a smile, letting out a laugh, and I'm mesmerized by the way his eyes seem to twinkle when he does. The dim lighting in the restaurant takes my mind back to last night...and the way he looked when we were nose to nose. So achingly beautiful. And it's like he doesn't even know.

"I figure my agent can take care of most of the shit for now," he says, leaning over the table, his hand coming down to rest on mine. "He's already hounding me about some endorsement deals, and I know that's all part of the package, but all I really want to do is play baseball."

I smile, tangling my fingers with his. "That's all most of us want...just to play baseball, just sing, just act...the rest of the shit is like our punishment for following our fucking dreams."

We both laugh, the feeling of being understood thick in the air.

CHAPTER 13

Bo

LISTENING TO THE BAT CRACK DURING BATTING PRACTICE IS LIKE MEDITATION FOR me.

It centers me, grounds me.

Everything about a baseball diamond is so familiar to me. It can calm me when nothing else can, and I need it today. After my date with Charlotte last night, we made out like horny teenagers in the front seat of my car, complete with fogging up the windows.

She asked me to come in and I wanted to—God knows I did—but for the second night in a row, I put the brakes on.

I will have Charlotte.

I'll have her nice and slow.

I'll have her fast and furious.

But when I do, I want to be able to savor it—savor her—and I knew since we have an early game today, I'd need to be at the field by seven to make it through my normal pre-game routine.

It was almost midnight when I made it back to the apartment last night, much to the dismay of my roommates. Luis and Jorge looked at me like I'd grown an extra head when I walked in the door. I also got the Spanish Inquisition.

Where was I?

Who was I with?

Did I know what time it is?

It's like they're my parents and I missed curfew.

But this morning, when I woke up with the worst case of morning wood I've ever had in my entire life and Charlotte front and center on my mind, I wished I had stayed.

I wished I had taken her up on her offer.

Responsibilities be damned.

I wished I had spent the night wrapped up in Charlotte.

And that thought freaks me the hell out. A month ago, I was determined to not have any distractions. I've made it. I'm here, living my dream, and I've never let anything or anyone stand in my way. As much as I'd like to deny it, Charlotte is definitely a distraction. Just the fact that I'm regretting not sharing a bed with her last night is a big glaring sign—a fucking neon light.

But it's too late. She's under my skin. And this thing between us feels like a locomotive. It's taken a while for us to get going, but now that we are, it'd take a force of nature to stop us.

Fortunately, I worked out most of the tension I woke up with during warm-ups. The lingering buzz under my skin is reminiscent of the way I feel before any given game, but this time, I know it has everything to do with a dark-haired beauty and less to do with a game I've loved my entire life.

"Rook," Davies says, clasping his hand on my shoulder. "Heard you were out a little late last night."

These fuckers gossip more than old women. "Is there a curfew I didn't know about?"

He gives me a sly smile. "I'm hoping this means what I think it means."

"Don't get your hopes up," I tell him, not willing to give away anything about me and Charlotte when it comes to sex. When it happens, and it *will* happen, it'll be between us. No one else.

"Dude, how can you be in town for a month and already be making it on TMZ?" Phil asks, walking up to a group of us standing around waiting on our turn to bat.

My heart drops at the question, then starts beating double time.

"Give me that," Davies says, snatching the phone from Phil. Davies inspects the photo, moving his fingers on the screen to zoom in on it. Mack walks up and looks over his shoulder. It's when Mack's gaze moves from the phone to me that I really start to worry.

He knows.

He knows about Charlotte.

"It's not bad," Mack says, trying to smooth over the situation. "It's grainy...I wouldn't even know it was you except for the fact you're a fucking giant."

Just because he measures in at around five-foot-eleven, one of the shorter guys on the team, he thinks the rest of us are abnormally tall. The fact is, he's kind of short for a baseball player.

When Davies walks over with the phone, showing me the screen, my stomach drops.

It's definitely me...and Charlotte.

I have my arm wrapped around her waist and she's tucked into my side.

The moment is ingrained in my memory from last night. Something about her laugh mixed with the warm New Orleans night made it feel damn near perfect. We'd just shared a fantastic meal and hours of conversation. It was normal and something I haven't had in a long time, if ever.

"Must've drawn a little attention...taking out someone like Lola Carradine," Davies comments, partially in awe and partially in disapproval. "I said get laid. I didn't say get caught up with a rockstar and land yourself on the cover of every gossip rag in the supermarket."

"Well, I didn't get laid. I went on a date," I correct, not wanting them to think mine and Charlotte's relationship is anything less than what it is. "And her name is Charlotte."

A whistle has me turning my head to look who's standing behind me. Jason Freeman, Golden Glove winner and last year's MVP, is listening in on our conversation. "Lola Carradine, huh?" He shakes his head and smirks. "Damn, Rook, that's a fine piece of ass."

At this comment, my blood turns to lava.

Davies must see this fury on my face because he steps between me and Freeman, handing the phone back to Phil. "You want him talking about your fine piece of ass...what's her name? Alicia? She was on the cover of that magazine a month or so ago, right? Lacy black number, if I remember correctly."

"Shut the fuck up, man," Jason seethes.

Davies nods, taking a step back. "That's what I thought."

And that was the last anyone talked about Lola Carradine.

Ross Davies has been on this team for five years and is under a ten-year contract, one of the longest in the league. If there was a designated captain for a major league baseball team, he'd be it. He keeps this team motivated and running smoothly.

Later, when we're walking out of the dugout for the National Anthem, he turns to me and talks quietly, where only the two of us are privy to the information. "A high-profile relationship is never easy. I've seen it ruin a guy's career, but I'm not saying that to talk you out of it. I'm just saying it so you're aware of what you're getting yourself into. There will be guys like fucking Freeman who will love to get under your skin by making comments about her...you...your relationship. If you can't rise above it, you might reconsider. But whatever you do, let that shit go and get your head in the game."

The game doesn't go our way and we end up losing by three runs. Being our first loss of the season, the locker room is quiet, everyone taking quick showers and tossing their shit in a bag.

"Drinks at my house," Mack says. "For anyone who needs to drown their sorrows."

"I'm gonna pass," Davies groans, tentatively stretching out his left side. He slid into home, missing by an inch, and walked away with a nice bruise he'll feel for a few days. "I'm going home to ice this and hit the hay. I suggest y'all do the same. We've got another early game tomorrow and we need to show them who owns this field."

There are a few mutters of agreement from guys around the locker room.

The atmosphere is downright stoic compared to the other post-game locker room sessions since I've been here. No beers and beignets tonight.

All I want to do is get to my car and call Charlotte. I left two tickets for her and Casey at Will Call, but the few times I sought them out, I didn't see anyone in the seats. I'm assuming she's seen the photo and maybe decided to lay low for the night.

When I step out of the locker room and into the long corridor that leads to the player parking, I hear them before I see them—people, cameras.

"Bo!" someone calls out making my head snap up and flashes blind me. "Over here, Bo!"

My head is spinning as I look around, thankful for the gate at the end of the corridor keeping them at bay, but feeling like a caged animal. I could retreat back to the locker room, but I'd rather get the hell out of here.

"Bo, is it true you're dating Lola Carradine?" one yells.

"Bo, tell us about your relationship with Lola."

More clicks of a camera paired with flashes of light.

"Do you know if she's been in rehab recently?"

What the fuck?

"How long have you been dating?"

"Is it serious?"

A hand comes up on my shoulder, scaring the shit out of me, but when I turn around, it's Davies standing behind me with a scowl on his face. "Fucking vultures," he mutters, guiding me to a narrow hallway to our left. "No comment."

Twisting the knob, he shoves me into the dark space. "Keep walking," he instructs. "There's another side entrance at the end of this hallway. You can ride with me and I'll drop you at your place. You can catch a ride with Luis or Jorge tomorrow."

I swear, the theme song to the Twilight Zone is playing in my head. I have no idea what just happened or how I ended up here. "Thanks, man," I mutter, feeling like I owe him for coming to my rescue. I'm not a fucking damsel in distress, but I was not prepared for that.

"Always tell them no comment," Davies instructs as we start to see light coming from a closed door ahead of us. "Keep your head down, don't make eye contact. They can smell fear."

Once we get to the door, he pushes it open and we're immediately bombarded by a couple rogue photographers. When the questions start flying, I duck my head and follow Davies to his car, muttering, "No comment."

CHAPTER 14

Charlotte

"LOLA, ARE YOU LISTENING?" TERRY ASKS. I'VE ONLY HEARD HIM DRONE ON AND ON about my career for the last fucking hour, so long I missed any chance of seeing Bo play today.

After a long night and half the morning in the studio—needing something to keep my mind off of my building sexual frustration—I had finally decided to pull myself up and go catch the last half of Bo's game. But before Casey and I could get out the door, Terry called.

I let it go to voicemail at first, but when he immediately dialed me back, I knew I had to answer. His level of persistence knows no bounds.

At first, I thought it was just a typical call, some other publicity stunt he wanted me to participate in or some rumor he'd heard, but then he dropped the bomb.

Another photo surfaced earlier today. But this time, instead of showing me doing a line of coke in a grungy club, I'm on the arm of one of the best rookies in baseball. I felt like my heart stopped beating. It's the last thing I wanted to happen. The bubble I felt like I was floating in since coming back from L.A. burst in a spectacular fashion.

"Listen," Terry continues. "Musicians and athletes make great couples. The media will eat this shit up. I mean, I can't believe I didn't think about it myself...kudos to you, kid. For once, you've made a choice without consulting me first and it actually turned out in your favor." He sighs and I know, secretly, he's pissed as hell.

The first rule he ever set for me, back when I was barely old enough to sign my own name, was I don't do anything without contacting him first. Never sign, speak, or agree without running it past him first. Shit, when I was younger, I felt like I couldn't fucking sneeze without his permission. The older I got, the more of a backbone I grew, the less I consulted Terry.

If you ask him, he would say that was my demise.

According to him, he's been trying to dig me out of a hole since I was eighteen years old and disappeared off the face of the earth. That time of my life is one I don't like to think about, even though I do, every fucking day. I also don't like to talk about it. It's done. Over. There's nothing I can do about it, so I've been trying to move on...for the last eleven years.

Eleven years, two months, and seventeen days.

I've been counting.

When I still don't reply to his self-indulgent monologue, he continues to talk. "So, here's what you do," he instructs, changing his tone to one of pure business. "You and Bo Bennett, you go out, you be seen. I'm going to need you to schedule at least two public appearances a week. We'll cultivate a relationship, at least in the eyes of the media. We'll play it up, showing you with this wholesome, boy-next-door type. To everyone else, it'll seem like you've really made the turn toward home, coming back to your roots. People who were your fans during the *Life with Charli* days will be eating this up with a fucking spoon."

His excitement would be contagious if it weren't for the fact that every word he spews makes me want to fucking hurl.

"No," I tell him, my voice unrecognizable.

"No what?" he asks with an incredulous laugh, like how dare I contradict him.

I clear my throat, conviction heavy in my chest.

"No, I won't parade Bo Bennett around like a fucking prize trophy. No, I won't exploit him. No, I won't ask him to go under the microscope with me. He didn't ask for this. He doesn't want it. And I refuse to be the reason he's distracted from playing the game he loves." Swallowing, I bite down on my lip to keep my emotions in check. "So, here's what you're going to do, Terry," I say, as calmly as possible. "You're going to go to your people and you're going to tell them this was two acquaintances having dinner. We were discussing a charity event, that's all it was. And I'm going to lay low until people forget about it and move the fuck on."

"You're not thinking clearly," Terry says, exhaling loudly over the phone. "Think about it." Each word is over pronounced like I need help understanding the English language. There's a long pause and I wonder for a second if he thinks I'm going to change my mind.

"Look, I can tell you like this guy. I'm not sure what's going on, but if you really do like him, why not play it to your advantage?"

It's like Terry can't wrap his mind around someone not using someone else to get ahead. He's lived his whole damn life that way, using people like rungs on a ladder, stepping on people's heads to get to the top.

"Talk to him," Terry encourages. "Have him talk to his publicist—"

I roll my eyes and groan. "He doesn't have one. That's what you don't get—Bo isn't like everyone else."

Terry's cynical laugh sends chills up my spine. "Oh, Charlotte."

He only uses my real name when he's being a condescending prick.

"Still so naive after all these years."

My back stiffens and I grip the phone tighter.

"Think about it," he repeats. "Get back with me." His famous fucking line which translates into *when you see things my way, call me.*

After that, the phone goes dead and I wish I had a receiver to slam mine down into. I need to physically hurt something.

"What was that all about?" Casey asks, her voice low and timid. She hates it when Terry tries to interject himself into my life. If it were up to her, I'd leave this life behind. She wants to see me happy...loves that I'm following my dreams, but like me, hates the rest of this bullshit.

"Terry," I say, knowing that one word will explain everything.

She sighs, coming into the kitchen to lean against the counter. "We missed the game."

Glancing down at my phone that I still have a death grip on, I realize she's right. It's much later than I thought, which means I've been on the phone with Terry for over two hours.

"They lost," Casey says.

I wonder if Bo has seen the photo.

I should call and tell him, give him a heads up while I figure this shit out, but I don't want to add to his shitty day. Knowing Bo, he's taking his first loss of the season hard. He doesn't need me to add to it. Even though he's the only person I really want to talk to right now, I can't. I wouldn't be able to not tell him.

If he texts me, I'll text him back, of course.

But if he doesn't, I'll wait it out...give him a day before I unload this on him.

"What are you going to do?" Casey asks.

I let out a sigh and lean against the counter beside her. "I don't know, Case. I...I think I thought for maybe the first time in my life I was going to be able to have a normal relationship outside of the public eye. But now I realize that really was naive of me..." I hate that Terry is right, but I didn't really think there was a chance I could keep Bo all to myself. Hoped? Yes. Unfortunately, I know how this works. "Living here gives me a false sense of security sometimes. Everything has been so quiet since we moved, but then I remember that I haven't put an album out in two years and the closer we get to the next one, the more media attention I start to get, it probably won't be like that for long."

We stand there in silence for a few moments, letting all of it sink in.

"Bo's a good guy," she says. "He really likes you."

Biting down on my lip, I nod. I think she's right...on both accounts. So, now I have to figure out what to do about that. Do I let him decide on whether or not he's willing to be scrutinized by the media? Or do I make the decision for him and put an end to this before it goes too far?

"I think he'll choose you," Casey says quietly, already knowing where my thoughts are.

If I give him that choice, I think to myself, but don't say out loud.

"You've been happier this last month or so than you've been in a really, really long time," she continues, turning to face me. "And, Charlotte, you deserve to be happy. So, don't let them steal this from you too."

Her words sit heavy, like lead in my stomach.

Don't let them steal this from you too.

She's right, they—the media, the label, my management, people who profit from me and my name—have taken so much. My childhood, my youth, my freedom...choices. They've also given me a lot. I have a comfortable life. I get up every morning and do what I love. It just sucks that to make a living at what I do I'm forced to live out my life on the cover of every gossip magazine out there. That's the part I didn't ask for.

But it's the sacrifice you make when your craft depends on the approval of the masses.

CHAPTER 15

Bo

"CAN YOU TAKE ME TO CHARLOTTE'S?" I ASK AS DAVIES DRIVES AWAY FROM THE stadium, taking a few side streets until he's confident we've left behind any straggling paparazzi.

He lets out a stunted laugh. "You sure about that, Rook?"

"Yeah, I need to talk to her."

He makes another turn, slowing as we enter an empty side street, free of traffic coming from either direction. Pulling over to the side, he parks his car, which is a sick, white Aston Martin. When he kills the lights, I glance over at him. "What are we doing?"

"Making sure none of those cock-sucking bastards are following us," he says, his eyes on the side mirror of his car. "And I need a second to make sure you know what you're doing."

"Of course, I know what I'm doing," I scoff, but even I know that's a bold face lie. I don't have a fucking clue what I'm doing.

"You need a publicist," Davies says. "I know you have a good relationship with your agent, and he's great, but you need someone who can handle this media attention and use it to your advantage."

I groan and run a hand down my face, leaning back in the plush, leather seat.

"I know you hate this side of things," Davies says. "I can see it on your face anytime anyone mentions endorsements and shit, but it's part of it. Plus, you want to make all the money you can while you have a chance to make it."

I know he's right. My agent, Daryl, says the same thing, and I've been made offers. I even have a deal going right now with a clothing line and one in the works for an athletic line. But just the thought of banking off of publicity that involves Charlotte feels cheap.

"You need a publicist to watch your back, if nothing else," he continues when I don't comment. "Your agent can only do so much."

Clearing my throat, I sit up a little straighter in the seat. "Do you think this thing I have going with Charlotte is a bad idea?"

Davies is quiet for a minute, thinking before he answers. "No, it's not a bad idea, not if you really like her." Letting out a deep breath, he rests his hands on the steering wheel. "Every relationship has challenges, so don't let these fucking paparazzi keep you away from your girl. If you like her, she's worth it. End of story."

"Not everyone can have it as easy as you," I tell him, trying to lighten to mood in the car. Ross Davies has been married to his college sweetheart for seven years. They got married at the end of his rookie season. She's at all the home games and leads several local charity organizations. The only thing that's missing is the two-point-five kids.

"Everything's not always as it seems," he murmurs, his thoughts obviously drifting from the topic at hand. I start to pry, but he turns his headlights back on and slowly pulls back out on the road. "Where to?"

I direct him to Charlotte's house and cringe when I see a car parked about fifty feet from her gate with the lights turned off. Davies flips them the bird as we drive by and when we get to the gate, I give him the code Charlotte gave me yesterday.

Before he even has a chance to put his car in park, the side door opens and out walks Charlotte and Casey. They both look a little worse for wear and I want nothing more than to wrap Charlotte in a hug and tell her everything is going to be okay.

"Want to meet her?" I ask him. His eyes are focused on the two women who are dressed in their Revelers t-shirts and jeans, Charlotte looking a far cry from her stage persona. They were obviously planning on coming to the game, but never made it.

When he opens the door and unfolds his tall frame from the car, I do the same. Walking over to Charlotte, I hesitate for a split-second, wondering if

I can just hug her anytime I want, but she answers the unspoken question by closing the gap and leaning into my chest. "Hey," I murmur, placing my lips at the crown of her head and breathing in her sweet scent, honey and lavender hitting my nose and easing the frayed edges of the last hour.

"Sorry about the game," she says, wrapping her arms around me. It's the best feeling in the whole damn world. Not the losing part, but being here like this with her.

Davies clears his throat and I remember that we're not alone.

"Sorry," I say, taking a step back while keeping an arm around Charlotte. "This is Ross Davies," I start, but Casey finishes for me.

"Ace pitcher," she says, giving him a shy smile.

"This is Casey," I tell him, "Charlotte's little sister."

The look on Casey's face says she doesn't like something I just said, maybe the little part.

"Nice to meet you," she says, turning her attention fully on Davies and offering him her hand to shake, which he does.

"Nice to meet you," he replies, giving her a smile.

"And this is Charlotte," I tell him.

"Ross Davies," he says, dipping his chin. "I've heard a lot about you."

Charlotte lets out an exasperated laugh. "I'm sure."

"All good, of course," Davies says, a wide smile growing on his face, showing his mischievous side.

The way Charlotte relaxes tells me she appreciates that he's not going straight for the celebrity card, for either of them. Ross Davies is a household name in his own right. So, they're probably even on that front.

"Well, I better get going," he says, shoving his hands in his pockets and taking a step back toward his car. "You good, Rook?"

"Yeah, I'm good."

He nods and turns for his car. "Call me if you need a ride."

When he's halfway down the drive, Casey excuses herself back inside.

"Where's your car?" Charlotte asks, a hint of dread in her tone.

"Back at the stadium."

"Why?" she asks, her eyes focused down the drive to where Davies is exiting the gate. "What happened?"

"Uh, there were some...people," I say, unsure of how much I want to tell her, knowing she'll take all the blame and I don't want her to.

She groans and leans her forehead onto my chest. Instinctively, my hands come up, gently stroking her hair. "I'm sorry," she says, her hands coming up to grip the sides of my t-shirt.

"Don't worry about it," I soothe. "It's not your fault."

"You didn't want this...a distraction," she murmurs. "And all of this is definitely a distraction."

I sigh, resting my chin on top of her head and hugging her to me. "That was before I knew you," I tell her honestly. "I didn't know what I was missing, but now I do. And I like you, Charlotte Carradine. You're worth the distraction."

Her body sags a little, her grip on my shirt loosening. We stand like that for a few more minutes, her leaning into me and me holding her, until she finally whispers against my chest, "Are you sure?"

"Positive."

"You wanna come inside?" There's weight in her words, not just a casual invitation, but it's like she's giving in to something—desires, her better judgement? I'm not sure, but I immediately take her up on the offer.

"Yeah, unless you want me to call Davies back to come get me, I'm kinda stuck here."

Charlotte tilts her head back until our eyes meet and she gives me a slow, easy smile. "I like that," she says, closing the short distance to my lips, kissing me fully. "Let's get inside before we give people even more to talk about."

As I follow her into the house, she turns and stops. "I'm sorry I didn't make it to your game."

I chuckle and shake my head. "That's the least of my concerns, but I did miss seeing you up there in the seats," I admit, my face feeling a little warm. "But it's probably better that you don't come until we figure out a better way to get you in. I don't want you to have to deal with those fuckers."

She sighs and walks the rest of the way in the house, closing the door behind us and arming the alarm. "You're stuck here for the night," she says with a sly grin. "Guess you're sleeping with me."

Those last words—with me—sound like an invitation and my dick stirs at the thought of being wrapped up in Charlotte. The night we spent on the couch was great, but I haven't stopped thinking about what it would be to have her in my bed, or me in hers, since then.

I'm pretty sure the temperature in the room goes up about fifty degrees. I clear my throat as Charlotte walks around the island of the kitchen and reaches up into a cabinet for a glass. Her shirt pulls up, showing a stretch of creamy skin, and my fingers twitch to touch it.

I've kissed Charlotte.

I've kneaded her ass.

She's ground herself on me.

But I've yet to get my first touch, something beyond what's typically exposed.

"You really didn't have to come over," she says, turning around and walking to the refrigerator to pour a glass of water. "I know you have another game tomorrow."

"Yeah, and I leave late tomorrow night for New York," I tell her, feeling the pinch in my chest from the thought of not seeing Charlotte for days at a time, but I know that's coming. "We're headed to New York, then to Boston. We won't be back home for eight days. I wanted to see you."

"We better make the best of our time," she says, her tone dipping. When she takes a sip of her water, her eyes stay glued to me, like she's drinking me in instead of the cool liquid.

"It won't get any better," I warn, needing her to know what she's getting herself into, like she's always warning me. "I'll be gone eight of the next ten days with only a small window of time when I'm back in town."

She sighs, leaning a hip against the counter across the kitchen from me, using the island as a barrier, allowing us this time to talk and air our concerns without the temptation of touching each other and forgetting about talking all together. "Well, I have an album to finish," she says thoughtfully. "And maybe the talk of us will die down with you out of town. Paparazzi get bored fast. When there's no story, they usually move on to their next prey."

"Even if they don't," I tell her, needing her to know I'm not going anywhere, "I don't care. Every relationship has challenges...ours just happens to be a little unique."

"A relationship, huh?" she asks, quirking an eyebrow, her lips turning up into a soft smile.

I stare her down. "Yeah, a relationship."

She nods, pursing her lips like she's rolling the idea of it around in her head, trying it on for size.

"I just have to get used to people yelling at me and asking me questions about you," I tell her, crossing my arms over my chest and leaning my back against the wall behind me. "I've never dealt with that before. I don't want to say the wrong thing."

"No comment is the best comment," Charlotte says. "Never give them any ammunition. You give them an inch, they'll take a mile."

I nod my head in agreement. "That's what Davies was saying."

"Davies is wise and he's been there and done that," Charlotte adds. "Also, don't ever make them feel like you owe them shit...not pictures, not statements, not comments...because you don't."

Her words carry weight, sounding like they're coming from her soul. She talks about Davies being wise and how he's been there and done that, but so has she. I have an intrinsic desire to share this burden with her, take some of it off her and give her someone to lean on. I want her to know she's not alone in this.

I want to protect her, which is crazy. She's the one who knows this business and she's tough as nails, but I can't help the way I feel.

Instead of going all caveman on her, I simply tell her, "I'm here for you Charlotte...I know that it's not going to be easy, but even when I'm not physically around, I'm still here. You can call me anytime, text me whenever. I won't always be able to answer right away, but I'll be better about keeping my phone on me." Pausing for a second, I let my words sink in, not just for her, but for me. The only thing I've been committed to in the past five years is baseball. So, standing here, in Charlotte Carradine's kitchen, telling her that I want a relationship with her is a lot for me.

"You're a good person," she whispers, setting her glass down on the counter and crossing the kitchen to stand toe-to-toe with me. "Probably way too good for me."

I shake my head, refusing to even acknowledge that statement. On no level in the universe am I too good for Charlotte Carradine. If I had to name one thing about her that's a fault, it would be that she doesn't see herself clearly. I think over the years, she's let everyone else's perception of her muddy the waters.

"You, Charlotte Carradine, are good," I tell her with as much fervor as I can muster. "You're kind and caring. You put other people above yourself all the time." Bringing my hands up to cup the sides of her face, I tilt her head until she's looking me square in the eyes. "You're funny and smart and so fucking talented."

When I pause to lean in and kiss her nose, then brush my lips over her cheek, she whispers, "I think you bring out the good in me."

The air around us shifts as I move my lips closer to hers, our breaths becoming one.

"Have I showed you my bedroom?" she asks, her words coming out choppy.

I laugh lightly, dropping my mouth to her ear. "I don't think so. Is there something interesting in there I should see?"

"Uh huh," she murmurs against my lips as I begin to walk her backwards. "Show me."

CHAPTER 16

Charlotte

FOR THE FIRST TIME, SINCE THE NIGHT HE BRUSHED HIS LIPS AGAINST THE CORNER of my mouth when we were sitting outside at the crepe truck, Bo's walls are completely down.

Everything about him, from the way he's looking at me to the way his touch feels, tells me he wants me and he's not going to deny himself this time. Thank goodness for that. Not that I wanted to rush things. I'm glad we've progressed slowly, but I'm ready. All I think about is what it would be like to be completely owned by him—claimed by him.

With his hands on my back and his eyes glued to mine, I watch the muscles in his jaw tick as he breathes deeply through his nose. Pure, unadulterated attention from Bo Bennett is intoxicating.

There's no time, no space.

It's me and him and desire.

He continues to walk me backward until we reach the stairs. Like a switch has been flipped, his mouth comes down to claim mine, needy and demanding, and I realize in that split-second that this is a different Bo.

Long gone is the guy who blushed at our first shared sexual innuendo and in his place is a man who knows what he wants and knows how to get it. When my back presses against the wall of the stairs, I moan. Bo's mouth leaves mine to drop hot, wet kisses down my neck, his hands cupping my ass and lifting me off the ground.

Gripping his biceps for support, my eyes roll into the back of my head as he licks the base of my neck and trails his way up to the sensitive spot behind my ear. "Aah," I cry, squeezing his torso with my legs and being fully aware of the hard body I'm wrapped around.

Hot.

Hard.

Honed.

And playing me like a fucking violin.

I can't help the wanton moans that continue to spill from my lips as Bo's hands claim my ass and he grinds into me.

"You're so beautiful," Bo murmurs between tastes of my skin. "So fucking delicious. I've wanted to touch you like this since the first night we met." Pausing, he pulls back to look at me, our breaths heavy and labored, not from effort so much as desire. "You scare me, Charlotte. I've never wanted anyone like this."

His confession is quiet and honest, full of vulnerability, and it makes my insides clench. "We can go as slow or fast as you want," I tell him, meaning every word. If all we do is make out again like horny teenagers and go to bed early, I'll be happy because I'll be with Bo.

"Which way to your room?" he asks, his expression darkening.

I don't speak for fear of sounding desperate, so instead, I motion over my shoulder, signaling that my room is up and to the left. Without another word, Bo turns and begins carrying me up the stairs.

We spend the few moments it takes to walk to my bedroom just drinking each other in, a silent conversation passing between us. This isn't just about getting off or a random fuck. It's more than that. Bo doesn't do casual, I already know that. And I used to, but it hasn't been my style for a long time.

This is more.

We're more.

I wouldn't want to label it because I'd fail miserably and probably jinx the good thing we have going, so instead I'm just going to roll with it and let it happen. For once, I feel like I'm making choices for Charlotte, not

Lola. Even though Bo has become a high-profile rookie, this isn't about that. If he was flipping burgers at Krystals, I'd still want him, just like this. I want what's on the inside just as much as I want what's on the outside.

"Which one?" he asks, not even a little out of breath.

So. Fucking. Hot.

"Second door on the left," I instruct, my arms still wrapped around his neck, loving the way his body feels pressed to mine.

Thank God Casey's room is at the opposite end of the house and she's on a Netflix binge right now. She probably won't even come out of her room until morning, which buys us some privacy.

When we reach my door, Bo steps inside and kicks the door closed behind us.

"What was it that you wanted to show me?" he asks with a crooked smile, a hint of the reserved guy I met that first night coming out to play. I like it. I like the combination of shy and confident. He's got the goods to be a cocky bastard, but he's not. The way he balances his God-given attributes and talents while staying humble and real is one of the sexiest things I've ever witnessed. When he lets go of my ass and I slide my way down his body, feeling every ridge of muscle beneath me, my breath hitches. Every cell in my body is firing on all cylinders.

When I take a step back and reach for the hem of my shirt, I notice the way Bo's eyes take a trip down my body and he visibly swallows. Once the article of clothing is tossed to the floor, I make eye contact with him and lick my bottom lip, an open invitation—*Touch me, take me, have me.*

Taking a few slow steps forward, Bo reaches out, tentatively at first, slipping an arm around my waist. Then his grip tightens and he pulls me forward, burying his head in the crook of my neck and breathing me in. Gentle kisses start assaulting my neck and shoulder, and then across my collar bone, sending charges of electricity through my body.

His audible breaths against my skin are like an erotic love song, permeating my soul.

Slowly, he kisses his way down my body. Kneeling at my feet, Bo begins to unbutton my jeans, his mouth now devoted to the skin just above the waistband of my panties.

Close—*so close*—to where I want him, but then again, I want him everywhere. My knees feel weak as he touches and tastes, taking his time. I run my hands through his hair, gripping the strands when his tongue darts under the thin fabric. My pants aren't even all the way off and I feel like I could come at any moment. The build-up is making me physically ache with need.

"Bo." I moan his name, my fingers tangling with the soft strands of his hair. When I pull a little too hard, he hisses, looking up at me through the longest eyelashes I've ever seen on a man.

It should be against the law.

"What do you want, Charlotte?" he asks, his voice rough with need.

Staring down at this beautiful man who's basically worshipping at my alter, I feel like crying and laughing at the same time. It's the weirdest rush of emotions I've ever felt during a sexual encounter.

Everything.

It's on the tip of my tongue, but I refrain, opting for the second best answer. "You. Just you."

A deep, guttural growl comes out of Bo as he stands and grabs me, tossing me to the bed. My hair flies around, falling in my face as a laugh escapes my lungs. The look of wonderment on Bo's face as he hovers above makes time stand still.

"What do you want?" I ask in return.

"You," he whispers, a shadow of some unspoken words passing behind his deep blue eyes. The lazy grin he's giving me grows a little before his tongue darts out to wet his lips, and I think I come a little at the gesture. A low, seductive chuckle vibrates through him, shooting straight to my core.

When he presses his hard cock against me, showing me just how much he wants me, I really begin to lose control.

"Oh, God," I moan, when he repeats the movement with a little more pressure. Even through the denim, I can feel his length and hardness and it's hitting at just the right spot.

"You can call me, Bo," he muses. "But if we're doing nicknames already…"

Kneeling between my legs, he discards his own shirt, putting his beautiful body on display. His muscles flex beneath his golden skin, kissed by the sun. I want to ogle him for hours, memorize every inch, but I don't get the chance. Before I even make it down to his happy trail, he's lowering himself onto me, the weight of him glorious. When I drag my nails up his back, he moans and it's all I can do to not dig into him, marking him, letting everyone know he's mine.

The intense kissing from the stairway reconvenes, but this time there are less barriers. Our hands explore each other's bodies, learning every dip and curve. Bo's fingers skim lightly over the sensitive skin at my waist, silently asking permission to move lower.

In an effort to answer any questions he might be having about where this is going, I break away from him and push my jeans down my legs. After I kick them to the floor at the end of the bed, I lie back and stare up at him, panting from desire. Now, all that stands between me and him is two sheer pieces of material. And his jeans, which seriously need to go. Like, right the fuck now.

Bo swallows hard, slowly shaking his head as he takes me in and I feel like I'm on top of the world, floating on a cloud. "Fuck," he mutters, rubbing a hand over his mouth and then through his hair, letting a low, seductive chuckle rumble through his chest.

"Is this what you want?" I ask.

Instead of answering, Bo dips down, bringing his head to my chest, and latches onto my nipple, sucking it through the flimsy fabric of my bra and sending me into orbit. My hips buck up under him on their own accord, my thighs falling open.

"You taste so good," Bo murmurs, turning his attention to my other nipple, giving it equal amounts of attention while his hand tugs on the other one, keeping it stimulated and my body wanting more...more touching, more sucking, more *him*. "I knew you would. Ever since I got a taste of you that first night, I've had dreams of tasting every inch of you."

The timber in his voice, paired with his words of what he's dreamt of doing to me stokes the fire building in me, the tightening in my stomach intensifying from the friction he's giving me.

"I'm going to savor you," he whispers, kissing and licking a path down my torso.

"Please," I beg, squirming under him.

He places open-mouthed kisses along the edges of my panties, right at the juncture of my thighs where I want him. When he licks my slit through the fabric, I can't help grinding into him, begging for more. Looking down, I see him peering back up at me, his long lashes hitting me full force as his mouth is latched onto my pussy, bringing me pleasure, and it's the hottest fucking thing I've ever seen.

"Oh, my God, Bo," I groan. "If you don't touch me, I might die. And while fucking a corpse isn't against the law in the state of Louisiana, I frown on it."

He stops what he's doing, which displeases me immensely. When I glance back down, he's looking at me with wide eyes and a humorous grin. "You are so weird," he says, a light chuckle escaping, his breath fanning the sensitive skin beneath him. "Like, in the best way," he adds, his tone dropping. "And touching you would be my pleasure, Charlotte."

Always the fucking gentleman.

But I'd like that to be in the literal sense.

The break in tension with my crass comment seems to have released whatever was holding Bo back, because he pushes himself up and sits between my legs, gripping the edges of my panties with both hands and tugging them down. His eyes are glued to me, drinking me in and I feel myself getting even more aroused—if that's even possible—under his scrutiny.

"Beautiful," he murmurs, before lowering himself back down. I prop myself up on my elbows, wanting a front row seat to the show that is Bo Bennett zeroing in on my pussy. His strong biceps and forearms are braced on either side of me. His head blocking me from seeing exactly what he's doing, but when his tongue darts out and licks, I lose my damn mind.

It's been a while, like a long fucking while since I've been with anyone. A year ago, I was with a random guy I know from the music industry, but it was a quick fuck in a back room at a studio in LA. Before then, it'd been a year since my last semi-serious boyfriend and he wasn't really into oral. And I wasn't really into him.

"Oh, God," I squeak, trying not to completely lose my shit as his tongue traces the sensitive skin.

Bo's moans of pleasure, paired with his talented tongue dipping and swirling, bring me to the edge in record-breaking time. My hands instinctively go for his hair, tangling with the short strands, pulling and pushing as I lose myself under him.

Writhing on the bed, I feel my body begin to shudder with pleasure. My legs want to close around him like a vice grip, holding him to me and never letting him go.

"Oh, my fucking...Ah," I scream in pleasure, my hips coming off the bed to meet his mouth, begging for more and less all at the same time. It's too much and yet somehow not enough.

I look down to see him pull back, his mouth glistening with a smug look on his face as he slides a finger inside, then two, matching the pace his tongue was keeping. When his thumb begins rubbing circles around my clit, my head falls back, and I give in to the tidal wave—my legs shake, my walls spasm, my mind is blown. I cry out in pleasure. And then I see fucking stars.

Somewhere, in the midst of my orgasmic fog, I'm vaguely aware of soft, tender kisses and then a movement on the bed. When I eventually open my eyes back up, I'm rewarded with the vision, and I do mean fucking *vision*, that is Bo Bennett—naked, hard. His gorgeous cock is standing at attention while he digs in the back pocket of his jeans, coming back with a condom.

A second later, he has the package ripped open and is rolling the latex down his length.

How is it that putting a condom on can be sexy?

His forearms flexing and his hands on his cock has me clenching my muscles in anticipation. Bo's not scary huge, but he's well-endowed. I'm in the camp that cocks can be beautiful, and Bo's is in the running for top honors. I want to touch it and taste it, but for now, I'll settle for it being inside me.

"My turn," I tell him, getting up on my knees, and motioning for Bo to get on the bed.

His eyebrows raise and he smiles—sinful—but obeys my command, slipping back on the bed and lying on his back. In a bold move, I straddle him and collect some of the wetness from my center and rub it onto his cock, stroking him from base to tip before I line myself up and slowly sink down.

When he's completely inside and I feel impossibly full, I pause for a second, letting my breathing catch up.

"Fuck," Bo groans, gripping my hips in his strong hands as his head buries into the pillows behind him. "Just a sec," he begs, holding me in place. "You feel so fucking good and it's been too long."

That.

That confession.

It's one I've wondered, but haven't had the chance to ask about. We've talked about past relationships, but I wasn't sure if Bo had been with anyone recently. Shamelessly, I love that he hasn't. I want to be the only one who knows him like this, feels him like this, and that realization scares the shit out of me.

But I scratch it from my mind by leaning forward and placing open-mouthed kisses on Bo's exposed neck, relishing in the strength of his muscles and toned body. It's a masterpiece. He's a masterpiece.

"Move, Charlotte," Bo finally commands. It's the most demanding thing I've ever heard him say. He begins to move my hips for me, setting a slow, steady pace. "So, fucking good...better than I dreamed."

"So much better," I agree, my lips just a fraction of an inch from his, sharing his breath as he pushes into me. From this position, I get the pleasure of his cock while my clit rubs against him. It's a perfect combination and like he just said, so much better than I've dreamed. And I have dreamed. Bo's starred in every dream and fantasy I've had since the day I met him.

We fall into a rhythm with the sound of our bodies offering the melody. "Feels so good," I say against his cheek, sucking in a breath when he begins to thrust faster, his fingers digging into my ass.

"Do you like it like this?" he asks, bringing one hand up to swipe the hair out of my face, our eyes locking onto each other's. "Can you come like this? I want to see you come."

"Yes," I reply, on the verge of tears from the intense pleasure and connection I feel with this beautiful man. "Yes."

Pushing up on his chest, I brace myself as he picks up the pace and I meet him thrust for thrust.

"So fucking perfect, Charlotte," he mutters, one hand leaving my ass to slip up my stomach, between my breasts, and then to my collar bone.

When his long, deft fingers wrap gently around the column of my neck, he brings me down to him, claiming my mouth.

CHAPTER 17

Bo

HAVING CHARLOTTE ABOVE ME, WATCHING HER PERFECT TITS BOUNCE AS MY COCK slides in and out of her, it takes everything in me to not come. I want to, I want to explode inside her, but I also don't want this to end.

She's all I've thought about for weeks and now that I have her, like this, I don't ever want to let go. The sight of her and the perfect sounds she makes are invading my senses and I've forgotten everything else. My mind is only filled with Charlotte.

When she tosses her head back, her hair brushes my thighs and everything that is Charlotte is on full display—tits...smooth, soft skin... long, lean neck. Gripping her hip with one hand, digging my fingers in, I pick up my pace, pushing up into her, while I reach down and find her clit. When my thumb begins to circle the sensitive spot, Charlotte cries out, not holding back. "Ah! Oh, my God...Bo." Her words are choppy and my name falling from her lips while in this position is the most gorgeous thing I've ever seen or heard in my entire life.

Better than the sound a bat makes when you hit the sweet spot of a ball.

Better than thousands of fans cheering you on as you round the bases.

Better than an ump yelling "safe" as you slide into home.

"I'm gonna come," she breathes out, tilting her head back down to look at me, our eyes locking. She braces her hands against my chest, riding me and seconds later, her orgasm. As her walls clench around me, her thighs squeezing my hips, I let go, a roar breaking free from my chest as I completely lose myself.

Holding Charlotte to my chest, we both continue to breathe heavily, my body on a high like I've never felt before. I kiss the top of her head and she wraps her arms tighter around me.

"That was...amazing," I tell her. There's no need to try to save face or pretend like that wasn't the singularly most incredible sexual experience of my life.

"The fucking best," she mumbles, sounding sated and like she's somewhere between awake and asleep. "Like, honest-to-God, the best I've sex I've ever had."

I chuckle lightly, stroking her hair. "Come on," I tease. "You're Lola Carradine...I'm sure you've had—"

Her head pops up from my chest and she clamps a hand over my mouth. "Stop. Don't do that. Don't ruin it." The expression on her face is nothing but serious, so I stop talking. "I'll never lie to you, Bo. If I say it's the best sex I've ever had, you can take that to the bank."

I kiss her palm and then nip at her fingers as she finally starts to pull her hand away. "Okay, Charlotte...I believe you."

"Good," she whispers, a small smile on her beautiful lips. When she leans forward and kisses me, it's soft and sweet. I'm beginning to love every kiss we share for a different reason. I fucking love the hot and heavy kissing we were doing in the stairway. And then the ones where we were basically mouth fucking. Those were great. But these tender kisses she gives me feel important, like something I want to remember and take with me when she's not around.

"I'm gonna need to go take care of…" I drift off, but Charlotte knows what I'm talking about.

"Condom," she finishes with a smirk, slowly lifting her hips. And holy fuck, I think I could be ready to go again with a few more slow strokes like that, sheathed in her warmth. The second I'm no longer inside her, I miss it.

Lifting her the rest of the way off of me, I slide off the bed and head for the bathroom connected to her bedroom. "I'll be right back." Turning my head over my shoulder, I catch Charlotte's eyes drinking me in—hooded and approving. When she sucks in her bottom lip and bites down, I know we're not done here.

Later, after we've had another round of mind blowing sex, visions of Charlotte beneath me, over me, and beside me are running through my mind on replay, keeping me semi-hard.

"I have to tell you something," Charlotte mutters sleepily. I actually thought she'd dozed off due to how quiet she'd been for the last fifteen minutes or so. My hand stops stroking her hair and pauses at the middle of her back.

When she lifts her head from my chest, I see worry etched on her brow.

"What's wrong?" I ask.

"Terry called me earlier." Her words sound ominous, but I kind of figured he'd called her before I'd made it to her house. "He wants me to play up this thing between us," she admits, her gaze falling to my chest and her voice dropping with it.

"Okay," I say, letting her know I'm listening, but giving her space to get whatever she needs to say off her chest.

She huffs and rolls her eyes. "He thinks you're good for my career."

"Am I?" I ask. "Good for your career?"

Her smile is sweet and endearing. Shaking her head, she brings her arms up and folds them across my chest, leaning her chin on them, putting us right at eye level. I decide right here and now, this is how I want to have every serious conversation with Charlotte from now until eternity—naked, in bed with her, looking deep into her soulful brown eyes.

"I never want you to think I'm using you in any way," she states. "That's not me. I see people do it every day, all around me, but that's never been me."

We sit there for a moment and the realness of her words sinks in. If I had a magic eight ball, and asked it: would Charlotte Carradine ever use me? Its answer would be: no.

"I believe you," I say emphatically. "I know you, Charlotte. I haven't known you long, but during the time we've spent together, you've only ever given me the truth. So, whatever Terry wants you to do, us being an us, I'm all in."

The small smile on her lips grows.

Leaning forward, I pull her into my lap and my semi-hard cock brushes against her, earning me a quirk of an eyebrow, as if to ask me if I'm serious. I shrug and let out a chuckle. "What can I say?" I ask nonchalantly. "I've been in a drought and you are my oasis."

Her arms wrap around my neck as she settles on my lap.

Brushing her lips against my cheek, she whispers, "I like the sound of us...being an us." When her mouth skims the line of my jaw, I'm suddenly very aware of every slight movement she's making. A shift of her hips and I'd be sliding into home without anything between us.

I want that, someday.

"So," I tell her when she leans back up to look me in the eyes, her forearms resting on my shoulders, "we'll be an us and if it's good for your career, that's bonus."

"Are you sure you're ready for that?" she asks, seriousness back in her tone—concern for me. It's not the first time. Actually, Charlotte has been trying to warn me since our first night together, but I'm not afraid of her or her reputation or anything the media wants to throw at us.

I nod my head silently, licking my bottom lip. "Don't worry about me. I know what I'm getting myself into and I can handle it."

She swallows and her eyes grow hooded. "That's maybe one of the sexiest things you've said to me yet, and you've said some pretty sexy things, Bo Bennett." When she shifts and drags her warm, wet slit up the base of my cock, I groan.

"Charlotte," I warn.

"Did you bring another condom?" she asks.

"No." I swallow, wanting to kick myself for not being more prepared. "Sorry," I tell her. "Because I want you...again and again..." pausing I nip at her jaw and then her ear. "And again."

"How many days until you'll be back?"

"Eight."

Eight days too fucking long when it comes to seeing her.

"Wanna shower with me?" she asks, pulling back and sitting further back on my lap, removing her sweet pussy from the vicinity of my dick. "Then we can get some sleep and I'll have Frank drive you to the field in the morning."

"You twisted my arm," I muse, leaning forward to place a kiss on her chest.

Showering with Charlotte was distracting, but also soothing. She washed her hair and then I washed her. When it was my turn, I got a nice rub down, exactly what I needed after the game and extracurricular activities.

Now that we're out and dried off, we're lying under the cool sheets and a thick, fluffy blanket. Charlotte is tucked into my side. It's the most relaxed I've felt in months. She sighs contentedly, snuggling deeper into me, and after a few moments, I feel myself drift off.

Sleep comes easy.

The soft breathing next to me, a lullaby.

Hours later, I feel movement to my side and crack an eye. Charlotte is slipping out of bed and I'm rewarded with her gorgeous sleek back, but what I really want to see is her beautiful face.

I dreamt about it while I was sleeping.

"Good morning," I murmur causing her to turn to me, a bright smile on her face and my heart lurches forward. How long will she do that to me? How long will my first sight of her, in the morning or after a few days apart, cause me to lose a heartbeat?

"Good morning." Her voice is raspy and sexy from sleep. It's always a little raspy, but even more so this morning. Once she finds what she's looking for in her dresser drawer, she pulls a loose t-shirt over her head and then goes back for some pants. Tossing her messy hair up on top of her head, securing it with a rubber band, she walks back over to the bed and kneels beside me.

"I thought it was a dream," she says, an uncharacteristically shy smile on her face. "When I woke up, for a split second, I wasn't convinced you were really in my bed, but then I felt you...smelled you...and I knew it was all true." She twists her lips to hide an even wider smile. "Kinda felt like something that belongs in a song."

I laugh, pulling her to me, loving how she feels falling against my chest. "You're gonna write a song about me, huh?" I ask, tickling lightly at her sides and being rewarded with a hearty laugh.

"I already have," she says, a bit breathless. Turning in my arms, she brushes her nose against mine and whispers, "It's probably gonna be my number one release."

Swallowing, I push my head as far back as I can so I can get a good look at her. "Are you serious?"

She nods, biting down on her lip. "Yeah, *Hard Hitter*."

Hard Hitter.

"I want to hear it," I tell her, not sure how to feel about the fact that Charlotte wrote a song about me.

"Well, it's not completely finished yet," she begins. "And everyone won't know it's about you...it's kind of symbolic, but I'll know—"

"I want to hear it."

Her eyes go wide with my demand. "Okay, I'll, uh, send it to you while you're gone."

"And then promise me you'll sing it for me live one of these days," I insist, because God, what I wouldn't give to hear Charlotte sing a song for me...inspired by me.

"Promise," she says with a soft kiss to my cheek. "Want some coffee before you have to leave?"

I gently push her back and slip out of bed, grabbing my boxer briefs and jeans, pulling them up my legs and making quick work of the button and zipper. "I'll come down with you."

Charlotte's eyes are on me and a dreamy smile is on her lips. "I don't know if I'll ever get used to that," she muses.

"What?" I ask, looking down to make sure I'm fully contained.

"That," she says, painting the air with her hand, motioning to me—my chest, torso. "It's a little overwhelming."

"You're quite the eighth wonder of the world, Miss Carradine." I don't miss the way her breath hitches or the way her eyes flutter. But it's the truth. I'm kind of gone when it comes to this woman. I don't know how it happened. My feelings are inexplicable. But they're there and there's no going back from here, only forward.

After a cup of coffee and a banana and a quick goodbye, Charlotte's driver, Frank, picks me up at the side door of her house and gets me out without much notice. There's a car camped out a few feet from her gate, parked on the side of the road, but they don't seem to move when they drive by. I kind of wish they would. That would mean they wouldn't be around to bother Charlotte. I hate that I won't be around for the next eight days. But maybe with me being out of town, the media attention will die down.

When Frank pulls up at the player entrance, I pop my head out the window so George knows it's me and he opens the gate. Thankfully, I have everything I need either in my bag or in my locker, so there was no need to go home before coming here, which bought me another hour with Charlotte.

"Thanks, Frank," I tell him as he pulls up to the entrance.

"Any time, Mr. Bennett," Frank says from the driver's seat.

I poke my head back into the car. "Just Bo," I instruct with a smile.

Frank nods, "Bo."

I give him a smile and a wave before disappearing into the clubhouse.

Walking down the long corridor, I feel lighter, which is weird because leaving Charlotte standing in her kitchen, knowing I'm not going to see her for more than a week felt wrong, yet right. I can't explain it, but knowing she's here, and by here, I don't mean in a literal sense, just here—wherever she is, I know she's with me. It's what makes committing to this relationship and all the bullshit that comes with it easier.

Once I'm in the locker room, I'm relieved there's only a few people in here, mostly relief pitchers and coaches. The veteran players usually show up about an hour after everyone else. Davies and Mack, being the dynamic duo they are, show up half an hour later. It's not that they're slackers, they're just a well-oiled machine.

Going about my business, I change into some warm-up gear and head out to the field to get some batting practice. A whistle from behind me has me turning to see who's here.

"Rook," Davies says with a cheesy ass grin on his face. "Did you get laid last night?"

What the fuck?

"What the fuck?"

"Yeah, fuck...fucking," he continues. "Is that what I'm sensing here?"

I roll my eyes and turn to grab my batting gloves. "I..." I start, but stop, because how the fuck?

"You," Davies reiterates. "Your shoulders are looser, like visibly, and your stance is relaxed...less of a stick up your ass." He smirks, arms crossed over his chest. "You got laid and if I'm reading the signals right, more than once...and it was good."

Narrowing my eyes, I silently warn him to stop, because that shit is off fucking limits.

Ross casually unfolds his arms and puts his hands up between us. "Hey, I'm happy for you. And when you play your best game today, I'm going to be there to tell you I fucking told you so," he says with a cocky smile.

Groaning, I brush past him and head out, ready to crush some balls.

"Don't even say it," I warn, shaking my head at Davies as we walk to the locker room.

"Say what? That every game we've played this week has been better than the last? That this has been the best week for a rookie, or any player, really, this entire season so far? Or is it that you don't want me to remind you that I was right and all you needed to do to hit your stride was get laid?"

"Fuck off, man. If you spent as much time worrying about your game as you do my love life, you might be able to keep up with me."

Ignoring my dig, Davies focuses on exactly what I hoped he'd missed.

"Your *love* life, huh? Damn, Rook, you move fast...on the field and off."
Bastard.

We reach our lockers and I quickly grab my bag before flipping him off and heading to the showers. His boisterous laugh behind me lets me know he's not pissed I told him off. It also tells me he won't be letting up on giving me shit anytime soon. Not that I really expected him to.

I consider Ross Davies to be one of my best friends on the team and

I know when he's busting my balls it's just his way of checking in on me and making sure I'm handling things all right. He's looking after me, like a big brother would, and I appreciate it. Being an only child, I can't help but look up to him in that way.

Stepping into the shower, I let the hot water pound against my muscles, coaxing them to relax and loosen. Davies was right; this has been the best week of my career. With twelve hits, five RBIs, eight runs, and three homers, hopefully I'm on my way to an invite for the All-Star Game, in addition to bringing a lot more attention to the team.

It's also been the worst week, though, because I'm away from Charlotte. I know I sound like a sad, love-sick sap but I can't help it. Finally having her the way I'd dreamed about for so long, only to be separated for eight fucking days is enough to drive any man insane.

And, it's not just about the sex. Being with Charlotte like that is beyond anything I'd imagined up until that point, but it's everything else—spending time with her, laughing with her, the smell of her on my t-shirt, those brown eyes, that voice. It's the quiet times and the loud, the funny and the sweet—in addition to the amazing fucking—that all add up to her being the total package. And I fucking miss her.

On our way back to the hotel, I pull my phone out of my bag to see if I missed any calls or texts since the last time I checked, but there's nothing there. With my thumb hovering over the text box, getting ready to shoot her a short message to let her know how the game went, a text pops up on the screen.

Charlotte: Where are you?

I smirk, wondering if she's trying to sext me. By the way, I'm totally down with that.

Bo: Just finished our first game in Boston. On the bus headed back to the hotel…where are you?

A few seconds pass, the three little dots telling me she's typing a reply and I'm *this* close to asking for a photo, anything. I'm literally jonesing for a fix—a Charlotte fix.

Charlotte: Boston

CHAPTER 18

Charlotte

WALKING UP TO THE ROOM NUMBER BO TEXTED ME HALF AN HOUR AGO, I FEEL butterflies take flight in my stomach. It's not a completely foreign feeling. I get them from time to time on stage, especially if I haven't performed in a while. But never over a guy. He does that to me, though. He makes me feel things I thought would never be a possibility.

I've been jaded when it comes to love for so many years. I've watched my parents have a loving, successful marriage. I've seen people I know find love. But I've always felt like that was asking too much for myself.

When I was younger, on the set of *Life with Charli*, I had a friend in the industry. She and I had similar backgrounds and lifestyles. She was a childhood actress too and was homeschooled. She knew what it was like to live under the microscope. We'd spend afternoons laughing and joking around on set, when things were simpler. We hadn't even got our period yet, but we'd spend hours reading through Cosmo magazines she stole from her mom. There was a quiz in one issue about finding love, predicting when it would happen for you.

My results were always along the lines of "*you're gonna have some trouble.*"

We decided that it was unfair to have everything. No one person deserves to be pretty, talented, skinny, funny, *and* in love. It was just too much. And we'd laugh and laugh, making ourselves feel better with juvenile rationalizations.

Being with Bo makes me feel like I can have it all...everything.

I've missed him this past week. Eight days felt like entirely too long to go without being in his presence, which is why I'm now standing in front of his hotel room door.

That, and the fact that the paps have been atrocious since he left. I thought I might get a reprieve with him out of town, they'd assume there were no photos to be had or juicy gossip to obtain. But no. It's been worse. It's like they're waiting on me to screw up.

At the grocery store.

And the restaurants.

Outside my gate.

Everywhere.

Feeling like a prisoner in my own home is something I used to feel when I lived in L.A., but not in New Orleans. My hometown has always been my safe haven, a place I can be myself and blend in, but not lately. I knew it was coming, I could feel the storm brewing, but it didn't mean I had to stick around like a sitting target.

So, Boston it is.

Knocking lightly on the door, it takes a few moments before it cracks open and then further when he sees it's me. One second, I'm standing in the hallway. The next second, I'm being pulled into the dim room, Bo's strong arms around my waist and his soft lips on mine.

"What the fuck are you doing here?" he growls, low and rough. "God, I missed you."

When his nose goes to my neck, breathing me in and his arms wrap tighter, I melt into him.

"I kinda missed you too." With my arms around Bo's neck, I soak him in, immediately feeling the tight strings that have been wound up since he left loosen.

Leaning back to look me in the eyes, he laughs lightly, shaking his head. "What's with the get-up?"

My hand instinctively goes to my head, covered in the blonde wig.

"Oh, ha," I laugh, tugging and pulling it off, exposing what I'm sure is a rat's nest beneath it. "Uh, well, it's my way of going places under the radar. The last thing I want is for the fucking paps to figure out where I am. I'm sure they have a good enough guess, which means I won't be leaving this hotel room for the next two days."

Bo's brows shoot up and a pleased expression spreads across his face. "Now, that sounds like a good idea...also, a terrible one," he says, brushing his lips across my cheek. "How am I supposed to leave, knowing you're in my room?"

"I'll be here waiting on you," I tell him, twisting my arms tighter around his neck. "It'll be a reward for playing good ball..." Pausing, I return the soft kiss, feeling the heat start to build under my skin and knowing these sweet, gentle kisses will only last for so long before things turn heated. "You've been playing *really* good ball lately."

Bo smirks. "Davies seems to think I have you to thank for that."

"Oh, really?" Biting down on my lip, I fight back a smile. "Well, I guess you owe me a thank you."

"I do," he says, nodding his head with all seriousness. "And I have an idea of how I could do that...at least a start." When I latch onto him even tighter, partly in anticipation and partly because I'm just so fucking happy to see him, he pauses and pulls back a little. "Did you really come all this way just to see me?"

I offer a wicked smile, pushing back a little to swat playfully at his shoulder, which is solid and hot as fuck. "Don't let it go to your head," I tease. "Either one of them."

The instant blush on Bo's cheeks reminds me that he's not like other guys. He's different. He's equal parts reserved and confident, and it's sexy as hell. The sly smile that spreads across his face and the way his hand tightens at my waist tells me that even though my crassness catches him off guard, he likes it.

"What else is going on?" Bo asks. "Have you had any trouble since I've been gone?"

When I stiffen a little at that question, he dips his head to get a better look at my face. "Charlotte?"

"It's fine," I tell him, and it's not a lie. I'm fine. I've been better, but

I'm not letting them win. Letting them win would've been me hiding out in my house and turning into a hermit, but instead, I'm here...in Boston... with him. "I'm fine."

"More rumors?" he pushes. "Anything you want to talk about?"

Is Lola Carradine using again?

What is Lola Carradine hiding from the media?

Are Bo Bennett and Lola Carradine already on thin ice?

With Bo out of town, will Lola be stepping out?

Lola Carradine hasn't released an album in over two years.

Will her next one live up to the hype of her last album?

The rumors are vast and wide, some of them so far-fetched and others hitting too close to home. They're tapping into my fears and pulling them to the surface. Can I live up to my last album? Will I be able to finish this one in time to release it on its anticipated date? Those are all things I lose sleep over at night lately. Add all of that on top of missing Bo like an amputated appendage, I knew what I needed to do.

I had to escape the madness and calm the one storm I knew I could tame.

"That's why I came to see you, to get away from all of that," I confess. "So, no, I'd rather not talk about it."

Bo's brows pull together as he considers me thoughtfully. "I'm here for you, you know that, right? Any time, for anything. Don't feel like you can't dump that bullshit on me," he says in a low, quiet tone—steady and dependable.

"I know," I tell him, turning my cheek and pressing it to his chest. "I promise if it gets to be too much, I'll talk to you, but since there's nothing you can do, I'd rather just forget about it for a while."

"I can help with that too," he says, his lips brushing the top of my head. "Have you eaten?"

I sigh, loving the way his arms feel around me. "Yeah, Case and I ate on the plane."

"Oh, right," Bo says, like something just hit him. "Casey. Where is she?"

"Our room, two floors up," I tell him. "She checked us in under her name and we dumped our bags up there. She's ordering room service and movies."

Walking a few steps backwards, pulling me with him, Bo turns me until my back is pressed against the wall. "So, I have you all to myself?"

"Uh, huh," I murmur, feeling heat immediately pool in my belly, anticipation flooding my body.

His voice is low and raspy when he says, "I was hoping you'd say that."

Using his body to keep me pressed against the wall, he drops his grip on my waist and brings his hands up to cup my face. His thumb brushes across my lips and then he hooks his fingers under my chin, tilting it up until our mouths are practically touching. I need them to be touching. I need to taste him, feel him.

Like he can read my thoughts, he closes the sliver of distance. The slow sweeps of his lips against mine make me feel warm and tingly all over. When he licks and then lightly bites down on my bottom lip, I groan into his mouth, opening mine for him to have complete access. His breaths come in quick pants against my skin as he devours me and I allow him to do so, giving it back as good as I'm getting.

When I feel his hard cock pressed between us, I run my hands down his chest and to his torso, eventually finding the waistband of his pants... elastic waistband, which gives me zero resistance when I push them down his thighs.

"Wha...What are you doing?" Bo asks, sounding like he's a few drinks in, but I know he's only drunk on me and that's an empowering feeling. I did that. To Bo Bennett.

Giving him a grin, I bite down on my lip and proceed, ridding him of his pants and boxers. "You seem a little tense," I tell him, even though it's a lie. He seems more relaxed right now than I've ever seen him, except for the night after we had sex...made love? That's a contemplation for another time. Right now, the only thing on my mind is Bo Bennett's cock. "I thought I'd help you out with that."

Dropping to my knees, I come eye-to-eye with one of the most glorious sights I've ever seen. It's long and completely erect, girthy, but not scary. Quite perfect when it comes to cock, if you ask me. The bead of precum on the tip is begging to be licked, so I do. Running my hands up Bo's thighs, I pull him to me and take my first taste.

Bo's hands instantly find my hair. He doesn't force my actions. He just tenderly tangles his fingers into the strands, holding me to him as he elicits the hottest fucking groans I've ever heard in my life. Licking from base to shaft, his breath hitches and he secures his stance. But when I take him fully in my mouth, easing down as far as I can go and bringing my hands up to encompass what doesn't fit, that's when he really loses it.

Bracing his hands against the wall behind me, he begins muttering a stream of cuss words, ending with an elongated, "fuck." When I swirl my tongue around the tip, Bo slams a hand against the wall, making me jump and then laugh, which just works him up even more.

"Charlotte." My name sounds like equal parts warning and prayer.

I speed things up, working my mouth up and down the shaft, one hand cupping his balls while the other is planted on his firm, tight ass. "Mmmmm," I hum and Bo jerks.

"Charlotte," he repeats, his hips trying to pull back, but there's a reluctance there, like he's fighting his natural instincts. Sitting back on my heels, I keep as much contact as possible while I remove my shirt, creating a canvas for what's to come.

Pun fucking intended.

After a few more quick strokes, Bo comes with a roar, painting my chest with his release. Looking up, I swipe a finger across my lips, licking a small drop off, and make direct eye contact with Bo, who is now hovering above me, chest heaving.

His jaw clenches and he visibly swallows before picking me up off the floor and manhandling me onto the bed. When my back hits it, I bounce, causing my already messy hair to fan out and cover my face, making me laugh with the sudden change of location.

Before I can say anything, Bo disappears into the bathroom and comes back two seconds later with a warm washcloth, which he uses to clean up his mess. "That," he says, making a second pass across my chest to make sure he got it all, "was the hottest fucking thing I've ever experienced."

"You liked it?" I ask, already knowing the answer.

The crooked smile on Bo's gorgeous lips is all the confirmation I need. "Get naked," he demands.

The next morning, Bo leaves early to head to the field. The Revelers are playing an early game, which I'm kind of pissed about because I was sleeping so well before Bo left the bed and took my pillow with him. As hard and chiseled as his chest is, it makes a great landing spot for my head. The few times we've slept together, I've woken each time practically wrapped around his torso. He doesn't seem to mind because every time, his arms are always caged around me, keeping me in place.

"You'll be here when I get back?" Bo asks standing tentatively at the door.

"Where else would I be?" I ask in return, stretching as I turn over to face him, drinking in the sight of a freshly showered and ready-to-play-ball Bo Bennett.

His slow, easy smile sends a jolt of electricity straight to my core, which is ridiculous, because after going three rounds last night, my lady bits should need some recovery time.

Once Bo is gone, the door closed behind him and all signs of life outside of the hotel room gone with him, I slip out of bed and make my way to the bathroom. Taking my time, I shower, using Bo's body wash and inhaling it like it's the essence of life. After I dry off, I find one of Bo's t-shirts and slip it on, tying it in the back at my waist so it doesn't swallow me whole.

In one of his duffle bags, I notice a wide selection of shoes, which makes no sense, seeing as though when he's at the field, he's in baseball cleats and when he's in his room, he's usually barefoot. But I make a mental note to ask him about this new discovery.

Bo Bennett is a shoe whore. Who would've thought?

Slipping my blonde wig back into place over my partially dried hair and securing my large sunglasses over my eyes, I pick up my dirty clothes and stuff them into one of those disposable dry cleaning bags. Before leaving the room, I give it a once over and make sure to not leave any identifying traces of myself behind, just in case, and then I crack open the door, checking to make sure the coast is clear.

As I step out, I hear the elevator ding and freeze, thinking about scurrying back into the room, but whoever it was must go the opposite direction, so I let out a sigh of relief and head for the stairs. I need the exercise and the anonymity.

Casey is still snoozing when I open the door to her room, slipping both her room key and Bo's into my back pocket. "Rise and shine, sleepyhead," I call out, startling her awake. What can I say? Sometimes, I'm a pain in the ass, but so is she, so we're even.

"God, Charlotte," Casey moans, rolling over. "What the frak has you so chipper this morning? Never mind, don't answer that."

I sigh in contentment, sprawling out on the bed beside her. "I feel like going for a run or scaling the Eiffel Tower or maybe sneaking out for coffee...take your pick."

Her glare tells me that none of my fun suggestions appeal to her.

"I take it your Lothario has left the building?"

I snicker, turning to her and giving her a playful shove. "You're just jealous you're not getting some."

Finally, she sits up in bed and scrubs at her adorable face to wake herself up. Her blonde hair is in a mess on top of her head, somewhere between a bun and a ponytail. It's funny, everyone has always thought we look nothing alike, and we don't, not really. We do, however, share our mother's eyes. But she looks identical to her—hair, stature, skin tone, the whole nine yards. Whereas I look like my father—dark hair and a more olive complexion. But the brown, deep set eyes, those are the same. Although, with this blonde wig I've been bonding with lately, we probably come closer to passing as sisters than we ever have.

"We should take a selfie and send it to mom," I tell her, sliding up in bed and pulling my phone out of my back pocket. Leaning against the headboard beside her, I press my face next to hers, hold the phone in the air, and take the photo. Immediately, diving into a fit of laughter.

"Holy fuck, Casey." Holding my stomach, I can barely catch my breath. "This has meme written all over it." She's not laughing, which makes it even funnier. But looking back at the picture, I laugh even harder.

Her crazy, wild hair paired with her expression of complete and utter disgust is priceless. I wish I could post it on social media and make it go viral, but alas, I cannot. However, I can send it to a few choice people. Typing out a quick message, I shoot the pic to Mom, Dad, and Bo...not in a group text, of course, that'd just be weird. We're not at that level...yet.

"Woke up like dis," I text Bo with a cheesy emoji attached.

"The apple doesn't fall far from the tree," I text Mom and Dad with a few appropriate emojis.

All the while, Casey is shooting daggers at me.

Ahhh, sisterhood. Where would my life be without it?

Sailing down shit creek, that's where. Seriously, without this little ray of sunshine sitting next to me, I would probably be sequestered to my house and never leaving. My life would be boring. I'd be lonely. It would be horrible. But with her, I have someone who's always on my side and who willingly fights my battles at the drop of a hat. She's my sidekick. Without her, I wouldn't have made this trip. It's scary traveling alone, not knowing what's waiting around the corner, but with Casey as my travel buddy, I feel confident. We can tackle anything as long as we're together. I know one of these days, she'll leave the nest, and me, but I'm grateful for this time in our lives.

"I love you, Case," I tell her, leaning into her shoulder.

"I love you too, weirdo," she says, sighing as she leans her head over onto mine.

"Thanks for coming to Boston with me."

"I've always wanted to see the inside of a Boston five-star hotel," she teases.

With that, I sit up. "You know what?" I ask, suddenly feeling a rush of bravery. "We're getting out of here today."

"No," Casey says, sounding more awake than she has since I burst through the door. "No, Charlotte. We're staying here. That was the deal. I'd check us in, you'd have your fun, we'd leave...no harm, no foul, nobody knows. The last thing we need is the paps picking up on your scent. This far away from everyfreakinbody? Does Terry even know you're here?"

My stomach sinks at that thought, because the answer is no. I didn't tell anybody, well, except for our parents. We called them on our way to the airport yesterday. But other than them, no. No one knows we're here. And even I can admit that's playing with fire.

"You're right," I admit, sinking back into the bed.

Casey repositions herself next to me and pats my leg. "Hey, it's fine. We'll order all the junk off the room service menu and all the Julia Roberts movies we can find. It'll be great."

"I'm sorry I dragged you all the way here," I tell her, feeling the guilt settle in. "It was impulsive and selfish of me."

She scoffs, slapping my leg. "Shut up," she says, putting heavy emphasis on each word. "I've never done anything I don't want to do, you know that."

I do. Casey is a strong person, stronger than most people give her credit for. She's determined, committed, and loyal to a fault. Sometimes, I wonder where she got her strong moral compass from. Growing up in the environment she did, surrounded by celebrities and affluent people, you'd assume she'd be a spoiled, entitled brat, but she's nothing like that. She's an old soul. And although she's still unsure what she wants to do in life, I know one thing for sure, she'll be amazing at whatever she chooses.

And I love that she has choices.

When my phone rings in my hand, I about piss my pants. Looking down at the screen, hoping it's Bo, I'm super disappointed and somewhat hesitant to see it's Terry.

"Might as well answer it," Casey says, staring off into space. "You know he'll just keep calling."

She's right, he will, so I do. "Hey Terry," I say, putting the call on speaker and setting it in my lap.

"Lola," he says, my name sounding like a reprimand, forcing me to roll my eyes. I catch Casey doing the same. "Where are you?"

The funny thing is, I'm sure he knows where I am. He tracks my phone. But he wants me to say it. He needs me to be reminded that he basically runs my life, whether I want him to or not. "Boston," I reply in defiance.

"Why?"

"Sounded like a good place to be," I retort.

His huff holds no humor and I can picture him fuming as he paces his office with all the windows, living large off my success. "What have we discussed about you running off without telling me and why, for God's sake, aren't you in the studio finishing up this album. Do you realize we're down to the wire on this? If you don't get the last few tracks laid, we'll never be able to make the deadline with the label and I don't think I need to remind you that you're skating on thin ice here. They're going out on a limb for you with this album. If it tanks, your career is over."

Geez, thanks for the vote of confidence.

"Relax," I tell him, knowing it'll just piss him off even more than he already is, but not caring. "I finished up the last two songs before I left. After I make a few tweaks, I'll have the files uploaded and sent over by the middle of next week." Just in time to meet the deadline, I think, but don't say.

"And then you'll need to come to L.A. so we can put the finishing touches on everything," he insists. "I was even thinking about getting Blaine Wilson to pop in and do a collab with you. Wouldn't that be great? I think it'd really make the album sell. I've always thought the two of you would sound great together, not to mention, he's single again. We could definitely spin this in our favor."

This is classic Terry. Not too long ago he wanted to exploit my relationship with Bo...now, he's moved on to Blaine Wilson. It's whatever works for him—whatever he thinks will pad his pocket.

Fuck that.

"I don't want a collab. I don't need it. And I've already told you, I'll do whatever needs to be done from my studio. If you need to send people to me, that's fine, but I'm staying in New Orleans until the album is ready to drop. Then, I'll see you in L.A. for the release and the two week radio tour."

I'm so tired of people dictating my life.

Terry sighs, obviously giving up for today. "We'll discuss it later. But for now, we need to talk about security while you're out of town. I'm sending someone over to the hotel."

"I don't need him," I insist, feeling my hackles raise.

"Do you plan on never leaving the hotel?" he asks.

Deep breaths, Charlotte.

"Those are my exact plans." The details of my stay are not necessary nor pertinent to this conversation and none of his goddamn business. "I'll call you when I'm back in New Orleans."

"I hope you know what you're doing," he warns. "I'm sending him over whether you want him or not. He'll be at your disposal when and if you need him. And trust me, you will."

His overconfidence at me needing a bodyguard does not sit well with me. "Terry, this isn't a fucking publicity stunt. If my location is leaked, there will be hell to pay, do you understand me?"

There's a long pause before he speaks again, a little more reserve in his tone. "Understood. Safe travels, Charlotte."

Is it crazy that when he uses my real name it grates on my nerves? I hate it, actually. Without a parting greeting, I push end on the call and shove my phone onto the bed.

"Gah, I hate him," Casey groans. "Like with a fiery passion. After this album, you have to fire him. You know everyone in the industry, surely you can manage your own career. I feel like he's just sitting up there in his shiny L.A. office getting fat off your hard work."

That's Casey, always on the same wavelength.

We spend the rest of the day watching the Revelers beat up on Boston while eating our weight in chocolate cake and French fries. After the game is over, instead of hurrying back to Bo's room, Casey and I watch *My Best Friend's Wedding* and part of *Pretty Woman*. It's basically a perfect afternoon—no paps, no calls, no rumors—just me and my sister, living our best.

My two days spent with Bo wasn't a total fuck fest. We did spend plenty of time in bed together, but we also spent a lot of it just relaxing and watching movies. He's decided *Notting Hill* is his second favorite Julia Roberts' movie, which I couldn't be happier about, so we did a rewatch.

The Revelers swept Boston and I wish I could've been there to watch it in person, but I didn't want to risk it. Laying low for a few days was exactly what I needed. Casey has been religiously checking the gossip blogs and none of them have mentioned me since we left New Orleans, except to speculate where I've been, most of them guessing L.A. I'm sure they'd eventually put it all together and find me here, but it's too late, because in a few hours, we'll be on a plane headed back to New Orleans.

"I'm so glad you came," Bo whispers, his lips on my hair. "Having you here was the best surprise ever...I want you with me at all the road games."

I laugh, wrapping my arms tighter around his midsection, wedging my head under his chin. I wish I could follow him around God's green earth, but this was an indulgence I can only allow myself occasionally. The last thing we want is for the media to catch on to me tagging along to away games. That would create a shit show of mass proportions.

Bo and the team will be flying out in an hour, but Casey and I will be on a commercial flight a couple hours behind them. Knowing that we're headed to the same city is making this goodbye easier to take, but even knowing that, I still don't want to let go.

When there's a knock at the door, we both jump a little. Looking up, I see Bo's eyes widen and then cut to the door.

"Shit," I whisper, dropping my arms and looking for a place to hide. It's not that I'm breaking any rules or laws, but we've managed to keep this on the downlow and I really don't want to blow that at the last second. This has been our happy little bubble for a couple days. I'd like to keep it that way. My wig is laying on the table across the room, so I run as quietly as possible over to it and slap it on my head, glancing briefly in the mirror on the dresser to make sure it's somewhat in place.

"The bathroom," Bo whispers. "I'll get rid of whoever—"

"Rook," a familiar voice booms through the door and now we're both wide-eyed as we freeze in place. It's Ross Davies, so not the end of the world if he figures out I'm in here. Not great, but not horrible. However, I still scurry into the bathroom and silently close the door behind me, leaning against it and breathing as quietly as possible. Catching a glimpse of myself in the vanity mirror, I have to stifle a laugh. I look ridiculous. My wig is sitting a little off center and looking thoroughly fucked, even though it's not seen any action in the sack.

Hmmm. Maybe we'll do a little role play the next time I have to go undercover to see him.

"Hey," I hear Bo say from the other side of the door.

"What took you so long?" Ross asks, sounding suspicious.

"Oh, uh...I was in the bathroom," Bo replies. Yeah, not suspicious at all. One thing is for sure, my guy is not a good liar. Which is good. I like that about him. I like that he's honest to a fucking fault. It's refreshing.

"Bathroom, huh?" Ross still doesn't sound convinced and I swear if I could see him, he's probably peering around Bo's shoulder to see what he can see. "You got somebody in here, Rook?"

"What?" Bo asks, entirely too quick on the draw. "No, wh—why would you ask that?"

There's a pause before Ross continues. "Oh, I don't know, other than the fact that it smells like lavender...and girly shit...maybe some honey or sugar. Are you into that sort of thing, Rook? Something I don't know about you? Are bath salts your secret weapon?"

"You got me," Bo says with a chuckle, a very very guilty chuckle. "Yep, bath salts. Trick of the trade, loosens up those muscles every damn time. My mom, uh...sends them to me. I keep telling her to quit with the lavender shit, but she never listens. I mean, moms...whatcha gonna do?"

Oh. My. Good. God. Bo Bennett, shut your fucking mouth. Laughing, silently, I drop my head to my hand and wait for it.

"You're a damn liar," Ross says. "A fucking horrible one, but a damn liar." His laugh tells me his thinks this shit is as funny as I do, but Bo is still trying to cover.

"What? No...I'm—" he starts, but Ross cuts him off.

"Look, Rook...you do whatever and whoever you want, but I thought you had something special with you know who," he says, his voice dropping an octave to keep their conversation private, since the door of the hotel room is still open. "So, don't go fucking that up, just because you got your dick wet for the first time in years...don't become a manwhore like Wilson. I don't know if you've noticed, but he's got pussy in every city. But you know what he's also got?" Ross asks, waiting for Bo to catch up. "Three kids, all different mamas, paying child support out his ass. Don't be Wilson."

"I'm not," Bo says firmly. "And I'm not stepping out on...you know who," he says, adopting the same lower, private tone Ross was using. "She's here," I hear him whisper. And there must be a silent conversation going on between the two men, because I don't hear anything else for a long moment.

Then there's a *hey, Charlotte* against the bathroom door and I die. "Hope you enjoyed Boston."

Sighing, I focus my attention out the window, to a sky of nothingness as we fly from Boston to Louisiana, and lean against the glass.

"Already missing him?" Casey asks, most of her attention on the book in her lap. "You've got it bad."

"Shut up."

"Just callin' it like I see it."

"Shut up."

"Just sayin'."

"Shut. Up."

Humming to herself, she flips a page. "I'm guessing you're not regretting this trip."

"Nope."

Never. This was the best trip I've taken in a long time, maybe ever. My time spent with Bo was time well-spent and well-deserved. I feel strong and confident flying back to New Orleans and diving into my work, getting ready for this album release. Whatever is headed my way, I can take it. There's a quiet strength in knowing how solid I feel about my relationship with Bo, one I never knew I needed or wanted, but it's giving me a much-needed fresh perspective.

"How are we getting home from the airport?" Casey asks, flipping another page.

I let out another sigh. "I sent Terry a text from the airport. He's supposed to have Frank meet us near the baggage claim, just in case."

"Good ol' Frank," Casey muses.

He's really the best. I've never feel uneasy when I know Frank is around, but he's also at Terry's beck-and-call. Maybe one of these days, when I kick

Terry to the curb, I'll make sure Frank stays. More than likely, the day Terry and I split, will be like a divorce. There will probably be negotiations and mediations—his and hers.

Once the plane lands in Kenner, Louisiana, Casey and I grab our carry-ons and are the first to disembark, due to being in first class. It's the only way to fly, the only way I can fly, without being noticed. As we make our way toward the exit near the baggage claim, my phone rings.

"Hello?" I say, shuffling my bag to my other shoulder, pressing the phone to my ear.

"Listen," Terry starts and I inwardly cringe. Anytime he starts with that, I know he's up to something. "There will be people outside the airport. You know your job. Look disinterested, keep your head down, sunglasses up, and no comment your way to the car. Frank will be there waiting."

"Terry," I grit out, wanting to reach through my phone and wring his fucking neck.

"Hey," he starts, verbally backtracking. "It's not me...I just happened to be on the phone with Frank and he said there are a few cars he recognizes, so I'm giving you a heads up. Would you rather I let you walk into the lion's den without warning?"

Yeah, you're just a fucking saint, aren't you?

"Fine." I leave it at that and hang up on him. We've almost made it to the doors and I know there's nothing I can do about it now, so I grab Casey's hand and tell her, "Stay close."

Terry was right, and more than likely to blame, for the throng of cameras and people who bombard us as we exit the doors. With the paps attention comes other people's attention, turning to see if they recognize whoever the media is making a big deal about. Thankfully, I have my wig and sunglasses in place, but that does nothing to keep them from yelling out my name, blocking our path to Frank and the car.

"Lola, why the disguise?"

"Lola, over here, were you with Bo?"

"Lola, did you just land from Boston?"

"Lola, how's the album coming?"

"Lola, what will be your first single?"

"Lola, is it true you're pregnant?"

That last one stops me in my tracks and if it wasn't for the firm grip Casey now has on my hand and the extra squeeze when she hears the question, I might trip and fall over the words. "No comment," I mutter, dipping my chin to my chest and pushing my way around the man who asked, his camera right in my face.

"Is that why you've been seen in baggy sweatshirts recently? Are you hiding a baby?"

"Is it Bo's?" another paparazzi asks. "Does he know?"

"I'm wearing fucking sweatshirts because I want to, they're comfortable, and sometimes I eat too much chocolate cake and French fries. What the fuck is it to you?" That's what I want to say, but I don't. I just keep my head down, and Casey as close to my back as possible, and push my way to the car.

"Miss Carradine." Frank's familiar voice and gentle hand on my shoulder makes me look up. I'm sure the look on my face is one of pure gratefulness.

"Frank," I say with a smile.

"Right this way," he says, a little more force in his tone, as he uses his big body to make a path for us, right to the open door of the car.

Yeah, I totally get Frank.

CHAPTER 19

Bo

"OH, GOD," I GROAN, WIPING MY EYES ON THE SLEEVE OF MY SHIRT.

Charlotte tsks from across the kitchen, facing me on the other side of the island. "Don't rub your eyes, it makes it worse."

I laugh. "Well, it's either wipe my eyes or cut my fingers off with this big ass knife you have me using," I tell her, making out her beautiful face through the blurriness of tears. "I kinda need my fingers."

"Damn right, you do," I barely hear her mutter under her breath. "We can switch jobs," she says.

Oh, hell no. "Huh uh," I say, shaking my head and getting back to my task at hand—chopping onions and peppers. "I'm not de-pooping shrimp."

Charlotte's laugh is contagious. "It's not that bad."

Once I have a nice pile of onions, I turn to the sink and wash my hands, feeling that familiar warmth in my chest every time I'm around Charlotte, especially when she's laughing and happy. The past couple weeks have not been easy for her. If I thought the leaked photos were bad, they were a drop in the bucket to the relentlessness of the paparazzi since we got back from Boston.

I still get pissed when I think about her and Casey being swarmed as soon as they got off the plane last week. Thank God Frank was there. But the gut feeling about Terry is getting stronger and stronger. He's a weasel of the worst kind. I know Casey is on to him and I think Charlotte is too, but according to her, her hands are tied until after this album is out.

My goal this past week has been to make her life as easy as possible. I snuck her in the players' entrance a few days ago and up to a private box so she and Casey could catch a game and get Charlotte out of the studio without worrying about cameras and reporters.

The rumor that seems to be bothering her the most is about her being pregnant. It's laughable. We know that. Everyone close to us who matters knows that. So, I'm not sure why she's letting it get to her so bad. I tried to talk to her last night, but she ended up seducing me instead.

Which isn't hard.

Charlotte Carradine is my kryptonite. I'm completely weak when it comes to her. And that scares the shit out of me more than what's getting ready to happen in this very kitchen.

Charlotte is meeting my parents.

They're in town for the Mother's Day game tomorrow. They both took off an extra couple days to enjoy New Orleans and my mother is dying to meet Charlotte. Instead of subjecting us all to the paps, we decided to cook dinner...me and Charlotte...cooking in her kitchen. It feels so domestic and a far cry from what my life was like just a few short months ago, but I'm not complaining. It's nice. Better than nice, actually. I love it. I love the change of pace from being at the ballpark. Having these moments with Charlotte—cooking, eating, sleeping, watching Netflix, arguing over who makes the best bacon—helps me enjoy the other side of my life even more.

I'd always thought a relationship equaled distraction, but what I didn't realize is that distraction was exactly what I needed. Davies was right. I reluctantly told him as much, which has made him nearly impossible to deal with lately. His head is so fucking big, it barely makes it through the locker room door.

"Did you say they'll be here at six?" Charlotte asks, drawing my attention back around to her. "If so, we should go ahead and start sautéing the vegetables."

Who would've thought it? Charlotte Carradine, on-stage badass, seductress in the bedroom, Netflix aficionado, and amateur chef. I thought I was capable in the kitchen, but she can pretty much run circles around me. However, real running is not her forte. I laugh to myself at the thought. She showed me her home gym the other day and I got in a quick workout to keep from having to leave. She wanted to race on the treadmills, but that didn't end so well for her.

According to her, she was dying and begging me to show her mercy, which I did not.

She went back to her Pilates machine and yoga. I stayed on the treadmill with the best view of my life. That was a routine I could get used to.

"Yeah, six," I confirm. "And my mom is never late." I huff a laugh just thinking about it. "Probably the teacher in her, but if you say six, she'll pull up in your driveway at five-fifty-five and sit there for four minutes before knocking on the door at precisely six o'clock."

"Well, in that case, bring your fine ass and your fine work over here and we'll get this show on the road." I thought the show was already on the road, but a few minutes later, the amazing smell that starts filling the kitchen lets me know *this* is where it's at...like go-time. The peppers and onions, mixed with garlic and melted butter, have my mouth watering.

Eventually Charlotte shoos me away to set her dining room table, which I happily oblige. A few minutes later, Casey joins us and starts pulling out glasses and coordinating napkins.

The Carradine girls are quite the hostesses.

"Meeting the parents," Casey teases when we're all reconvened in the kitchen. She laughs, bumping Charlotte's hip on her way by, to which Charlotte shakes her head and continues stirring.

Crab and Shrimp Creole—that's what's on the menu. My parents are the least picky people on the planet, so I'm not worried they'll love it...and Charlotte. Mom has already asked a million questions, wanting to know what Charlotte is really like, but other than setting her straight on some of the rumors, I told her she'd just have to wait and see for herself.

Charlotte doesn't need me to sell her to my parents. She'll do that with a five-minute conversation. They'll see what I saw that first night—a genuine person who is kind and caring and so much more than her onstage persona or anything the media would try to get you to believe. Sure, she's done some stupid shit in her life. I never said she was perfect, but who is? I might've lived a squeaky clean existence for the last twenty-five years, but that was by choice, because I was trying to push my body to extreme limits.

My past and Charlotte's are on two completely different realms, but we fit. I've always heard opposites attract, but I never knew what that was like until her. We're different, yet the same in a lot of ways.

"Can someone get the bread out of the oven?" Charlotte asks, cool as a cucumber as she sips wine from a glass Casey poured for her.

"Got it," Casey says, grabbing an oven mitt.

I look around the kitchen and take inventory—large pot of rice cooked and ready to go, salad tossed, table set, wine glasses ready. "What can I do?"

"I would say just be handsome," Charlotte muses. "But you do that so well without being told, so…"

Casey's gag makes us both laugh. Even though Casey and I are closer in age, she still feels like the little sister I never had.

When my phone rings, I pull it out of my pocket and immediately answer. "Hey, Mom."

"Uh, I think we have the right address," she says hesitantly. "But there are two cars at the gate."

I groan, forcing down a growl bubbling up from the pit of my stomach. "Just go around them. I'll buzz you in…and make sure the gate shuts before you continue up the drive."

Her audible sigh is full of annoyance. "Isn't there something you can do…or the police?" she asks. "I mean, this is harassment."

I couldn't agree more. But apparently, the fucking paps have rights, too. The only thing the authorities can do is keep them off Charlotte's private property, but that's even questionable. They're sneaky mother fuckers.

Charlotte catches my attention and motions to the keypad, the happiness she'd found in the kitchen falling away for a split second.

"Okay, Mom," I say, ignoring her question for now. "Drive in and then to the left, you'll see the side door."

A few moments later, my parents drive up in a rental car, which looks oddly like the one they have at home—a newer version of the Toyota Corolla I drive. I bought mine from my dad for five hundred bucks, which was basically just him keeping me responsible and teaching me the value of a dollar. I appreciate it. I appreciate everything they've done for me. When my dad runs around to open my mom's door, I smile.

Yep, got that from him, too.

"Hey," I say, walking out into the drive to greet them. First, my mom latches onto me like she hasn't seen me in years. Then, my dad is beating the shit out of my back. "Great game yesterday," he chirps into my ear. "You've been looking really solid lately. Proud of you."

I pull back, giving him the once over. He looks good. Even at fifty-five, he's in tip-top shape. A lot of people comment on how much we look alike, but I have to laugh at that. The only thing we have in common when it comes to appearance is that we're both in great physical shape.

"Honey, you look good," my mom says, coming up to pat the side of my cheek. "Like, really really good." Her obvious approval makes me smile, like always. What can I say? Deep down, I'll always be that little kid who wants his mother's approval.

"Thanks," I tell them both, turning my attention to Charlotte who's standing in the doorway behind me. "Uh, this is Charlotte." Not that they don't know who she is, but I have manners and I always use them, especially when my mom is present. "Charlotte, this is my mom and dad, Brenda and Greg Bennett."

She steps out and walks up beside me, stretching her hand out to my mom first. "Hi," she says, but she isn't going to get by with that. My mom instantly pulls her in for a gentle hug, much more subdued than the one she just gave me, but sweet nonetheless. "Hello," Charlotte says in surprise, hugging her back. "It's really nice to meet you. Bo has only had the best things to say about you."

"What about me?" my dad asks, cocking his head to the side. "Does he say the best things about me, too?"

I laugh, shaking my head.

"I mean, because he wouldn't even be here if it wasn't for me," my dad teases. "Did he tell you that part? Did he tell you I taught him how to snag a fly ball and swing his bat?"

Charlotte laughs. "Yeah, he might've mentioned that."

"Nice to meet you," he finally says, cutting off the dad talk...for now.

"It's really nice to meet you, too," she says, peering up at him. My dad is also freaking tall, which is another reason people think I look like him. "I see where Bo gets his height."

I swallow the thought, deciding to leave that conversation for another time.

"Something smells amazing," my mom says, always having perfect timing.

"Crab and Shrimp Creole," Charlotte offers. "Bo said you like pretty much everything and I thought since you're visiting, we'd give you some authentic Cajun food. It's one of my mom's recipes."

That makes my mom smile even wider. "Sounds wonderful."

When we all walk into the kitchen together, Casey is just finishing moving all of the food to the table in the dining room. "Mom, Dad, this is Casey, Charlotte's sister."

I almost said little sister, but now that I know her, I know she hates that label, even though it's true. Apparently, it makes her sound like a kid and at twenty-three, she's trying to separate herself from that phase in life.

"Casey," my mom says with a layer of sweetness she reserves for people she really likes. "So nice to meet you...officially." When she pulls her into a hug, Casey goes willingly.

"Yes, we sat next to each other the last time y'all were in town for Bo's game," Casey says. "It's nice to officially meet you." Turning to my dad, she offers her hand. "Mr. Bennett," she says.

"Greg," my dad corrects, shaking her hand and giving her an endearing smile. "I remember you. You were really passionate about the game."

Casey and Charlotte both laugh.

"Do you want to know the truth?" Charlotte asks, giving Casey a side-eye, like she's getting ready to deliver some dirt. "She doesn't know much about baseball...or football...or tennis or golf or figure skating, but she loves yelling at refs and umps."

Casey sighs. "I think I have some pent up anger, and it's just nice to let it out at people who deserve it."

We all get a laugh out of that and now I wish I had a video of Casey watching baseball. I might have to make that happen somehow. She's always so damn nice. I can't imagine her getting all worked up like that over a sport. I mean, baseball is life to me, but I know it's not as life and death to other people.

"Shall we eat?" Charlotte asks, motioning to the table. "It's best served hot."

After we're all seated and plates full of delicious food, the light conversation picks up.

"This is a beautiful house," my mom comments, passing my dad the basket full of crusty bread. "I love all the white and the openness."

"Thank you," Charlotte says. "I didn't design it, but I bought it while it was still being built, so I had some say in wall colors and flooring...stuff like that. When I moved back to New Orleans, I knew I wanted something that looked like the houses on St. Charles Street...old mixed with new. Have y'all been on St. Charles?"

My mom's eyes light up. "Yes, we took the streetcar down it the last time we were in town. I was just telling Greg we needed to go back tomorrow, if we have time."

"It's beautiful, one of my favorite places in New Orleans," Casey chimes in. "Charlotte and I used to ride that streetcar for hours, just people watching."

I see my dad's curiosity spike. "You grew up here?" he asks, glancing from Casey to Charlotte.

"Yep," Charlotte says. "We lived here until I was eleven, Casey was five. Then we moved to L.A."

"Completely different from this LA," my mom says, making the contrast between Louisiana and Los Angeles.

Charlotte rolls her eyes and huffs. "Like night and day."

We tiptoe around Charlotte's profession and celebrity status, sticking to safe topics like their other favorite places in New Orleans and recipes their mother and grandmother passed down to them. I've already warned Mom and Dad that everything regarding the paparazzi and the album are touchy subjects right now, so I'm appreciative of them avoiding going there.

Once we're all stuffed like fat pigs and leaning back in the comfortable chairs at Charlotte's dining room table, my mom asks to be directed to the powder room. Casey offers to show her, and Charlotte announces she picked up dessert from La Boulangerie, also excusing herself from the table, leaving me and my dad.

"She's great," my dad says, nodding his head thoughtfully and letting me know he's not finished.

When he takes a minute, I prompt him. "But?"

He turns his attention fully on me, leaning his elbows on the table. "But nothing," he says. "She's great and I think she's great for you."

I'm skeptical. I figured he'd come here to warn me, give me some lecture about not letting my heart get in the way of my success. He's given me that speech so many times over the years, it's literally ingrained on my DNA.

Don't let a girl ruin your career.

One forgotten condom leads to eighteen years of responsibility.

No one-night stand is worth being tied to someone you don't really care about.

I've heard it all. Except this. "She's good for me?" I question, trying to process what he's saying.

"Listen," he says with a sigh, leaning a little closer and lowering his voice when the chatter in the kitchen picks up as Casey, my mom, and Charlotte laugh about something. "Up until now, your life revolved around getting to the majors. That was a huge endeavor, one most people never succeed at, but you did. I always knew you would. But now, you're here. You made it...you made it farther than I ever did," he says with a proud smile, his eyes coming up to meet mine. "I'm proud of you."

It's no secret that my dad—Greg Bennett—was a promising athlete. He played for the Kansas City Bluebirds minor league team. He put in his time and years, headed to the majors, if not as a player, then as a manager... at least a hitting coach. But then, things changed. He met my mom and his dreams shifted to match hers. After another year in the minors, he left and started teaching and coaching. They wanted a family and my dad didn't want my mom's life to be on hold while he lived his. Sure, they could've made it work, plenty of people do, but he wanted something different.

I admire that. I admire him.

"Baseball is now your profession," my dad continues. "And you don't have to put your personal life on hold to be great at your job. You can do both...have both. I thought I couldn't, but looking back, I think if I had wanted it enough, I could've done it." He swallows, his gaze turning introspective. "But you want it enough..." He drifts off and I feel the double meaning in his words.

I want it enough, meaning baseball, but I want her enough too. I can have both.

Before I met Charlotte, I didn't think that was possible or that it would ever be true for me, but that was before. After Charlotte, well, there's only

Charlotte.

And baseball.

They're kind of competing for first place and I like it. It keeps me on my toes. I think clearer. I run faster. I try harder. "She's good for me," I tell him, repeating his opening line.

CHAPTER 20

Charlotte

FOLLOWING A FEW STEPS BEHIND BO'S MOM AND DAD, I DUCK MY HEAD, HIDING behind my new wig—auburn and curly—since my blonde one is no longer able to hide my identity thanks to the airport a week or so ago. Between the hat, wig, and glasses, I'm pretty well hidden, but I can't help feeling exposed no matter where I go and how much of a disguise I wear these days.

They're getting to me—the rumors, the photos, the cameras in my face, the questions yelled in my direction. On the outside, I'm trying to stay positive and unaffected, but I can't help it.

It was something about the pregnancy rumors that started at the airport that pricked the surface. Since then, every misguided report about me or Bo or us as a couple digs a little deeper.

"You coming, Honey?" Brenda asks, pausing to stretch an arm out to me.

"Coming," I say, taking her outstretched hand and jogging to catch up.

"You okay?" Her concern is sweet and motherly and it makes me miss my own mom, who has been worried sick about me lately, which makes me feel a tremendous amount of guilt.

I give her the best smile I can muster. "I'm fine." Now that we're through the doors of the players' entrance, I take my sunglasses off and hope I'm convincing in my act. "I'm good...just hate that y'all have to sit up in the box instead of down in the stands. I know how much you love being as close to the action as possible."

"Nonsense," she says, swatting at my hand that's now looped around her elbow. "I've never sat in a fancy box. I'm actually looking forward to it." Her brown eyes, reminiscent of mine, go wide in excitement. "And Greg is just beside himself. He's always wanted to see the game from up here. I promise, we're not missing out at all."

Smiling, I breathe a little easier. "Casey's excited, too," I tell her. She had to run an errand and is taking an Uber over here. I told her to text me when she leaves the house and when she gets to the stadium...basically every five minutes until I see her. I know she's not me, but I would feel horrible if something happened to her because of me.

"She's a delight," Brenda says as we take the private elevator to the box seats. Greg holds the door for us, ever the gentleman—just like his son—then pushes the appropriate floor number. The passes Bo gave us allow us clearance to everything in the stadium. I'm sure he went through a lot of trouble to make today happen and I kind of feel bad about that too, but I also kind of love it. I love that he wants me here bad enough to jump through these kinds of hoops.

"Yeah, she's great," I finally answer, wondering something and speaking it out loud at the same time. "I'm kind of surprised Bo is an only child." I want to shove my foot into my mouth as soon as the comment is out. That's a rude thing to say. I don't know these people enough to delve into their personal lives. "I'm sorry," I say, shaking my head at my stupidity. "I shouldn't have said that."

"No," Brenda says, blowing it off and giving Greg a small smile when he turns around to look back at her. "We wanted more. It just wasn't meant to be."

And now I feel even worse. "I'm sorry," I mutter, feeling horrible that I obviously brought up a sensitive subject, and also showed how much I still don't know about Bo.

"But we've been fortunate. Bo is the best son a mom could ask for." She beams, her gaze turning upward like she's fighting back emotion. "And I have my kids at school...and Greg's kids." She laughs, squeezing my arm a little extra. "Things work out the way they're supposed to."

I give her arm a squeeze back. "They do."

When the elevator opens, we follow Greg to the designated seats and I smile at the view...and the spread. Okay, this is pretty awesome. There's food and drinks and a guy dressed in a uniform standing by the bar, obviously waiting to take our orders and bring us whatever we'd like.

By the time we're settled in some seats, Casey texts me to tell me she's inside the stadium safely, no issues and I breathe a sigh of relief.

Half an hour later, she's sitting on one side of me, Brenda on the other, and Greg standing near the ledge for the view of his life. The Revelers take the field and we all sit a little straighter, taking it all in. It's a beautiful day at the ballpark. Spring is in full swing and it's nice and toasty in New Orleans. If I was sitting in a regular seat, I wouldn't be able to tolerate this wig, but with the shade and cool air of the box, I'm good.

Everything is good.

Great, actually.

I could never have imagined this weekend with Bo's parents going any better. And as much as I've felt like my insides are in turmoil, they've helped to balance everything out and keep me from diving too far into my head. I'm grateful. It's been the perfect distraction from all of the media and gossip.

"And now, ladies and gentlemen, a word from your home team for today's special game. Happy Mother's Day to all you moms out there. Thank you for spending your special day with us."

"Bo didn't say anything about this," Brenda says with a look of anticipation and awe. "I wonder what they've done?"

About that time, the jumbotron directly in front of us comes to life and Mack Granger appears on the screen in an obvious pre-recorded message.

"Hey, Mom," he says with a cheesy grin. "I just want to say Happy Mother's Day. Sorry I can't be with you today, but I hope you see this and know how much I love you." It's short and sweet, just like Mack. We're actually about the same height, but for a pro baseball player, he's kind of short, but really cute and a great personality to boot. Except, he's known to romance the ladies, a bit of a love 'em and leave 'em kind of guy.

"Awe," Brenda sighs beside me, her hands clasped under her chin.

The screen fades out to a field of flowers, very Mother's Day-ish, and then Ross Davies is on the screen.

"Mom, you're the best woman I know. Thank you for being such a great role model and taking such good care of us. I love you." Ross's Hollywood good looks don't go unnoticed and I think I hear a few women in the crowd swoon when he blows a kiss to the screen.

"He's easy on the eyes," Brenda comments, earning a low "mmm hmm" from my sister. I can't help the laugh as I split my attention between the two of them.

"Oh, my God," I say, shaking my head.

A few more players come on the screen sending their love and gratitude to their mothers, grandmothers for some, and I wonder if Bo made a video and if it'll make it into the montage. The screen fades again, but just as I think we're not going to get to hear Bo's message, his gorgeous face comes up on the screen along with his usual shy smile.

I peer out over the ledge, begging for a glimpse of the real him, but I can't spot him.

"Hey, Mom," Bo starts with a wave to the camera. "Thanks so much for being here today. You've always been the best mom I could've ever hoped or dreamed for. You've supported me, loved me, taken care of me, and best of all...you chose me. So, thank you, for everything."

My heart stops for a second, putting together what Bo just said and getting a vibe from Brenda as she clutches her chest, her focus dedicated to her son on the screen in front of us...the same one thousands of fans are watching from their seats and living rooms across the country.

He pauses, hesitating for a moment, and then continues. "I also would like to send out a message to my birth mother. We've never met, and that's okay." He pauses again. "I just want to say, thank you. Thank you for choosing to have me."

The entire ballpark is silent, glued to Bo's face on the screen and the message he's delivering. My thoughts are everywhere. My head feels like there are a million little bees buzzing around and my skin feels prickly hot. Casey's hand on mine is the first thing I register when I try to regain my composure as Bo's video comes to a close.

"Happy Mother's Day," he says and the screen goes blank, the commentators voice coming back on to again wish all the moms a Happy Mother's Day.

"You okay?" Casey whispers to which I can only shake my head.

Nope.

Not okay.

I don't think it's just the knowledge of Bo being adopted. It's everything. It's the rumors, the pressure, the prying, the secrets. There's something I haven't told Bo and with this latest surge of interest in my life, I've been worried that it'll surface somehow. This entire week, ever since the airport, I've been meaning to tell him, but haven't worked up the nerve or had the right opportunity.

And now, I just feel like I need to get away. This awesome box feels claustrophobic, the seats too close together. I feel like everyone is watching me, when for the first time in over two weeks, everyone is certainly not watching me.

They're all still focused on Bo's message.

Greg is now sitting beside Brenda, offering her a shoulder to let out her quiet sobs on. "It was just so beautiful...my beautiful boy," I overhear her say.

"Char," Casey whispers, leaning close. "Charlotte." My eyes are kind of zoned out like my mind and I'm feeling queasy. All of this is just too much.

"It's too much," I whisper back to Casey, squeezing her hand in a silent plea for help. "I just...I can't breathe and it's...too much."

Casey abruptly stands, drawing Brenda and Greg's attention and she doubles over, gripping the arm of my chair. "Oh, God," she says, panting. "I think I...I don't know, maybe I ate something bad?" Her groan is Oscar worthy and if I didn't know better, I'd think she needs to be rushed to the emergency room.

"Casey?" I ask, trying to mimic her concern, reaching for her hand and standing to support her. I want to kiss her. I could kiss her, but I'll save that for later, when we're away from Brenda and Greg...Bo's adopted parents... and Bo's heartfelt message...and the rumors and the public's interest in my life.

I've got to get out of here.

"I'm taking her home," I announce, turning to offer Brenda and Greg a regretful, but worried smile. "Maybe to the emergency room. I'll just see how she's feeling once we get her out of here."

"Yeah," Casey agrees, now putting most of her weight on me and she can tone that shit down, because if she thinks for one damn minute I'm carrying her ass out of here, she's badly mistaken. Ten years ago, maybe. But not now. "I...I feel like I'm gonna be sick."

"Oh, Honey," Brenda says, springing into action and coming to Casey's other side, her hand immediately going to Casey's forehead. "Well, good news is it doesn't feel like you're running a fever, but you do feel clammy." Turning to the guy who's been waiting on us hand and foot, she calls out, "Roger, do you have a wet towel...and maybe a plastic bag, just in case?"

Roger snaps to attention and scurries off.

"Greg," Brenda says, turning to her husband. "Walk the girls down and make sure Frank is outside waiting on them." Turning back to us, she gives us a sad smile. "Don't worry about us, we'll catch a ride with Bo and we'll call to check in after the game."

I want to spill my guts right there, laying all of my burdens at Brenda's feet, but I can't. I won't. Instead, I offer her a grateful smile and accept the towel and plastic bag Roger brings over.

"Please—" I begin, but Brenda finishes for me.

"We'll let Bo know," she says. "And text us when you've made it home safely. I know it's just a short drive, but with all this crazy media attention, I'll worry if I don't hear from you."

"Right," I say, gathering the few wits I have left. "Yeah, I'll text you. And thank you."

Greg walks us downstairs and makes sure we get in the car safely. Once Casey is inside, I slide in behind her and Greg closes the door. Frank gives me a questioning stare through the rearview mirror, but my expression must say it all—don't ask.

"Home?" he questions, starting the engine of the car.

"Yes, please."

"So, are you going to tell him?" Casey asks, sitting up in her seat and looking as well as can be. I don't miss the look Frank gives her as he pulls out of the parking lot and onto the road.

I let out a deep breath, the first one I've been able to release in a good twenty minutes. "I've been meaning to."

"Really?" she asks, arms folded over her chest. "I mean, I know things are getting serious between the two of you, but you've never told anyone else before, so I wasn't sure."

"He's different," I tell her, my eyes turned to the window. "I shouldn't let it bother me this much, but with everything else going on, I just…" I let out another deep sigh. "I think I need a break…I've been thinking about flying to L.A. and staying with Mom and Dad until the album is finished."

"You hate L.A." Casey's tone is even, but there's a bitterness there. She hates L.A. We both do, and I know this will look like a win for Terry, but I don't know what else to do. Everywhere I turn here lately has been torture. "At least in L.A. I know what I'm up against. My armor will be in place." Biting down on my lip to keep my emotions in check, because I know being in L.A. means not seeing Bo for a few weeks, but I think it'll be good for him too. I know all of this has been a lot for him to take and even though he's put on a strong front, it's getting to him too.

"Being here," I continue, "being in New Orleans…with Bo, I think it's given me a false sense of security. I've been living in a bubble, but that's not the real world, or at least not mine, not right now. I need to go to L.A. and do what I need to do. Bo needs to focus on making it to the All-Star Game and then we'll see where we're at."

Casey's laugh holds no humor, and she doesn't even look at me when she speaks. "I can't believe you."

"What?" I snap. "What can you not believe?"

My tone is sharp, and I feel one of our old-time, childhood fights coming back to haunt us.

"You," she says with a huff. "You find someone amazing, who is so into you…just for you—Charlotte Carradine—and things get hard and you push him away, put that thick f—" For a second, I think she's actually going to say it…just let that fucking word fly, but she pulls back and collects herself. "Put that thick wall back up, blocking out anyone from getting through."

"I'm not doing that," I argue. "You don't know what it's like—"

"See," she says, cutting me off. "I do know what it's like. I've lived this life with you. I've sat back and watched you be used over and over again. I know all you really want in life is for someone to see you...not the rockstar or the childhood star. Just you. And he's giving you that. If you walk away from it, you're...crazy," she whispers.

"He deserves better than this," I tell her. "The first thing Bo ever told me was that he didn't want distractions. He's on a mission to be the best fucking baseball player he can be and all of this shit I've brought into his life is ruining it."

"You should let him decide that," Casey quips. "And stop thinking that you're not good enough for him, because that's the stupidest thing I've ever heard." It's funny that the thing that pisses her off the most is me devaluing myself. She's always been that way. We can tease each other and cut each other down, but we never let other people talk about us, even ourselves. "You're good enough...and you deserve someone wonderful like Bo Bennett."

I want to believe her. I really, really do. But I can't help thinking this relationship is seriously off-balance, and not in the I'm Lola Carradine sense, but in the I'm taking a lot more than I'm giving sense. And that doesn't settle well with me.

Sometimes, you care for someone so much that you're willing to let them go for their own good.

"I don't like what you're thinking," Casey says with a huff, crossing her arms over her chest as Frank pulls up into the drive. I don't miss the black car that's been permanently parked along my street for a fucking month sitting about ten feet from my drive.

"And what would that be?"

"You're thinking about Bo and what's good for him...and you're thinking, somewhere deep in that messed up head of yours, if you tell him the truth that he'll think badly of you and you can't take that, so instead of taking the risk and letting him make up his own mind, you're going to do it for him."

We sit in silence as Frank parks the car near the side entrance.

"And just for the record," she says, opening the door and stepping out. "I think that's...*bullshit*."

CHAPTER 21

Bo

MY CALL GOES STRAIGHT TO VOICEMAIL. AGAIN. I DON'T BOTHER LEAVING A MESSAGE because I'm pulling into her driveway and will hopefully be seeing her beautiful face very soon.

I was disappointed to learn that Charlotte and Casey left before the game even started but that quickly turned to concern when my mom explained that they left because Casey started feeling sick. It's weird that Charlotte isn't answering her phone, though. I hope it doesn't mean she's up to her elbows in Casey's puke.

I'm kind of a sympathy puker, so the thought alone has my stomach rolling a little.

After punching in the security code and driving through the gate, I park and quickly jog to the side door. I ring the bell twice before finally hearing a woman's voice yell that she's coming.

I was expecting and hoping to see Charlotte open the door but instead, it's Casey. Her eyes are red and, maybe, a bit swollen but she doesn't look ill. She also doesn't look too happy to see me here.

What the hell is going on?

"Casey, hey, my parents told me you were sick. Are you okay?"

She's looking everywhere but my face and I notice her jaw twitching a few times before she speaks. "Yeah, I'm fine…" she says, stumbling over her words a bit. "I, uh, guess I just needed some…fresh air. But thanks for checking on me." She moves to close the door but I block it with my foot.

Fresh air? Like there isn't plenty of that at the ballpark? Nope. No way.

"Casey, what's wrong? Is Charlotte okay? Where is she?"

Casey's shoulders sag in almost what looks like defeat. "She left." Her words are short and swift, matching her second attempt to shut the door. This time, I grab the door with my hand and stop it by pushing my way in front of it.

"Casey, what the fuck is going on here?" I ask, feeling like I've stepped into the Twilight Zone. "Did I do something wrong? Is Charlotte upset with me?" My questions come out sounding a little like pleas, but I'm not above begging; I have to know Charlotte is all right.

My thoughts turn immediately to the fucking paps, but now that I think about it, they weren't even at the gate or on the street, like they have been recently, sitting like fucking vultures. And the last time I saw her, which was last night when we cooked dinner for my parents, things were great so, it doesn't make sense for her to ghost me like this.

Casey finally looks me in the eye and I can see now that she's definitely been crying. Actually, I think she still is.

"You're not sick, are you?" Dread and unease settle into my stomach and I think I might be the sick one now.

"No, I'm not sick," Casey sniffles. "I'm pissed. I'm also sorry because I can't tell you anything. So, you should just go home, Bo."

Anger builds in the pit of my stomach, mixing with the nauseous feeling that just came over me and it's a bad combination. "That's bullshit and you know it. What happened to Charlotte? Surely, you don't think I'm gonna accept this and just go on my merry way? Fuck that."

"Charlotte isn't here and I don't know when she'll be back. That's all I can tell you," Casey says, regret lacing her words. "I'm sorry, Bo."

Stunned, I take a step back. Casey uses the opportunity to grab the door again, shutting it in my face and leaving me completely dumbfounded.

She's gone?

Charlotte just took off and left without saying goodbye. Without saying anything. That doesn't make sense, and quite honestly, I have no idea what to do. My body feels numb as I turn and walk back to my car.

I don't even remember driving home.

One minute I'm standing outside Charlotte's house and the next, I'm sitting in my car in my apartment's parking lot. I'm at a total loss—

confusion, hurt, and worry are all swirling inside me and I don't know what to think.

Did I do something wrong?

Does she want to break up with me?

Those thoughts sound so juvenile for what we are, but they're definitely there, nagging, like little demons with claws, latching onto my brain. But what I desperately want to know, more than anything, is if she's safe. That's what is most important to me.

I grab my phone and dial Charlotte's number for a third time and for a third time, it goes straight to voicemail. This time I leave a message because I can't sit here and do nothing.

Clearing my throat, I will my voice to stay strong. "Charlotte, hey, um, it's me. Look, I don't know what's going on but I just talked to Casey and she said she can't tell me anything...but that you're gone. It's driving me absolutely fucking crazy not knowing you're okay. If I did something to upset you, please give me a chance to make it right. Just talk to me, baby, I'm worried sick about you. Please let me know you're safe, even if it's just a text. I won't be able to sleep until I know you're alright. Okay? Please, Charlotte."

I hang up and toss the phone onto the passenger seat before rubbing my hands over my face, trying to clear my mind. I have to act as if everything is normal when I go into my apartment because I don't want Jorge and Luis suspecting anything's wrong. Rumors running rampant around the team would just make things worse. For now, until I can figure out where Charlotte went and why she left, I want to keep it to myself.

I just want to go to my room and wait to hear back from Charlotte. Surely, she'll throw me a bone at some point. She's not a hurtful or vengeful person. Even if I did something to piss her off, I know she'll do the right thing and at least message me, I just don't know when.

It's three hours later when my phone buzzes, startling me out of my video game stupor. Succumbing to the stupidity of electronic entertainment was the only thing to keep me from obsessively checking my phone every ten seconds. When I glance down at the screen, there are only a few words there and they don't make me feel great, but at least they're something.

Charlotte: I'm okay. I'll call you later.

I want to press her for more of an answer, but I'm afraid in doing that I'll somehow push her farther away...she feels far enough as it is.

Bo: Where are you?

Charlotte: L.A.

L.A.?

L.A.

Maybe she had to leave to do something important on her album? But if that's the case, then why was Casey so pissed and crying? My mind starts to spiral again with all the questions and worries, but I can't let it. It's now after eleven o'clock and I have an early game tomorrow and then we'll be traveling to Minnesota.

I need to get my head on straight and somehow compartmentalize all of this, keeping it locked away until Charlotte calls me and we can talk it out. Tossing my phone onto the nightstand, I turn off the television and the lights and try to force myself into sleep.

But it doesn't happen. I lay there for hours, tossing and turning and thinking of Charlotte. I even pick my phone back up and scroll through our last few text messages before the game. All good. She told me she was so excited about finally getting to see another game. Since the media has been breathing down her neck, she hasn't taken any chances coming to the ballpark. It's like they can sniff her out from miles away.

She also said she had a great time with my parents and that she and my mom had a talk. Whatever that means. Maybe I should call my mom tomorrow and see what their talk was about?

The last thing I do is open a search tab and type in Charlotte's name. Photos from only three hours ago are all over social media: Charlotte in her new auburn wig showing up at the airport, Charlotte checking into the airport, Charlotte hiding her face from the cameras when she arrives in L.A., Charlotte looking distressed and completely out of sorts as she fights her way through what I can only imagine are a group of assholes begging for a piece of her. The last photo is of her in the backseat of a black SUV, driving off. It's that one that allows me to finally fall asleep, knowing at least she got away from them. Hopefully, she's tucked safely in bed in some posh hotel or maybe she's visiting her parents...or God forbid, Terry...but it helps me to think that she's not alone and that she's relatively safe.

It's the worst sleep I've had in my life...worse than the night before the draft...worse than the night before I signed my contract with the Revelers... worse than any night I've ever lost sleep combined.

CHAPTER 22

Charlotte

I DIDN'T LISTEN TO BO'S MESSAGE LAST NIGHT, I COULDN'T. I LET EVERY CALL GO TO voicemail because I didn't trust myself to be strong enough to do what I know is best for both of us right now, which is me in L.A. and Bo in New Orleans, or wherever the Revelers are playing.

Never in a million years did I expect a chance encounter with a hot baseball player to turn into this, whatever this is. I think I know what it is, but I'm scared to admit it. Admitting it means I'd have to tell my secrets and I haven't done that...ever.

When I texted him last night, I knew I owed him that much. Casey had already called Mom and Dad and told on me, basically. She didn't talk to me. She probably won't for a while, unless I apologize and make things right, but again, I can't do that.

But now, in the quiet of my old bedroom, I have my cell phone pressed to my ear and Bo's sweet voice sounds all kinds of worried and it's literally crushing my soul. My fingers are dialing his number before I can overthink it and the next thing I know, he's answering.

"Charlotte?" He sounds relieved and I hate I might be giving him false hope.

"Bo," I start, checking my voice when it cracks on his name alone.

Clearing it, I start again. "Hey, I, uh...sorry I didn't call you last night and for leaving like I did." I am sorry for all of that. I really, really am. "I didn't mean to make you worry. That was really shitty of me." But I had to, I want to tell him. I had to get the hell out of there and clear my head. It's crazy that the place I ran to is usually the only place I'm running from.

When I arrived at the airport last night, surrounded by paparazzi, I immediately regretted my decision, but it was too late. I'm here now and I need to somehow make all of this go away before it gets any worse. I'm not sure how to do that, but I'm praying I'll get some sort of divine revelation while I'm here.

"Are...are you mad at me?" he asks and my heart breaks a little more.

I shake my head to myself, hating that he's assuming responsibility when he's done nothing wrong. He's amazing. He's good...maybe too good, too good for this life and all the shit that comes with it. "No," I finally say. "No, you didn't do anything wrong."

For a second, I almost come completely clean, telling him what that final straw was that broke the proverbial camel's back, but I bite my lip to keep it inside. That's not a conversation I want to have over the phone. I'm just hoping and praying I get a chance to do it in person, when everything has settled.

"Then why did you leave?" he asks, confusion and maybe a bit of anger surfacing under that hurt that's so audible it's chipping away at my resolve. I'll take his anger. That I can deal with. "The last time we talked, you seemed fine...I know things have been bad with the rumors and media, but I thought we were dealing?"

"I was trying," I admit, I can at least give him this much. "I was...we were. But..." I pause, exhaling sharply and pulling at my hair. God, why does my life have to be so fucking complicated? What happened to just having a dream and living it? Can people not do that anymore? "It was just too much and I hated that it was becoming such a distraction for you...I never wanted all of this to affect you."

Some of that is bullshit. I know it. He knows it. Bo's actually handled everything like a champ. He's ignored the rumors, not even paying attention to gossip articles, even when he's mentioned in them. When people approach him, he tells them he doesn't have a comment and he moves on. It's me...the professional...the veteran, when it comes to paparazzi and living life in the public eye, who's breaking under the pressure.

"I just need to finish this album," I tell him. "In two weeks, this will all be behind me and hopefully after the album drops, someone else will do something scandalous and everyone will forget I even exist."

God, that sounds amazing.

"And when that happens," I continue. "Because it will." It's happened before. I have no doubt in a month's time, rumors of me being pregnant will be old news. And no one will care where I'm at or what I'm doing or who I'm doing it with. "I'll be back in New Orleans and we'll pick up where we left off." At least, that's what I'm hoping for.

Bo's quiet, too quiet for my liking, and I'm getting ready to tell him to say something when he finally speaks up. "Are we breaking up?"

Are we?

Would that make it easier on him?

I feel like I know Bo, but I don't know this, so I ask. "Do you want to break up? A break?" I offer, hating the way the words taste on my tongue—bitter and ugly and wrong.

"I…" he hesitates, sucking in a sharp, audible breath. "I want whatever will make you happy Charlotte."

If he had physically stabbed me, it would've hurt less than that statement, but I suck it up and try to make this as painless as possible. "I'm not looking to be in a relationship with anyone else," I tell him. "If that makes this easier...better. This isn't me telling you I don't want to be with you. It's just me telling you I need to figure my shit out and the only way I know how to do that is to be here in L.A., where I can focus on the album. When I'm here, I know what to expect. No one will get one over on me. I need that. I need to feel like there's something in my life I can predict right now."

He's quiet for another moment, but then I hear people talking in the background. Glancing down at the clock on my nightstand, I see it's almost ten o'clock in the morning here, which makes it almost noon there. The Revelers have a game starting in about an hour.

"I can give you that," Bo finally say, his voice barely above a whisper. "Whatever you need."

I have to swallow hard around the tears that are threatening to spill.

"I'm just a phone call away, Charlotte," Bo continues softly. "Anything you need, just call me."

I lose the battle with the tears and feel one slip down my cheek. Brushing it away, I tell him, "Okay." The fact that after all of this he still wants to be there for me makes me want to crawl through the phone and curl up in his lap. I could tell him everything and we could hide away from the world. It'd be like the bubble we were in back in Boston. But I can't do that, so I do the only thing I know to do. "Goodbye, Bo."

"Goodbye, Charlotte." Those last words from him sound more tortured than anything else he's said, like they were ripped from his body.

Closing my eyes, I fall back on my bed and curl up into a ball. I'd like to stay like this forever, but I know I can't. As much as I want to hide away from the world, I can't. Sighing, I bring my phone back up and dial Terry.

"Lola," he says, happier than I've heard him in months. But why wouldn't he be? I've played right into his plans. I'm here, in L.A. I'm exactly where he wants me. "I was just getting ready to call you. I have a driver scheduled to pick you up in an hour and some studio time blocked out at Venture Records. John and Sam will both be there to mix a few of those last songs you laid down last week. With you and them in the same studio, it will make all of it go much smoother."

This business-as-usual demeanor is actually making me breathe easier. Studio work is something I'm good at. Paparazzi can't follow me into a studio. "Sounds good," I tell him, rolling over to stare at the ceiling. "I'll be ready."

"I've also got you an interview on KXCA set for tomorrow."

"Fine."

"Encore would like a photoshoot," he adds. "I thought we could schedule that for the day after next. It would be great for you to get some hair and makeup done and make some appearances. These pregnancy rumors floating around are okay...I mean, no publicity is bad publicity," he says with a chuckle. "But I'd like to debunk those and get their attention directed in other areas. We could set you up to be seen leaving a few key places...with the right people...and in something form-fitting..."

His words become a drone of nonsense in my ear, so I tune him out, letting him talk because I know nothing I say will change any of this. I just have to suck it up and deal—pay my penance.

"Charlotte," one photographer yells, while another one thrusts a camera in my face.

"Is it true you're pregnant with Bo Bennett's baby?" another yells.

My hands go up to shield my face, while I keep my head down and pray I don't trip and fall on my way to the car. If this was New Orleans, Frank would be at the end of this torture, waiting to rescue me and help me in the car. But this isn't New Orleans and Frank isn't here. The new driver Terry assigned to me is waiting at the car with the backdoor open, but other than that, when I catch a glimpse of his face, it's a blank slate, showing no emotion.

"Does he know?" the guys yells again, snapping a photo.

"Did the two of you break-up?"

"Have you put on weight?"

"Are you seeing Cruise Salvatore?"

"What brings you back to L.A.?"

Their questions are rapid-fire and nothing new. I've heard them all. I'm gaining weight, according to them, but the truth is that I've lost nearly ten pounds in the last two weeks. The pregnancy rumors are the ones that always get me, but the more they ask, the less it stings.

I don't even waste my breath by telling them I have no comment any more. I just try to block out as much as I can and get to the car as fast as possible.

They're everywhere. I haven't been one place in L.A. without at least a handful of cameras following me or meeting me there. The worst of the recent questions and rumors are surrounding Bo. I actually thought about confirming that we're not together in hopes they'll leave him alone, but I couldn't say something like that knowing it would get back to Bo. That statement would hurt him more than any rumor ever could.

"Charlotte, over here," one guy yells.

"Come on, baby. Give us something," another yells from my right side, making my back stiffen at the *baby*. *Who the fuck does he think he is?* I know who I am and it's definitely not his baby.

"We know you're not a prude," the same guy jeers, laughing and getting a few of the others to laugh along. My heart rate spikes about that time, realizing there's only one of me and about half a dozen of them.

None of the photographers in the past have ever crossed the line between wanting to get the story and a personal attack. I've always been fortunate in that regard. But the tone this guy is using has me on edge.

"She spread her legs for Salvatore," he adds, snickering, like it's an off-handed comment between friends. "Wonder if she'd spread them for me?"

At that, I whirl, my breaths coming in quick harsh spurts. "Shut the fuck up," I yell, losing myself and my cool. "You don't know me. Stop pretending like you do and stay the fuck away from me."

Our eyes meet, his and mine, and I wish they hadn't, because in those eyes, I see no fear. He's unflinching and I've made this some kind of game or challenge. I know it's true when he darts his tongue out and licks his bottom lip suggestively.

Turning, I force my way through and stumble to the car. The driver shuts the door behind me like he's put out by the display, but nothing else. No care for what just happened, which I know he heard. How could he not? I think everyone in a two block radius heard that bullshit.

"Drive," I growl, pressing my head into the seat and taking some deep, cleansing breaths.

"So, tell me about this media attention," Cindy, the DJ for KXCA says from across the desk and I immediately begin to fidget, which is so not me. At least, it's not the Charlotte from a few months ago, but I find myself fidgeting more and more these days because I'm constantly put into uncomfortable situations...like this one.

"Uh," I stutter, knowing that's only going to make things worse. I need to come across as confident and unphased, don't give them anything to play off of...don't fucking bleed. "Well, I mean, it comes with the territory," I finally go with, trying to brush it off and under the closest fucking rug.

I came here to talk about the album. "Especially when you're getting ready to release your first album in two years," I add, hoping it will be a good segue into more comfortable territory.

"Yeah, but, I think even you can admit it's been a little much lately," she hedges. "Am I right? I bet you feel like you're being stalked. Do you even use the bathroom without a camera in your face these days?"

I know she's trying to be funny and relevant and give her listeners what they want—the juicy gossip, the dirt, the insider information—but I'm really starting to not like her.

"Pretty much," I reply, adjusting the headphones and giving her a tight-lipped smile.

"And what about Bo Bennett?" she asks with a lascivious smile. "Now, there's a hottie if I've ever seen one...baseball player...in the running for rookie of the year." Her eyebrows go up as if to say *impressive*.

I nod, but then swallow nervously when I realize no one listening on the radio can hear a nod. "Yeah, he's pretty...great."

"Are you two handling this long-distance thing, okay?" she asks, and I freaking want to strangle Terry. He promised me an interview about the album. He said nothing about being on *Unlocked After Dark*.

"Fine," I bark, a little too abruptly and give her a quick smile to try to smooth it over. "He's busy, you know, with baseball...and I'm busy with my album."

"What are your plans after the album drops? Will you be staying in L.A. or going back to New Orleans?" Thankfully, we're at least going in the right direction, so I try to sound a bit more enthusiastic with my answer, albeit vague. "I'm still unsure...kind of playing it by ear."

There's no way in hell I'm telling thousands of people my life plan.

"I can't imagine how difficult it must be living your life in the public eye...I'm sure you're used to it by now, what with growing up on *Life with Charli* and now being in the music scene. But even you must get tired of it."

Either her genuine interest or my exhaustion breaks down my walls and I reply honestly. "I do...I am," I tell her and the sad smile she offers me across the desk tells me she understands, or at least can empathize. Maybe this is my chance. I have a platform, I should use it. "No one tells you what it's going to be like, you know? You have this dream, but to live it, you have to be in front of people. And after a while, and with some success, people start feeling like you owe them for your fame...and the pay they want is your life...public and private. Some people are more innocent and only want to know more about their favorite singer or actor. But so many feel entitled. You know?" I ask, realizing that the entire studio is dead silent and all eyes are on me. I feel the blush creeping up on my cheeks and the on-air sign is glaring at me, reminding me I'm talking to millions of people. "I love what I do," I continue, searching for the right thing to say to make this less awkward. "I just would like to be able to do it without cameras breathing down my neck twenty-four-seven."

After the interview is over, I duck out a side door, headed to the waiting car and who is standing on the sidewalk? None other than the pervert from yesterday. When I climb into the back of the car, I can't help watching him walk to a similar black SUV parked a few cars behind us.

The weirdest part is he didn't have his camera. He was just standing there, waiting. I can't explain the feeling that washes over me, but it feels a lot like self-preservation and I suddenly just want to get back to my parents' house.

"Take me home," I instruct the driver.

"Mr. Carlson said to take you straight to the restaurant," he informs me.

I grit my teeth and chance a glance out the back window where I see the same black SUV following us. "I'm not feeling well. Take me home."

"Mr. Carlson—"

"Terry doesn't run my life," I yell, sitting up straighter in the seat. "Take me home. And lose the guy tailing us."

At this, he checks his rearview mirror and notices the vehicle following entirely too close. When he picks up speed, I sit back in my seat and try to keep calm. I just need to get home.

As we turn down a side road, I can't help checking, but the fucker is still there.

For a second, I think about telling him to drive to the nearest police station. My dad always told me to do that if I felt like I was being followed, but I have no clue where a police station is. Actually, I have no idea where we are. Looking out the window as business and buildings blur, I can't get my bearings.

The faster my driver goes, the faster the vehicle behind us goes, meeting us turn for turn.

"I can't lose him," the driver says and for the first time since he started driving me, he's actually showing some emotion and it freaks me out even more, because there's nothing but fear written all over his face when he looks over his shoulder at me. "Where should we go?"

"Police station?" I offer.

When he turns back to the road, I feel the car lurch forward and we have to be doing over eighty down the side streets of L.A., way over the speed limit. I'm about to tell him to slow down when a vehicle blows a stop sign on a perpendicular street. "Look out!"

I feel the car swerve, tossing me across the seat.

CHAPTER 23

Bo

"I KNOW WE'VE DISCUSSED THIS BEFORE," SKIP SAYS, SITTING DOWN BESIDE ME ON the bench in the locker room with a heavy sigh. "If you need our team publicist to handle this media attention, just give us the word."

We arrived in Minnesota yesterday and were greeted with photographers—at the airport, hotel, ballpark. Who would've thought my relationship or break-up would garner this much attention? Not me.

"I don't want to cause the team any extra cost or work," I say, adjusting the laces on my cleats. "And I'm sorry about it." Glancing up, I see Skip wince a little but then he shakes his head.

"It's not ideal," he says quietly, scrubbing at the scruff on his jaw. "I'm not in the *no-publicity-is-bad-publicity* camp...I tend to lean to the no-news-is-good-news when it comes to my players' personal lives."

I nod, blowing out a breath. "Again, I'm sorry," I tell him. "I had no idea—"

Skip holds up a hand to stop me. "No apologies necessary. I think this frenzy has caught everyone off guard. I've been around this business long enough to know that no one can predict what will catch the public's eye. Who knows why they're so obsessed with what you had for lunch yesterday or where you go after a game." Skip laughs, shaking his head again. "I just want you to know that if it gets to be too much, let us know and we'll see what the front office can do to diffuse the situation."

I appreciate his offer, really, I do, but I also don't know if what he or anyone else can do to put an end to this chaos. "Thanks, Skip." Standing,

I walk to the locker I've been assigned while we're here and close the door. "But I don't think it'll be a problem much longer."

The sinking, gut-wrenching feeling I get every time I think about Charlotte hits me.

"If you don't mind me asking," Skip says, "what makes you think that?"

I shrug, trying to play it off like I have every other time Davies or Mack have asked about me and Charlotte. "Call it intuition," I tell him. "She's back in L.A. ...I'm here." She said she'd be back. I want to believe that—believe her, believe in us—but my mind plays tricks on me these days, trying to convince me that what I thought we had was made up.

Skip nods, but the look on his face tells me he knows what I just dished was a large helping of bullshit. "Okay," he finally says, slapping me on the shoulder. "Good talk...I need you to get out there today and play a good game."

"Yes, sir." I'm going to try. That's the goal, anyway. I'll admit my mind has been elsewhere lately, but I've managed to play some decent games. So, hopefully today will be no different, and hopefully, in a few weeks, all of this will be a distant memory. Charlotte will be back in New Orleans and all will be right in my world.

All I have to do is ignore the way my heart squeezes every time her face pops into my head, which is basically every fucking second of the day.

If I had a penny for every time I've thought about Charlotte Carradine, I'd only have one...because I've never stopped. Since the first night, when she climbed into the passenger seat of my car, I've been lost to her, but also found. She unlocked a part of my heart I didn't think existed, giving my first love—baseball—a run for its money. She showed me I could play the game and have a life outside of it. And for that, I'll be forever grateful.

Shaking off the heaviness I keep feeling whenever I think about her, I walk out to the field, just in time to hit some balls. And then, I field some. The methodical nature of the sport, relieving some of the tension that's built back up in my shoulders, tension I haven't felt in a while, thanks to Charlotte.

Nope.

Keep your head in the game, Bo.

Davies, sensing my uptight demeanor, jogs over to me and I feel like

I'm in for a pep talk or some kind of Dr. Phil moment, but instead, he just slaps me on the shoulder and says, "Let's run it off." He motions with his head beyond the bases and we begin to make our way around the field, catching the eyes of a few of the early birds in the stands. Some of them holler at us, to which we smile and wave.

"Look," Davies says, pointing up into the stands. "Bo's Babes have taken their game on the road."

I look up into the bleachers as we pass by and sure enough, the purple and gold shirts with *Bo's Babes* emblazoned across the chest are well-represented, especially for an away game in fucking Minnesota.

"You're here a few months and you already have your own fucking fan club," Davies scoffs. "I've been here five years and nothing."

We both laugh, knowing he's gotten a lot out of his five years playing for the Revelers. Just last year he was up for the Cy Young Award, the most prestigious award for pitchers. Another solid season and I see no reason why he won't be the recipient, especially if we can make the playoffs again. Winning the pennant would put him in the top position, no doubt.

I get the feeling this little jaunt around the field is to help me clear my head and focus on what's right in front of me—baseball. It's a game I know and love, and it doesn't need a break or space. It needs me to be the best player I can be. My team is counting on me.

"Whatever, man," I say, blowing off his statement as we make our way down the left field, heading up toward the dugout. "I'm just here to play ball." We both know having your very own cheering section, especially one filled with pretty girls with your name on their chest, is kind of a big deal, but I'm not one to let shit like that go to my head.

"That's right," Davies says, slowing his run to a jog. "You're here to play ball."

The unspoken *don't forget that* lies heavily in the air around us. "You don't have any control over other people's actions and decisions, but you do have control over this," he says, thumbing over his shoulder to the diamond behind him. "Trust in that...and trust that everything else will fall into place."

I nod, squinting up at him and realizing for the first time that he looks a little weary himself. I want to ask what's going on, but I know Davies is a very private person. If he wants to talk about, he will. "Thanks," I tell him, not just for the run, but for everything. But I don't need to say that. He knows.

Slapping my shoulder, he jogs off to the mound, ready to throw a few practice balls with Mack, who looks my way and gives me his own nod.

After we warm-up and everyone is loose and ready for the game, we clear the field and head into the locker room to wait it out. One thing a lot of people don't realize is that there is a shit ton of waiting in baseball, especially at away games. Dress out and wait. Hit some balls and wait. Warm-up and wait. That's where all the video games and card games come into play.

Once we're all in the locker room, Skip gives us a good talk about Minnesota and game strategy. He lays out the batting order, which rarely changes much these days. After playing together for two months, we've become a fairly well-oiled machine. There will be some adjustments coming as we approach the All-Star break, but not many. We're playing good, solid ball. When he's finished, everyone breaks off to do their own thing and I settle in at one of the corners, leaning up against a wall and closing my eyes.

I need to just zone out for a few, clear my mind and be ready to play.

"Bennett," one of the other players says, drawing me out of my meditative state. "Yo, Bennett."

Snapping my head up, I look across the locker room to see Jay Dunavin staring down at his phone, obviously reading something. I swear to God, if he asks me about Charlotte's supposed pregnancy or how I feel about the break-up, I might lose my cool. Everyone in here knows it's off fucking limits, she's off fucking limits. Earlier in the week, back in our home locker room, Davies had set everyone straight on that matter.

"It, uh...it says here," he says, his voice sounding a little nervous... or maybe worried. "Man, it says that Charlotte's been in some kind of accident."

I literally feel the blood draining from my face, and then the rest of my body, as I jump to my feet and walk over to him, snatching the phone from him.

On the screen, a news article is pulled up, like one of those you see on social media websites.

Actress and singer, Charlotte Carradine, 29, was involved in a car accident yesterday evening. Police report that the celebrity was being followed at high speeds by an SUV. The driver of the vehicle transporting Ms. Carradine made a turn down a side road in downtown L.A., reaching speeds of over 80mph. A car crossing the road her vehicle was traveling down caused the driver to swerve and hit a light post. Early reports indicate the driver was taken to Cedars-Sinai in critical condition. Details of Ms. Carradine's condition are still unknown.

Ms. Carradine has been the focus of a recent media frenzy surrounding her relationship with baseball star, Bo Bennett, and her new album due to be released later this month...

The rest of the words on the screen blur as my vision goes hazy, my ears ringing.

I vaguely register a hand on my shoulder and someone taking the phone from me, voices speaking low, and people moving around me. But I can't think or breathe for what feels like minutes...maybe longer.

She can't be…

No.

She's...she's...

I can't think the words that are trying to force their way into my brain.

She's alive. I know she is. If she wasn't, I would feel it. I would know. Something as bright and wonderful as Charlotte Carradine can't leave this earth without the entire world feeling it.

"Bo," Davies' voice is close, the hand on my shoulder tightens.

"I need to go," I tell him, shaking myself out of the stupor. "I need to find her...see her," I tell him, swallowing down the razor blade in my throat. "I need to know she's okay."

Two hours later, I'm on a chartered flight to L.A. Thanks to Skip and whoever else is in charge of this shit for the team. I'll have to figure that out and thank them...somehow. No one even blinked an eye when I said I need to leave to go to Charlotte. It was understood. And I'll never forget that. Ever. Because they normally wouldn't do this, Skip informed the media I was due for a day off. They're letting Val Salito get some in some innings, buying me twenty-four hours.

I came into this season, this team, looking for success as a player, but what I found is so much more than that. I've found camaraderie, support I didn't even know I needed, and a family. Before now, I'd never given much thought about what my career would look like. As long as I was playing ball, that's all that mattered. But now, I can't imagine playing for another team. The Revelers have become family in a short period of time and I'm hoping to be here for the long haul.

The entire flight is spent scouring the gossip columns and celebrity news sites. When I left, I had no clue what to do or where to go, other than L.A. I figure I'll call Casey once I've landed and force her into telling me where Charlotte is, if I haven't discovered that information on my own before then.

Every website is buzzing with talk about the accident. Commenters on all the social media sites are furious about the paparazzi's involvement. They're outraged, calling for something to be done to protect celebrities. Normally, I'd shut this shit down, but their anger mirrors my own. For once, I want what they want. I want justice for Charlotte and people like her—people who want to live their lives, their dreams, without paying the ultimate price.

And I want her to be okay.

More than anything, I need her to be okay.

Mid-flight, I try Casey's number, but it goes to voicemail. I don't leave a message. Instead, open my texts, figuring she's more likely to reply through a text message than an actual phone call.

Bo: I heard about the accident. I'm on my way to L.A. Where is she?

There's no bubble, no indication she's responding, so I close it out and go back to the other tabs I have open. One of the news websites has updated their article and my heart jolts in anticipation.

Charlotte Carradine was admitted to UCLA Medical Center with unknown injuries.

What the fuck?

I squeeze my phone and think about launching it, but I'm on a plane and I need this phone. It's my only lifeline to information regarding Charlotte, so I reign it in. But seriously, they know what she had for breakfast yesterday and what color shirt she's worn for the past two fucking months, yet they don't know what the extent of her injuries are? That's fucking bullshit.

I need something, anything...I'm just looking for a little reassurance here that the woman I so obviously love will be okay.

Yeah, I fucking love her.

I knew I did three days ago when she basically told me we're on a break. I knew then that I'll wait for her as long as she needs me to wait. The way my heart felt when I found out she'd left for L.A. with no concrete plans on when she'd return, I knew.

Pretty sure I've never been on my phone as much as I am the four hours it takes to fly from Minneapolis to L.A. My thumb hurts from scrolling page after page, clinging to the one thing I've come to hate over the last two months—the fucking media—begging them for something...anything to let me know she's going to be okay.

When the plane begins its descent, I open my texts back up and make sure I didn't miss anything from Casey, but there's nothing. So, once we're on the tarmac, I take the offered mode of transportation and ask the driver to take me to UCLA Medical Center.

I have no idea what I'm walking into or if I'll even be welcome once I get there, but I have to try.

The forty-minute drive feels like pure torture, worse than the four-hour flight, because now I'm close. I'm in walking distance to her. If I had to walk, I would. I'd fucking crawl down the 405, if worse came to worse.

My knee bounces with nervous energy as I will the traffic to part like the Red Sea. Thankfully, the driver is great and he seems to feel the urgency bubbling off me. Once he pulls up to the hospital, I hop out with only my phone in hand. I didn't even fucking grab a bag. I just changed into street clothes and hauled ass to the airport. I figured I'd work the rest out once I got here.

Walking into the main part of the hospital, I realize that with Charlotte being who she is, there is no fucking way they're just going to direct me to her room. I mean, this is L.A., they're used to having well-known people in their care. I'm sure there are major protocols in place to keep their identities and conditions under wraps.

Turning around, I look through the faces of people waiting, hoping for someone I recognize, preferably Casey. She'd help me get to Charlotte. I know she would. But she's nowhere to be seen. Taking my chances, I walk up to the desk and collect myself before asking, "Could you tell me what room Charlotte Carradine is in?"

The smirk on the lady's face tells me she's not going to be easy. "And you are?"

"Bo Bennett," I tell her, hoping that maybe my name will ring a bell. If she hasn't been living under a rock for the past month, surely she's seen mine and Charlotte's name connected in hundreds of articles. There is a slight shift in her demeanor, but the no-nonsense attitude remains.

"I can't give out that information to anyone who isn't family," she informs and hesitates a beat. "I'm sorry."

I try to judge that sentiment and pick it apart. Is she sorry she can't tell me the room? Or is she sorry about Charlotte? Or me and Charlotte? Or the whole fucking messed up situation?

At my wits end, I run a hand down my face and then back up, gripping at the short strands of hair. "Listen," I tell her, trying to keep my fucking cool. "I really need to see her. And I know she's here...and I know she'll want to see me." *If she's conscious*, I think to myself. "Maybe you could get a message to her for me?"

I'm desperate.

She squints an eye, obviously thinking about my offer, but unsure, so I continue.

"I'll just write down my name and a short message. And then I'll wait over there," I say, turning to point at a waiting area off to the side. "I promise I won't try to sneak up to the floor or anything." Which I had thought about, but I definitely don't need a run-in with hospital security to go along with everything else. "Just a note," I plead.

She huffs and just as I think she's about to call the cops on me, she comes up with a small notepad and a pen. "This never happened," she says quietly, handing them over to me.

I nod, letting the pen in my hand hover over the paper. Now what? What do I say? Clearing my throat, I try to collect my thoughts and decide to go with the basics.

I just need to see you and make sure you're okay. Please. -Bo

I want to tell her I love her, but I don't want to put that on a piece of paper that could end up in a gossip column. Not that I think Nancy here will be selling it to the highest bidder, but when I tell Charlotte I love her, I want to be looking into her gorgeous brown eyes, not at a piece of hospital stationary.

Ripping the paper off the pad, I fold it in half and then in half again and hand it over to the lady behind the desk.

"Wait over there," she instructs and stands from the desk.

I let out a breath, blowing up my cheeks and expelling it, hoping that it won't be much longer. Walking over to the windows, I pace the small space and wait...and wait. Eventually, I find a corner chair, facing the direction Nancy walked, and set up watch.

When a man in a three-piece navy blue suit walks into my line of vision, blocking me from seeing the front desk, I lean to the side.

"Bo Bennett?" he asks, all business, causing me to whip my head back to him. And then it hits me, I know exactly who he is and what little hope I was clinging to begins to dissolve. "Terry Carlson," he informs, offering his hand to shake.

I take it, and I make sure to squeeze hard enough to leave an impression.

"Listen," he begins and I can already tell I'm not going to like what he has to say. "Ms. Carradine is in a...delicate situation…"

"Delicate?" I ask, unsure of what that even means. And Charlotte... excuse me, *Ms. Carradine* is a lot of things, but delicate has never been one of them.

"Yes," he continues, full-on bullshit mode. "What with the media attention and the accident. It's crucial we play our cards right."

"Are you fucking kidding me right now?" I ask, feeling my entire body heat up at the rage that's coursing through it. "She's in a fucking hospital and you're worried about playing fucking cards?" I grit out through my clenched teeth.

Taking a step back, his hands go up in mock surrender as he offers me a fucking condescending smile. Mother fucker. "Bo," he starts. "Can I call you Bo? Listen, I think we both know that you being here is not a good idea for Charlotte *or* her career. Right now, we need to redirect all of this focus to Charlotte's career. That's what's most important."

I bark out a laugh and run a hand down my face to keep from punching him in his. "I need to know," I say slowly, so this idiot can understand me, "that she's okay."

He sighs, placing his hands on his hips. "She's going to be fine." His face contorts like the words pain him. "She has a fracture in her left ankle, bruised ribs, a contusion on her forehead, and a laceration on her arm." The laundry list of Charlotte's injuries make me want to hurl, right here on the shiny hospital floor. "She's rather fortunate, the driver didn't fair as well."

It's then that I decide Terry Carlson is a soulless bastard and he has no business having anything to do with Charlotte.

"Now, if you'll run along...back to baseball. We'll sort this out and get everything back on track for her album release."

"I'm not going anywhere," I tell him, standing to my full six-foot-four, dwarfing him in his two-thousand-dollar suit that I have no doubt he bought with Charlotte's hard-earned money.

"I think hospital security will have a different answer."

Crossing my arms over my chest, I stand my ground. "Not going anywhere."

When he glares at me, jaw twitching, I offer a compromise. "Get Casey for me...I'd like to talk to Casey."

"Not gonna happen," he says, showing his teeth as he leans toward me, obviously trying to intimidate me, which isn't going to fucking happen. I'm not a violent person. I've never rushed the mound or thrown a punch in the game. Shit, I've never thrown a punch outside of the game, but right now would be the perfect time. Definitely justified.

"You think you're innocent in all of this, but you're not." His voice is lethal and low. "Charlotte was doing just fine until you came along. She was writing music, working on an album. Everything was on track for this to be the best year of her career." He pauses, laughing sardonically. "Then, you show up and everything falls apart. She's back to being stalked by the media, rumors start flying...do you know the shit I work day in and day out trying to cover up and keep from being leaked?" His face is now a vibrant shade of red as a vein begins to protrude in his forehead. "I haven't had a full night's sleep in weeks. Everything is on the line. Everything...her past, things she'd never want the media to get their hands on...everything would be for fucking nothing...and all because of you."

His words strike a chord, somewhere deep inside my chest where I'd buried the worry. Did I do this? Was her relationship with me what caused all of this?

She said she's used to it, but I know things didn't really get bad until we started being seen together. That's when the new photos started surfacing. That's when the pregnancy rumors started getting spread...the rumors that seemed to really mess with Charlotte's head. She tried to hide it, but I saw it. I saw the worry on her face and the obvious pain it caused.

He must see the change on my face because he takes a deep breath and smooths back his hair, like he's won this bout. And maybe he has.

"Now, go back to your life. Go play baseball. It's what Charlotte would want." Adjusting his suit, he clears his throat. "I'll tell her you came by and I'm sure when she's ready to talk to you, she'll know how to reach you." I watch as he practically slithers back to where he came from, disappearing into an elevator at the end of the long hall.

I know I should leave. As much as I hate to admit it, some of his words rang true. Regardless of all that, I still want to see Charlotte and hear from her own mouth that she wants me to stay away. It'll be the hardest thing I've ever had to do but I can't leave until I see her. If she asks me to leave, I'll do it.

Walking toward the sliding glass doors I entered through, I start to walk outside and get a breath of fresh air to clear my head and help me think of an alternate plan when my phone buzzes from my back pocket.

My heart beats a little faster when I see Casey's name on the screen.

Casey: Where are you?

Bo: Hospital. Where are you?

Casey: Thank God.

What does that mean? I'm about to text back when another text from her comes through.

Casey: Are you in the waiting room? I'm coming down. Wait there.

Bo: Okay, but Terry is on his way back up and he's not going to let me see her.

Casey: Terry isn't the effing boss.

Effing is a pretty strong word for Casey and somehow, it makes me smile in the midst of all the bullshit. I almost ask her if Charlotte even wants to see me, but again, I decide I'd rather hear that from her. Besides, I need to see her...with my own eyes. I need to know she's going to be okay.

A few more minutes pass before the elevator doors I watched Terry disappear behind finally open again. Casey steps out and briefly looks around the room before motioning me over, her hands waving quickly. As soon as I reach her, she grabs my hand and pulls me back into the elevator, pushing a button.

"I'm sneaking you in."

CHAPTER 24

Charlotte

"CHARLOTTE?" THE LOW, ROUGH FAMILIAR VOICE PULLS ME OUT OF THE SEMI-coherent state I've been in since everyone finally vacated my room, giving me the quiet I've been longing for since I got here.

UCLA Medical Center.

Seriously, the last place on earth I thought I'd be.

"Charlotte," he says again and now I know I'm not dreaming it. When Bo is in the vicinity, I can feel his presence. Slowly opening my eyes to keep my head from pounding, I glance over to see his beautiful face peeking around the curtain that was half drawn to give me some privacy.

He's here.

He told me if I needed him, he'd be here, and I do need him, even though I didn't call him. I need him. "Bo," I croak out, my voice raspy from not being used for a while.

"Hey," he says quietly, like he can read my mind...read me...and knows that I wouldn't be able to tolerate anything louder. When I'm able to fully focus, I see the intense concern etched on his face. "Hey." He repeats himself and takes another step closer. And that's when I see his eyes are glassy.

I want to reach for him, tell him I'm fine...everything is fine, but I can't. My arms and legs feel so heavy, every muscle sluggish. "You came."

It's then the fog begins to clear, and I realize Bo should be on a baseball diamond in Minnesota right now. "What are you doing here? Shouldn't you be—"

"I got the day off," he says with a sad smirk, his brows pinched together, like he's the one in pain. After a long moment of us staring at each other, he bites down on his bottom lip, running a hand through his hair. It looks like it's already been pulled a million directions, worried over miles, and along with everything else in my body, my heart hurts. What I wouldn't give to touch that hair, to feel him. I want to go back...I want a rewind button.

"Uh, I...I can't stay long," he says, stepping even closer, his leg brushing the side of my bed and his hand coming down to rest on top of mine. I watch as his eyes take inventory of me—everything from the bruises and cuts on my face to the bandage on my arm and down to my ankle. "I just needed to come and see you for myself. I needed to know that you're okay." He takes a breath and his fingers wrap around my hand, careful to not squeeze too tight, just enough to let me know he's here. "I was so scared when I read..."

His voice drifts off and I immediately feel terrible. I can't imagine finding out something like that about him through the media...the one thing we've both grown to hate. "I'm so sorry," I tell him.

"Don't," he says, shaking his head and staring down at our hands. "I'm sorry...I'm sorry it came to something like that. I…" he pauses, taking a deep breath. "I'm so fucking pissed." His words are thick with unshed emotion and it makes my eyes well up with tears. "I want to go out and hunt every one of those bastards down and beat the shit out of them."

I huff a laugh through my nose and immediately regret it, my ribs crying in outrage. "Ahh."

Bo flinches, drawing his hand back and nervously looking up and down my body. "Are you okay?"

"Fine," I say with another wince, trying to reposition my body to relieve the pain. Actually, I'm not. There's something I've wanted to tell him since the day I left New Orleans. Looking back, I should've just stayed and told him everything and let the chips fall where they may. But it's kind of too late for that now. So, I do the next best thing. "I need to tell you something."

Bo swallows, tilting his head to the side. "Okay."

"There's, uh, something I've wanted to tell you for a couple weeks now, but I just didn't know how...and then I never found the right time...It's... complicated."

His brows pull together, concern and worry etched on his face and I can only imagine where his mind is going, especially with all the bullshit he's heard and read. Which is exactly why I need to tell him, just in case what I'm about to say is somehow leaked to the media. Like the accident, I would never want him to learn this about me from anyone but me. It's my story to tell.

"When I was eighteen," I begin, drawing in as big of a breath as I can muster and refocusing my attention to my hands now knotted in the white, sterile blanket. "When I was eighteen, I got pregnant. It was unexpected, of course, and it was the result of a one-night stand. The guy wanted me to get an abortion...but I couldn't do it. So, instead, Terry made up this big lie about me needing to go to rehab. That was when my fictional drug habit started. He said it made for a better story. Doing drugs went with the rock and roll lifestyle he was trying to curate for me. A baby, not so much."

I pause, reflecting for a split second on how much of my life Terry has dictated, my stomach feeling nauseous, but I can't look at Bo. Not yet. So, I continue. "It wasn't like I wanted to keep it...I mean, I wanted to keep it... but I knew I couldn't give the baby the life it deserved and so many people can't have kids that want them...I was eighteen."

My voice gets smaller and smaller as I try to justify the actions of eighteen-year-old Charlotte.

"It was the hardest decision I've ever had to make. The hardest thing I've ever gone through. And I basically went through it alone, except for Casey, who was too young to really comprehend all the ramifications, and my parents. But they had to keep up pretense and carry on with their lives as usual. So, it was me, on a ranch in Ohio. Terry would come check on me once a week, but I lived alone and took care of myself for almost five months. Those were the longest days of my life."

It was hard, but it also made me grow up and assume responsibility. For the majority of my life I had people doing everything for me—managers, agents, parents, housekeepers, cooks. But to keep the secret, I had to go it alone. We couldn't risk inviting other people into the situation. Looking back, that baby was the best thing that ever happened to me and I think that's why Bo's video struck such a cord. I want that. I want to be able to get a glimpse into my child's life and know he's happy and taken care of. But I also want him to know that having him...and then giving him up... was the one thing that changed the trajectory of my life.

I must fall into my thoughts for longer than I realize, caught up in my own memories, because Bo finally speaks and breaks the silence. "What happened, Charlotte? What happened to the baby?"

"I gave it up," I say, the numbness I feel every time I relive that time of my life resurfacing. "It was a closed adoption. I never even saw the parents. But it was a boy...seven pounds and ten ounces...twenty inches long...all ten fingers and toes...dark hair."

That's when I finally look up at Bo, feeling a tear slip down my cheek and shocked to see a similar one trailing down his own chiseled face.

"I…" I start, trying to get out this last part. "I just needed you to know that...The day at the game when you—"

Bo swallows, wiping the back of his hand across his cheek. "I'm sorry," he says, again apologizing for nothing. "I didn't know."

"You couldn't have," I say. "Nobody does…"

He stands there, staring down at the bed and I wonder what he's thinking.

"Terry suspects some journalists have done their homework and might be getting ready to release an expose," I say. "He thinks with...everything going on, they're all trying to one-up each other...each one needing a bigger story than the last."

I use *everything* as a blanket for all the bullshit Terry's tried to feed me lately, about how Bo is the catalyst for everything blowing up in my face. Earlier today he told me none of this would've happened if I wasn't *attached to someone.*

"He thinks it's my fault," Bo says, his voice dropping.

"No—" I try to dispute but he cuts me off.

"Yes, he does. He stopped me downstairs...told me to go back to my life, go back to baseball and let you live yours."

When his shoulders straighten and I see the strong resolve in the set of his jaw, my stomach drops.

"I'm not so sure he's wrong," Bo says. "I think...I think what you said, about needing some time and space...I think that's good. I want you to get better and I want the media to forget all about this..." He drifts off, his fingers brushing my arm down to my hand, where he pauses and latches on for a moment. "I just want you to be happy."

I want that for him too.

I want to tell him that, but I can't force the words to come out of my mouth without breaking down, so I bite down on my lip and try to stay strong.

For Bo.

For myself.

"I'm gonna go," Bo says quietly, steadying his voice. "But, I meant what I said...if you need me, I'm just a phone call away. No matter where you are, I'll be there." Squeezing my hand one last time, he lets go, clearing his throat. "Take care of yourself, Charlotte."

When his broad shoulders brush their way past the curtain and out of my room, I let the tears fall...for this loss and for every loss that's come before.

CHAPTER 25

Bo

"STOP BROODING," DAVIES SAYS, SADDLING UP BESIDE ME AS WE LEAN AGAINST THE railing of the dugout. I grit my teeth to keep from saying something I'll regret. I've been doing a lot of that lately.

"You did this, you know?" Davies continues, his voice low and indiscernible to everyone else around us and in the stands. The way he occasionally spits a sunflower seed on the ground, you'd think we were shooting the shit over the game or the weather, both of which are horrible. It's hot as fuck and we're down by five runs in the seventh inning.

It'll take a gift from God to get us out of this with a W, and He hasn't been shining down on us much these days. We went from having a five-game winning streak to losing four in a row and I feel like I'm to blame. I know one person doesn't win or lose a game, but I definitely haven't been pulling my weight.

"You made the decision to walk away," he adds, spitting another sunflower seed onto the dirt at our feet, dipping his head between his arms and shielding his mouth away from any wandering eyes. "You could've stayed and fought for her...but you decided that walking away was the best thing for both of you." All of this is information I already fucking know, so I don't know why he's bringing it up again, unless he's trying to piss me off. "I'm a believer that everything happens for a reason...even the bad shit. So, trust in your instincts. Trust in what the two of you had together. And get your head in the fucking game." That last sentence sounds lethal, like a threat, like if I don't, he's going to kick my ass. I wouldn't blame him if he did.

The Revelers is Ross Davies' team. He's helped build this organization from the ground up. If I was him, I'd be pissed the hell off that some rookie is on a path of self-destruction and taking my team with him.

I don't want to be *that* guy.

I really don't.

But I'm also struggling to keep my head above water. When I'm at home, I think of Charlotte. When I'm working out, I think of Charlotte. When I'm trying to sleep, I think of Charlotte and occasionally surf the Internet looking for any news about her recovery. I also think about reaching out to Casey, but I don't want to put her in the middle. She's a good person and she really came in clutch at the hospital, but I won't abuse her niceness.

"Also, I don't want to see you ruin any chance you had of making it into the All-Star Game." He huffs, cursing under his breath as one of our batters strikes out, bringing the inning to a close. "You can salvage this... what you do from here on out is the difference between an average player and one that will go down in history." Turning to the bench, he picks up his glove and turns to walk out to the mound. "Make history, Rook."

Three-up-three-down brings the Revelers back into the dugout and me up to bat.

With Davies' pep talk still ringing in my ears, I try to tune out the crowd. Normally, that's not an issue, but today, every negative comment yelled in my direction sounds like it's coming from a fucking bullhorn.

"Get off your knees, Bennett, you're blowing the game!"

"Come on, Rook...don't be a rally killer!"

"No batter! No batter! No batter!"

As my walk-up song, *Work Hard Play Hard*, starts pumping from the speakers, the stands get louder, some trying to drown out the haters with words of encouragement, but nothing can quiet the chaos in my brain.

One game. My dad's reminder comes to my mind as I walk up to the plate.

This is only one game...one at bat...one swing.

Getting into my stance, I tap my bat across home plate, then again toward the pitcher, staring him down. Doing the sign of the cross, I send up a silent prayer before holding the bat up and over my right shoulder.

Deep breath in, deep breath out, and...*swing.*

Thankfully, I make contact, but it's a foul ball to the left.

Foul ball to the right.

Pop fly to centerfield.

It's a shitty at bat, but it's better than the no contact I've been making for the last three games. Dejected, I walk back to the dugout, tossing my batting gloves onto the bench and throwing myself down beside them.

"Fuck," I mutter, resting my head in my hands. *Fuck.*

"Shake it off, Rook," Skip says from his post at the railing. "Shake it off."

He doesn't make eye contact or come console me, but the fact he's not sending me back down to the minors makes me really fucking grateful. I've got to get my shit together.

We manage to get on base, but after Mack hits another pop fly, the game is over.

"Drinks on me," Davies says as he passes me in the locker room, which is quiet and somber. "We're going out."

A few months ago, I would've blown him off, but tonight, after the last couple of weeks, I agree to his invitation. I might not drink, but I'll go. Anything to keep me from obsessively thinking and rethinking my decisions regarding Charlotte Carradine and dwelling on my shitty playing.

"Maybe you need one of those sports therapist," Mack suggests as we wait at a table in a dimly lit bar for our first round of beers. I didn't plan to partake, but Davies had other plans.

I can nurse a beer for an hour. I used to do it all the time in college to keep from being harassed about never drinking. Being a part of a fraternity, it was kind of expected...and disrespectful if you didn't.

"He doesn't need a fucking therapist," Davies groans, leaning back in his chair. "He just needs to pull his head out of his ass and stop letting things that are out of his control affect his game."

"I thought you said it's my fault," I mutter, picking at a half-shelled peanut.

"Walking away was your call, but all the other bullshit...yeah, that's not yours or hers," Davies says, and I have to admit, I like him even more because he hasn't bashed Charlotte one time. Most guys have some smartass comment when it comes to her, probably trying to help me feel better about everything, but it only pisses me off. I don't want anyone talking bad about her. She didn't ask for any of this any more than I did.

"It's some fucking Romeo and Juliet bullshit," Mack says matter-of-factly. "Except for you being from the wrong side of the tracks, you're a baseball player...and she's—"

Davies laughs, scrubbing at his face, and cuts Mack off. "Shut the fuck up, man. Have you ever even read Romeo and Juliet?"

"Nope," Mack says, popping a peanut in his mouth and chewing it with a cheesy-ass grin. "But I saw the movie with Claire Danes." He raises his eyebrows. "Now, there's a hottie."

"What are you ladies crying about?" Freeman asks, setting down four shot glasses in the middle of the table. "You still wallowing over that rock star bitch?" he asks, picking up one of the glasses and motioning for us to do the same, but I can't.

I'm stuck on the bitch comment he just said and seeing red.

Davies goes to say something but I cut him a glare and speak up. "I'm gonna need you to shut your fucking mouth," I tell him.

He laughs, downing his shot. "Somebody's fucking touchy." Looking over at me, he takes the shot he'd sat down in front of me and lifts it to his lips. "Maybe you're the one with the vagina."

Mother fucker.

"Maybe that's why she left your ass..." he continues. "She needed a real man...one that can hit a ball and make her come."

Standing from my chair, it scrapes against the floor. I know people around us are watching. I can feel their eyes on me, but I don't give a fuck. I go toe-to-toe with Jason Freeman, slipping the full shot glass from his hand. Locking my eyes on his, I want him to see that I'm all business, so I throw the liquor back, feeling the burn down to my toes, and slam the glass back on the table beside us. "Don't talk about her again. Ever. Forget you even know her name."

"Kind of hard to do when she's all over the Internet...wonder if she has a sex tape?"

Grabbing the front of his shirt, I want to wipe the smirk right off his face. When his hands go up in surrender, I grit my teeth. "Shut your fucking mouth."

"Calm down, Rook," Freeman says, chuckling like we're sharing a joke among friends, but we're so fucking not. "It's not like I want to fuck her... sloppy seconds aren't my style."

"Alright, that'll be enough," Davies says, forcing his way between the two us with Mack standing to the side, glaring at Jason. "Walk away, Freeman."

The marching orders from Davies does the trick. Jason lifts his eyebrows, backing away with his hands still in the air. I want to kick his ass, but the logical side of my brain keeps reminding me that I don't need that kind of thing on my record. I'm not going to be *that* player. This is my career...*my life*...and I won't let someone like Jason Freeman ruin that for me.

"You good, Rook?" Davies asks, placing a hand on my shoulder.

"Fine," I tell him, my eyes still on Freeman as he makes his way back across the bar to a table where a few of the other guys are sitting. He glances back over at me and I don't back down, keeping my eyes locked on his.

Charlotte might not be mine, but I will always come to her defense...I will always have her best interest at heart. No matter what. Whether it's Jason Freeman or the fucking paparazzi, whether it's walking away so she can find some peace, I'll do whatever it takes for her to be happy.

CHAPTER 26

Charlotte

IT'S BEEN TWO WEEKS SINCE THE ACCIDENT, TWO WEEKS IN THIS FUCKING AIR CAST, two weeks since I last saw Bo...well, in person, that is.

Sitting in the green room, moments away from the release party for my album, I should be preparing—getting in the zone. But when my stylists left half an hour ago to give me my space, I immediately picked up my phone and opened up my MLB app that allows me to watch the games.

Most people in my position would probably be primping or praying, but I'm not most people. Never more so since the accident. That was definitely a wake-up call and it put things into perspective. The only reason I'm going through with this release party is because I have fans out there who I don't want to disappoint, and it's part of my contract.

I didn't go through all of the bullshit of the last two months to not get paid.

I deserve it.

I worked my ass off on this album, poured my heart and soul into, bled for it...literally.

Watching the screen of my phone, I bite my lip and hold my breath as Bo comes up to bat. The week after our talk in the hospital room, he played like utter shit. There were plenty of days I wanted to call him and ask him what the fuck he was doing, but I didn't. I knew if I reached out to him, it would hurt worse. Bo walked away and even though I know why he did it, it doesn't make it any easier. Not having him in my life has been the worst kind of torture. I can only hope that all of this will eventually work itself out...somehow, someway.

In the meantime, I get my fix by watching Revelers baseball.

I know what Bo and I had was real. I know it with every fiber of my being. Even when the little voices in my head try to convince me otherwise, deep down, I still feel it—that undeniable connection, our souls woven together. Our relationship might have come from left field and ended abruptly—let's call it a rain delay—but I'm hanging onto hope that it's not the final inning.

"Five minutes," someone says, popping their head into the room.

"Hmmm," I hum, giving them a head nod, but I'm not focused on what's out there waiting on me—two hundred people waiting to see Lola Carradine perform. All my attention is on the screen in front of me and the batter who's on his second strike.

"Come the fuck on, Bo," I mutter, my knee bouncing.

And just like that, as if he heard me...or maybe he still feels me too... he swings and makes contact, sending the ball soaring out into the cheap seats.

"Homerun, Bo *The Bat* Bennett," the announcer cries out. This moniker is a new one and it makes me smile every time I hear it. Ever since he made a turnaround last week and started slamming home runs and snagging impossible outs, the media has been going crazy with talk of *The Comeback Kid*, another nickname.

But to me, he's still just Bo...*beautiful* Bo, especially when he's dirty and sweaty and all smiles running the bases. It makes my heart happy to see him like that.

At first—back a week or so ago—when I saw him struggling, I was kind of happy about it, I'm not going to lie. I felt so shitty and missed him so bad, it was a relief to see that our break-up was affecting him as much as it was me.

It was like, if he could wallow, so could I.

Fortunately, we both managed to get our heads out of our asses.

A week ago, Bo hit two home runs in one game, one of them being a grand slam, his first of the season.

Also a week ago, I took my first steps toward removing Terry from my life.

It all has to be done in secret, for now. He holds too many keys to my life and if he wanted to ruin me, he could. But I'll bide my time and keep him at arm's length, until I'm able to pull the rug out from under him with no kick back.

Up until the accident, I still thought he was on my side, but with all of my extra time to sit and think, I started putting things together, with pieces of a very messed up puzzle coming into view.

I've always suspected that Terry was at the root of the paparazzi knowing my every move, but I couldn't ever prove it, until the accident.

When the police showed up on the scene, they saw the same photographer who chased us down running away from the scene. When they arrested him, they confiscated his phone and his camera, both of which had horrible, grueling photos of the wreckage and the driver who was unconscious.

Sick.

So fucking sick and twisted.

It still makes me nauseous to think about it.

Thank God the driver lived, but it could've been so much worse. My mom cried for hours over all the what ifs. She and my dad have basically held me hostage in my bedroom for the past week, not letting me go anywhere unaccompanied.

While the police had the photographer's camera and phone, they found texts messages between him and Terry going back over a month, where they were sharing information about my whereabouts. Thanks to one of the detectives, I have physical proof of those text messages and the photos from the scene of the accident. It's up to me whether I want to press charges.

My dad encouraged me to seek legal action, but all I really want is Terry out of my life.

If I have one regret, it's letting him control it for this long and not seeing him for what he truly is—a fucking selfish, self-centered, self-seeking asshole.

"You're on," the same woman with the wide smile says when she pokes her head back in the room. With the Revelers up by five runs, I turn the game off and send out my prayers to the baseball gods that they'll finish these fuckers off and continue their new winning streak.

"Let's do this," I tell her, grabbing my crutches and hobbling my sparkly ass out to the stage.

Casey, Mom, Dad, and fucking Terry are standing in the front of the audience with beaming proud smiles. Except for Terry, now that the cloak has dropped, I see everything for what it is. The only thing he's happy about right now is that my album debuted in the top twenty-five on the Billboard charts, which translates to dollar signs for him.

I smile down at them, an extra sweet one thrown in Terry's direction as if to tell him to soak it up, mother fucker, because this gravy train is coming to an end.

"Hello," I call out to the crowd and get an eardrum-bursting response. "Thank you so much for being here," I say, balancing on my crutches and adjusting my earpiece and mic, all while keeping my right foot from touching the ground. "I'm going to apologize in advance for my dance moves."

Everyone laughs and I love the energy I'm feeling in this small venue. It has me thinking that all of my shows will be in places like this. I'm not interested in packing out stadiums or even arenas anymore. I just want to play my music and feel this kind of vibe.

"How about a song?"

My band, Flight of Feelings, strikes up the first cord to *Hard Hitter* and the crowd goes wild. For a song that has so much grit and power, I can't help the lump I have to choke down before the opening lyrics. It's all Bo, every note, chord, and chorus. He oozes from every facet of this song and I fucking love it.

Eyes like the July sky
Couldn't forget you if I tried
I love looking at you...the spark in your eyes
Curved lips you can't disguise

CHAPTER 27

Bo

NOTHING FEELS AS GOOD AS PLAYING YOUR BEST GAME IN FRONT OF A HOME CROWD with your parents in the stands. The only thing missing in this equation is Charlotte, but I don't let that thought get to me. I'm here to play ball and that's what I'm doing...playing the best fucking ball of my life.

"Bo!" a few of the Bo's Babes girls call from the stands near the third base line. I smile politely and wave. Some players would be all over this cheering section, asking for numbers and having private parties in hotel rooms and shit like that, but not me.

I know I'm technically free to date or fuck whoever I want, but I can't... don't even want to think about it. Call me crazy or hopeless, but I'm pretty sure I'll hold out for Charlotte until I'm somehow convinced that she's no longer interested in me...and maybe even after that.

"Marry me, Bo!" Turning, I see a big white sign with a diamond ring in the shape of a baseball diamond and those exact words plastered across the cardboard. I feel the blush on my cheeks as the ump gets into position behind the plate, but that's where it ends.

Once that first pitch is thrown, I tune it all out.

A line drive my way has me diving for the ball and snagging it in the tip of my glove.

I'm back.

There's still a piece of my heart that resides with Charlotte Carradine, but everything else is fully invested in this game.

Davies throws some heat, painting the corners of the plate and sending the next batter back to the dugout.

After a pop fly to center field, the game is over and we go up two-to-one for the series.

The Revelers are also back.

Once I've showered and dressed, I head out to meet up with my parents who are waiting at the end of the corridor.

"Great game," my dad says, slapping my shoulder and gripping it tightly. "That last catch…" He smiles, shaking his head. "Best I've seen."

This time, when my cheeks heat up, it's from the praise from my dad. He's always been my number one supporter, but something about him being here to see me perform like I did tonight and then to have him tell me something like that, it's like it brings my entire life full circle.

"Thanks, Dad."

My mom comes up for a hug and I swear there are tears in her eyes. "You really were fantastic, Honey."

"Thanks," I say, squeezing her extra tight.

"It was a little lonely in the stands, though…" she adds with a shrug.

Leave it to my mom to bring up Charlotte, in a roundabout way.

"Brenda," my dad warns.

"What?" she asks, innocence thick in her tone. "I was just saying…I miss the girls."

I can't help the chuckle that escapes, my dad shaking his head. "I miss her, too."

"Yeah," she says, reaching a hand out to brush an invisible wrinkle out of my t-shirt. "Well, everything happens for a reason…and what's that saying? It ain't over, 'til it's over?"

Dad huffs. "Did you just quote Yogi Berra?"

"Or Lenny Kravitz," she offers with a smile only my mother can give.

We start to walk toward the players exit when something jogs my memory and I remember what I've been meaning to ask her since the night we all had dinner at Charlotte's. "Mom, what did you and Charlotte talk about? That night we all had dinner…"

"I just told her I'd never seen you that happy," she says with a sigh. "And I thanked her for showing you there's more to life than baseball." I don't miss the twinkle in my dad's eye as he leans over and places a kiss on the top of her head.

I want that, what they have, and I might not get it today or tomorrow or the next, but one of these days, I will. I feel it deep in my bones. My mom is right, Charlotte showed me that I could have a life outside of baseball...she showed me what true love feels like and I'll never forget it or her.

"Bo!" The photographer calls my name, obviously more than one time, as people buzz around like bees.

Taking the earbuds out, I offer him an apologetic smile. "Sorry." Ever since Charlotte's new album dropped, I've basically had it playing on repeat. *Hard Hitter* is just as amazing as Charlotte said it was—straight up rocker chick vibes...electric guitar, awesome opening riff, one hundred percent *her*—but I can't help the twinge of pain in my chest every time it comes on. I wanted my first time listening to it to be a live, private performance. She'd promised me an acoustic version, but never got the chance.

The lyrics are soulful, but it's not like a ballad or love song, even though there's so much emotion. Between the electric guitar, heavy bass, and up tempo, it actually pumps me up and makes me feel like running the bases.

Instead, I jog over to the grey backdrop, setting my phone and earbuds on a side table. "Where do you want me?"

My agent has been negotiating some endorsement deals over the past month. Today, I'm shooting my first ad for a men's clothing line. I still have no idea why they want someone like me representing their company. Most days, all I wear are jeans and t-shirts, but the paycheck makes up for the pretentious bullshit.

"Stand here," he says, positioning me in the middle of the backdrop that looks like a drop cloth with splattered paint all over it. I'm guessing they're going for an artistic vibe.

Davies' advice before I headed over here today was to keep my mouth shut, smile, and look pretty.

I told him to go fuck himself.

"Turn to the side," the photographer instructs, moving my arms around like I'm a toy doll. "Chin over your shoulder."

At some point, I zone out, my thoughts turning back to Charlotte's new album and wondering where she's at today.

What's she's doing?

Is there a chance she's thinking about me too?

Out of the radio playing in the background comes a voice I'd know anywhere, pulling me out of my thoughts. "Hey," I say, startling the photographer as he whirls around probably expecting a complaint or problem. "Could you, uh...could you turn that up?"

"The radio?" he asks, thumbing over his shoulder.

When I nod, he yells, "Mark! Turn the radio up."

CHAPTER 28

Charlotte

"TELL ME, CHARLOTTE, HOW DOES THIS NEW ALBUM DIFFER FROM YOUR LAST?"

I'm on day three of radio interviews and my brain feels like mush after answering the same questions over and over. I'm so thrilled to be talking about my music, though, that I have no problem answering as if it's the first time I've been asked.

"I think this album is edgier than anything I've ever put out. It's heart and soul paired with kick-ass music and perfectly represents who I am as an artist and where I'm at in my life."

"What's your favorite track on the album?" the interviewer asks.

Normally, when I'm asked this question, I say what I think the interviewer or the public wants to hear, whether it's true or not, but I'm not living that way anymore. I don't care what others read into my answer, I'm telling it like it is.

"Well, picking a favorite song is always so hard because each one is, like, my baby, you know? But, if I have to choose, I'd pick *Hard Hitter*. It's really special to me...it means a lot and it always puts a smile on my face."

I can tell the woman interviewing me wants to dig deeper and ask if it's about Bo, but she doesn't. In fact, most of the people I've worked with during this radio tour have been very respectful regarding my private life.

It's made doing promo for the album so much more fun than it's been in the past. I guess I have the accident to thank for that.

In fact, since the wreck, much of the paparazzi have left me alone. I still can't go many places by myself, but at least I don't have to push my way through a stampede just to get to my car anymore. It's a small victory for the pain I've suffered these last few weeks.

When the interview is over, Casey helps carry my bag as we make our way to the car that's waiting for us. I'm getting much better at walking with my boot on, but it's still really awkward, so having her with me for support has been awesome. Although, she's been relentless lately, calling me a duck then mocking how I walk. Fucking little sisters, man.

I'll have to wait for my air cast to come off before I can kick her ass properly.

The truth is, I'm just happy she's talking to me again, I'll let her make fun of me all she wants. She was really pissed when I left New Orleans and I don't blame her, but I think, once she saw how miserable I was—before and after the wreck—she realized leaving home wasn't easy for me. She knows I wouldn't purposefully hurt Bo or myself unless I believed it was necessary. And, although I wish I wouldn't have left so abruptly, I still think I did the right thing for myself, for Bo, and for us. I have to believe that or all of this was for nothing.

Another day, another city. But instead of being in a radio studio right now, I'm on my way to Wrigley Field. We just so happen to be in Chicago today and tomorrow, and it also just so happens to be where the Revelers are playing tonight...like in one hour.

It was by chance we ended up being in the same city, I had nothing to do with the radio tour schedule. But there's no way I could pass up the opportunity to watch them play and see Bo, even if it will be from a far, far distance.

He doesn't know I'll be there and I won't be seeking him out afterward.

I'm going to sit in the stands and watch my favorite team play, just like everyone else, albeit wearing a disguise.

The crutches are a bitch and the wig itches under my well-worn Revelers hat, but it's a small price to pay for anonymity. When we arrive at the park, our driver lets us out at the gate and Brutus, the bodyguard, basically carries me up to the Will Call window to pick up our tickets. I got online and bought them a few days ago, when I realized our schedules overlapped.

Again, Brutus strong arms me up the ramp, only sitting me down once we make it to our row. I'll have to remember to compensate him for his extra muscles. But when I hobble myself to my seat, that's when it hits me.

The green grass.

The wall of ivy.

The red dirt.

The familiar white uniforms with purple and gold.

The combined aromas of beer, peanuts, and hot dogs. It's all like a drug to me now, making me feel at home, just as much as gumbo and beignets... and Bo. Even after all this time apart, I still feel like he's my home. I just have to figure out how and when to make things right.

Before sitting down, I can't help but crane my neck over the side to search him out. And there, standing beside Ross Davies, near the visiting team dugout, is the other piece of my heart.

With Casey on one side of me and Brutus on the other, I eventually take a seat and try to just relax, feeling a tiny bit squished beside the big guy. "Sorry," Brutus says, pulling back his elbows as much as he can. "These seats are made for small children."

Laughing, I shake my head. "Not everyone is a freak of nature, Brutus." The name fits him well because the guy is huge. I made him stuff his torso into the biggest Revelers t-shirt I could find so he wouldn't stick out like a sore thumb, but the dude looks so uncomfortable. Fortunately, no one seems to suspect who we are and I'm praying it stays that way.

"When are you going to talk to him?" Casey asks, making it seem like it's such an easy question to answer. Her eyes scanning below us, obviously seeking out the same thing I was minutes ago.

"I don't know, Case..." I admit quietly, flipping through the program we picked up at the front gate. "I miss him so much, and we both seem to be doing really well...professionally...but now, I worry us getting back together would mess all that up."

"So what if it does?" She's sipping her beer while her eyes stay on the field, completely missing the look of shock I'm giving her.

"How can you ask that?" My voice raises a bit but I manage to reel it back in, glancing around us to make sure no one is listening. "You know how much is on the line, *for both of us*, and we *both* want the other to succeed, so why *wouldn't* we worry about that?"

Casey shrugs, still not looking at me. "Is your career more important than Bo?"

This causes me to sit straighter.

Is it?

I swallow, then grab her beer and chug half of it.

"Hey," she squawks, stealing the beer back.

Out of the corner of my eye, I see Brutus raise a hand to the vendor walking the stands, obviously trying to stave off a potential brawl between sisters over beer. Always one step ahead, this one.

My career has been the only thing that's been *mine* for as long as I can remember. However, if I'm being completely honest—which is all I've been trying to be lately—the minute I agreed to the rehab ruse eleven years ago, I lost a large amount of control, in addition to the hit it left on my soul.

"If you couldn't perform or record ever again," she whispers, eyes forward. "If he never played another inning of baseball? Would you still want to be with Bo? Would he still want to be with you?"

Sitting back further in my seat, my focus on the field in front of us and the men taking their places, I try to imagine what it would be like.

What if I wasn't Lola Carradine?

It's really not that hard to imagine. I thought about it many times during my darker days. Although, music is my passion and I thrive on stage, I could survive without it. I'd find a different outlet for the creativity that churns in my soul. I'm sure there are other careers out there where I could use my talents.

But, when I think of life without Bo, that's when my blood runs cold and my stomach feels sick.

This time without him has been hard enough, but I've had the hope of a second chance to keep me going. To consider a future that doesn't include him, to spend forever without his eyes, his smile, his touch...to never be in his strong arms or hear his laugh or feel his lips on mine...I can't do it. I reject that possibility.

"That's what I thought," Casey replies, smug as shit.

Sisters, man.

CHAPTER 29

Bo

WALKING OUT OF THE DUGOUT, I TAKE A DEEP BREATH, SUCKING IN THE HUMID NEW Orleans night air and letting it fill my lungs as I make my way to the plate. When my new walk-up song blasts through the speakers, everything feels... right...Charlotte's raspy voice belting out the lyrics to my new favorite song.

You're a hard hitter,
Breaking down my walls

"Bo Bennett," the announcer calls as the fans cheer.

Tapping my bat across home plate, then again toward the pitcher, I stare him down, already second guessing the pitch he's got in store for me. Doing the sign of the cross, I mutter to no one but myself, "This one's for you, baby," before resting my bat over my right shoulder.

Deep breath in, deep breath out, and...swing.

"And it's out of here," the announcer cries out. "Au revoir!" I didn't need him to tell me, I already knew. I felt it—the accuracy, the contact. Casually dropping the bat to the dirt, I take my trip around the bases, earning me a high five from Coach Simpson when I touch third, and the rest of my teammates huddled up around home plate, ready to strip my jersey off and douse me with water, but I don't care.

This is the shit I live for.

There's nothing like a walk-off homerun to win the game.

Except for one thing, but she's not here and this is a close second.

After beignets and beer in the locker room to celebrate our seventh consecutive win, I shower and dress, ready to call it a night and be ready for tomorrow's last game of the series. We need a sweep and I need to be at my best.

"Hey, Rook," Mack says, whipping his towel in my direction. "Drinks at my place."

"Nah, man," I tell him, picking up my duffle bag. "I've gotta call it. That last home run took it out of me."

He laughs, shaking his head. "You're so full of shit."

As I make my way out of the locker room, I stop for a few interview questions. This has become an every game occurrence lately, and it gives me a small taste of what it must've felt like for Charlotte. But at least these guys keep it pretty professional and they never follow me around.

"Bo, how good did that walk-off home run feel?" one reporter asks.

I didn't say every question was a smart question, but I answer him anyway, keeping the sarcasm out of my voice as much as possible. "Well, it was great…" I laugh, unsure of what else he wants me to say. "Felt great."

"What's the secret to your comeback?" another asks. "Sometimes rookies have a tough time coming back once they get down, but you seemed to bounce back pretty fast."

A couple answers run through my head.

I didn't want Ross Davies to kick my ass.

Losing fucking sucks.

"No secret," I say with a small smile. "I just needed to make a few adjustments." I know it's a little canned, but I only give them as much as I want them to have, another lesson I learned from Charlotte.

The unspoken part of that answer is that I realized playing like shit wasn't going to bring her back to me. Also, the reality that she would've been so pissed if I would've wasted this half of the season and missed my chance to play in the All-Star Game was enough to kick my ass into high gear.

After a couple more questions, I excuse myself and make my way down the corridor to the player's entrance. My Toyota parked on the second row looks out of place among all the sports cars and Land Rovers, but it makes me smile every time I walk out here and see it.

Call me crazy, but even with my new endorsements and contract, I have no desire to replace her. And yeah, she's a she, Tracy to be exact. Tracy the Toyota. I don't tell many people that because I don't want to catch shit for it, but Tracy and I have history together and I'm fucking loyal.

"Hey, girl," I say, sliding into the driver's seat and starting her up, pulling out my cell phone and putting it on the charger. When the screen lights up, I see I have a missed text.

It's just one line, from a number I haven't heard from in almost two months, but it makes my heart stop.

Casey: Good Times. 1300 Decatur St. 9:00

Good Times?

It's not from the person I want to hear from, but it's close...and it's the first interaction I've had with Casey or Charlotte since the day at the hospital. My mind begins to run crazy with thoughts as I glance at the clock and see it's almost nine now.

I have no idea where I'm going or what I'll find when I get there, but my heart tells me to drive. Pulling out of the lot and onto the street, I head in the opposite direction of my apartment, for Good Times.

The streets of the French Quarter are a little difficult to navigate. Twenty minutes later, I've managed to find a place to park not too far from the address. Before leaving my car, I dig out a ball cap and throw on a denim shirt I keep in my car. It might or might not be clean, but my goal is to blend in with the crowd.

Walking down the sidewalk, I hear the sounds before I read the location.

Electric guitar.

Heavy bass.

A familiar voice, full of timbre and rasp.

When I step up to the door of the dimly lit club, a man stops me. "Ticket."

I stop and stare. Of course I need a ticket. "Uh, can I buy one?" I ask, stretching my neck above the sea of bodies clustered around the stage at the center of the room. Charlotte's long legs poured into her signature leather pants, black combat boots, and a deep, V-neck tank top that shows off her amazing body. Not too much, just enough to make me literally stop in my tracks. My heart doing the thing it does every time I see her...losing a beat it'll never get back.

But that's okay, every one of them belongs to her anyway.

"Sold out," the man says gruffly. "Unless you're on the list."

List? Maybe Casey..."Bo Bennett," I say, dropping my voice to a whisper, not willing to be noticed and cause a scene.

He tosses his head to the side. "Go on in."

I smile my gratitude, pulling my ball cap down further on my head and finding a spot at the back of the room.

It's so fucking good to see her. For the first song, my eyes drink her in, every move, every step. I hang on every word and every note. She's working the crowd and they're eating out of the palm of her hand. It's then I notice she's not wearing a cast or anything...and her gorgeous face is perfect. The nasty gash on her arm is even completely healed.

She looks amazing.

My heart feels at home just being in her presence.

"Thank you so much for coming out tonight," she says, pulling the microphone she's been singing into off the stand. "As y'all know, this is for a great cause, something close to my heart. The French Quarter Collaborative is a nonprofit that helps place children with adoptive families, and all of the proceeds from tonight will be donated to the Boys and Girls Home of New Orleans." The crowd cheers and the smile that splits Charlotte's face is like the sun itself. "So, drink up...eat up...and let's bring this house down!"

The place erupts as her band cues up the next song and Charlotte grabs a hot pink electric guitar. My favorite song fills the room and I'm lost to her.

When the show comes to a close, I glance at my watch and realize it's almost eleven. Charlotte shakes a few hands of people who are next to the stage, signing some t-shirts and photos. She's in her element and looking completely at ease.

I love it.

I love seeing her like this.

And as much as I want to go up to her—wrap her in my arms, talk to her—I'm not sure I should. If she'd been the one to text me tonight, then yes, but she wasn't. I know Casey meant well, and I'm grateful to her. I'll find a way to thank her, but not tonight.

CHAPTER 30

Charlotte

"DID YOU SEE THIS?" CASEY ASKS, WALKING OVER TO WHERE I'M PERCHED ON THE kitchen island, drinking my first cup of coffee and jotting down a few lines in my journal.

Even when I'm not writing songs, I have to keep writing...something, every day. This journal is something I've kept up for over eleven years. I've paced myself, only putting in it the most important pieces of my life.

Last night was one of those.

I've been performing my new songs for the past month—the release party, radio studios across the country—but last night was different. I was back in my hometown, in front of a crowd who was gathered for a cause, something close to my heart.

It was one of those full-circle moments, and the only thing missing was Bo. I promised myself I'd reach out to him once I was back, but I haven't yet. Not sure what I'm waiting on...maybe some sign that he still feels about me the way I feel about him, but that's stupid, because I know what we have is real and it surpasses time and space.

So, why didn't I text him the second I was back?

I don't know.

"I don't want to see more puppy videos, Case," I tell her, taking a sip of my coffee as I place my pen and journal down beside me. "We don't have time for a puppy. If you want a dog, we need to go to the shelter and adopt one that's already potty trained."

She rolls her eyes, laughing as she sidles up beside me. "Not that, but we'll revisit the puppy debate later." Her eyes searching the screen, she halts, cocks her head...looks a little closer...and then a wide, knowing smile spreads across her pretty face. "This."

Holding the phone up for me to see, I recognize the landscape of the club I performed at last night, Good Times. What a great name for a club in New Orleans. And it really was good times. The crowd was so into the songs, belting back the lyrics, singing with me. The energy was amped—buzzing and unique, just like New Orleans. And for the first time in almost two months, I got to perform without an air cast or boot. When we landed in New Orleans two days ago, my doctor gave me the all-clear.

It's still a little tender, but surprisingly, my combat boots are the perfect support. I just had to forgo the four-inch heels.

"That was such a fun show," I tell Casey, peering over her shoulder as she zooms in on the photo. The first one is of me on stage and my hair is fanned out around my head as I strum a deep cord on my electric guitar. "We should contact the photographer and ask him to send that file to us. It would look great on my website."

Casey nods. "I'll email him later."

When her fingers scroll down to a wider shot of the crowd and she zooms in again, I know what the smile was about moments ago. She wasn't smiling at a photo of me, no...she was seeing what I'm now seeing. Tucked into the back of the dark, crowded room is a tall frame with a baseball cap pulled low down on his brow, and wearing a denim shirt I've seen countless times.

"Bo," I whisper and feel Casey's buzz of giddiness beside me. "How did he know? He had a game..." My words are to no one, but she answers.

"I texted him," she confesses, no regret or remorse to be had. "When I realized you weren't going to, I gave him the address, no details, and left his name on the list at the door."

"You little shit."

"You love me."

I do. So much. She has no idea. But now seeing him in the background of these photos, I'm kicking myself. I should've invited him. I should have called him, gone to him, the second I was back. What a fool.

Gingerly, I hop down off the bar, keeping the weight off my ankle that's still healing, and I walk across the kitchen to grab my phone.

"What are you doing?" Casey asks, excitement in her voice.

Taking a deep breath, I open up my contacts. "What I should've done two days ago."

Sitting in the box that Ross Davies secured for us, I feel like this is my first game...or maybe like I'm playing in the game. I don't know. The feelings are similar to what I experience before walking out onto the stage. Sometimes, the adrenaline is pumping so hard, my lips feel numb. It's like being drunk, but without an ounce of alcohol. My body is tingling with anticipation.

The game is getting ready to start and I feel Casey's eyes on me.

"Are you going to stand the entire game?" she asks, munching away on her popcorn like she doesn't have a care in the world...and she doesn't. That's the beauty of Casey. But right now, I'd like to choke her out with the rally towel they gave us at the front gate.

For the first time in months, I left the house without a disguise. I left the wig at home. But my trusty Revelers cap is in place, pulled down tight. It's become something of a good luck charm, and I know how baseball players are when it comes to finding something that works and sticking with it.

"Maybe," I finally tell her, twisting the towel in my hands. My eyes stay glued to the dugout, waiting on my first glimpse of Bo. After Mack grounds out to left field, I know he's coming up, my body and ears already anticipating his walk-up song, one I added to my own personal playlist because every time I hear it I think of him...see him so clearly in my mind.

It's funny how a song does that, creates a memory and holds it hostage.

But when *Work Hard, Play Hard* doesn't play and in its place is...me, mine...*Hard Hitter*. I slowly lower myself to the seat behind me, gripping the wall in front of me.

"Told you," Casey says full of cocky confidence and jubilant satisfaction. She's referring to my fear I had voiced to her: what if he doesn't still feel the same? What if he's moved on?

"I want to hear it, Charlotte," she goads. "I want to hear I was right."

You're a hard hitter,

Breaking down my walls

Bo Bennett

I've never been happier to tell my sister, "You were right."

My eyes stay glued to number thirty. He walks up to the plate and goes through his pre-batting ritual. I know it by heart. I actually play it in my mind when I'm feeling nervous or anxious, for some reason, it oddly calms me down. It's weird, I know, and something I'd never tell anyone, but it's true.

Feet shoulder width apart, knees slightly bent, one fist on top of the other. Tap the bat across home plate one time, then again toward where the pitcher stands. Then, the sign of the cross just before the bat comes to rest on his strong shoulder.

Deep breath in, deep breath out, and...swing.

"Bo," one of the reporters calls out from the back of the locker room. "How does it feel to be one of only two rookies playing in this year's All-Star Game?"

I watch Bo's face split into the biggest smile and it makes my heart flip in my chest. Holding my breath, with my hands clasped behind my back, I'm creeping off to the side of the locker room. A press badge around my neck gives people the initial idea I'm part of the press. Thankfully, no one has really paid me any attention. Most of the players are busy showering and getting out of here, ready to start their All-Star break.

"It feels great," Bo says with a light laugh, running a hand down his face and then through his still damp hair. "I mean, it was one of my goals for the season."

"Work hard, play hard, right?" the reporter asks, getting the mic a little closer as he waits for the response from Bo.

He nods, smiling. "That's right."

"Why the change of walk-up song?" another reporter asks and I find myself leaning closer, wondering what his answer will be. "Most players would never dream of changing something so influential in their game play at this point in the season."

Bo chuckles, shaking his head. "Uh," he begins and I notice the hint of pink creeping up on his cheeks and I want to jump in and save him and steal him away. "It's a song that resonates with me," he continues. "I needed something to inspire me and this song does that...I feel like I can climb Mt. Everest every time it comes on."

"Does the song choice have anything to do with your relationship with Ms. Carradine?" a tall, dark-haired reporter asks, her stilettos sticking out like a sore thumb in a locker room full of sweaty athletes and baseball gear.

"Is it true the two of you broke up?"

"Does that have any effect on your game?"

"How are you able to balance out the media frenzy with the grueling schedule of baseball?"

With the questions flying, Bo's expression softens, turning a little disconnected, and he pulls his brows together thoughtfully, those long lashes falling to his cheek. "Char—" he starts, but stops himself, his eyes flashing up to the people surrounding him, realizing he was about to bare his soul to strangers, people who don't deserve that piece of him. "I'd rather not discuss my personal life."

There's some muttering between the reporters and I feel one of two things is getting ready to happen—Bo was getting ready to bolt or they were getting ready to pounce. I couldn't let either happen. I came here for something and I'm not leaving without it...*him*.

"Bo," I say, stepping up into the mix and pushing my way toward the front, now within an arm's reach. "What's your strategy for the second half of the season?" I ask, my question really only having one purpose, which was to let him know I'm here.

I thought about what I wanted to ask and considered a few different options, but then decided it didn't matter, because the gesture should be enough to take him back to a different time and place...something the two of us shared, a moment in time when everything felt right.

I want that back.

I want him back.

There's a split second where he checks himself, his breath hitching... pulse probably picking up at being caught off guard...but he recovers, clearing his throat as his eyes bore into mine.

"Uh," he starts, licking his lips. "My strategy is to do what I always do—take it one day at a time...one game at a time." A small smile turns the corner of his lips up. "I'm hoping for less strikeouts and more homeruns." I swear my entire body responds to that statement, from the top of my head to the tips of my toes. "Take each opportunity I'm given and hold onto it."

The entire locker room quite possibly shuts down for those few seconds, but then again, maybe that's just me.

"That'll be all," Bo says, holding a hand up to dismiss the reporters while simultaneously pulling me by the arm and out into a private hallway, away from reporters and teammates, where it's just us. Our breaths echo off the concrete walls and when he turns me, my back against the cool, hard surface, I swallow hard. "Hey," I tell him, unsure of what to say, but also not feeling like talking.

Kiss me, I want to beg.

"Did you just *Notting Hill* me?" Bo asks, humor and light in his voice, so much levity, like a weight was lifted.

My laugh bounces off the space around us, my hand coming up to cup the side of his cheek, loving the new scruff there. I can't help running my fingers through it a few times, appreciating the change. "I did."

"God, I love you," he murmurs, like it's as easy as breathing. "Sorry, I didn't mean it to come out like that, but I've wanted to tell you for a while...and I promised myself that when you came back...because I *knew* you would..." he pauses, his hand coming up to caress my cheek. "I'd tell you." His rambling delivery is better than any eloquent soliloquy or rehearsed speech. It shot straight from his heart into mine.

"I love you too," I tell him, my lips brushing his when I speak. "I'm sorry I took so long."

"I would've waited longer."

EPILOGUE

Charlotte

JULY

WITH THE SUN BEATING DOWN ON MY BACK, A COLD GLASS WITH BEADS OF SWEAT dripping in my hand, and Bo Bennett lying next to me, this is paradise.

His eyes are covered by sunglasses, gorgeous, chiseled torso on display. Everything about his body screaming finely-tuned athlete, but right now, he's in full relaxation mode. It's well-deserved. The All-Star Game was a huge success, bringing the league their first win in over six years, and Bo was the star of the show. In three at-bats, he had one home run and three RBIs. His defensive game was nothing to blink at either. If he keeps it up, he'll be a shoe-in for Rookie of the Year.

As we lay here, in the Key West sun, on the beach, just the two of us, I've let my mind drift—ebbing and flowing like the waves crashing against the sand. Thoughts of me and Bo and our future, thoughts of last night—so completely wrapped up in him—and thoughts of the past. I've come to the conclusion it's no coincidence Bo Bennett walked into my life. The only explanation for finding someone like him—not perfect, but perfect for me—can only be the result of divine intervention.

"When did you find out you were adopted?" I ask, my voice raspy from not being used in a while. It's a question I've wanted to ask him since the day I found out we shared this connection.

Bo shifts on his lounger, angling his long body to face me and pushing his sunglasses up onto his forehead so I can see his gorgeous eyes. "Maybe when I was twelve or thirteen," he says softly.

"How did they tell you?"

He must know I need this, because he clears his throat as he slides up to a sitting position before answering. "Mom and Dad sat me down and basically told me how much they love me and that after years of trying to have a baby, they couldn't. Mom said they were able to choose their baby instead, that some families aren't blood-born, but heart-born. She said from the moment they saw me in the hospital, they knew I was theirs."

I swallow the lump in my throat and pull myself up to sit, facing him, knee-to-knee. "Were you mad?" I ask, voicing some fears I've held onto for all these years, things I've wanted to ask someone...anyone...Little did I know, Bo would be here, down the road, waiting for me. "At them or at your birth mom?"

Bo immediately shakes his head. "No, I wasn't...it was different, but it's like when she told me that this missing piece I'd always felt slid into place. I can't explain it," he says, gripping the back of his neck with his hand. "But it made everything make sense. I was glad they told me...I'm glad they didn't wait."

I lick my bottom lip, sucking it between my teeth. "That's what I'm afraid of," I whisper, my eyes drifting to the ocean twenty feet away. "What if they wait too long to tell him...or what if they never tell him?" Past pain threatens to strangle me, my throat tightening, until Bo's hand reaches out, taking my hand.

"You don't have any control over that...over other people's choices," he says gently. "I can only imagine how difficult it must be being on your side of things. You make me wonder about my own birth mother...who is she, what is she like, does she want to know me?"

My eyes come back to his and we sit there, locked in a moment, each feeling each other's burdens and pains, but they don't feel so insurmountable any more. Of course, they're still there. I'll always wonder, always worry, always hope and wish, but something tells me I'll never have to do those things alone anymore.

Later, after a lazy dinner on our private patio, Bo lifts me from my chair and takes me into his arms, walking me to the outdoor shower.

"Strip," he commands, setting me down on my feet and going to the knobs to turn the water on. I watch his back as he bends forward, lean muscles moving under his golden skin, and I want to pinch myself, just like that morning after Bo spent the night for the first time.

Like who is this guy?

And how did I get so lucky?

"Charlotte," Bo says, disappointment on his lips, bringing me out of my memories. With an arch of his eyebrow in the pale moonlight, I do exactly as I'm told. I strip my flowy dress off, exposing my body to the cool night air, only my panties left to discard, which I do.

"Better?" I ask, giving him a wicked smile.

"The best," he says, his eyes drinking me in and his tongue coming out to lick his full bottom lip. I've seen him do that on the baseball field and every fucking time, it makes me squeeze my legs together, just like right now.

Biting down on mine, I try to keep myself from falling apart before he even touches me. "You're wearing too many clothes," I inform him.

His hand reaches out to test the water and when he's satisfied with the temperature, he stalks toward me, reaching me in just a few steps. "Do you want to do it or do you want me to?" he asks, his breath hot on my skin as he dips his head to kiss a path from my neck to my breasts.

When his hands brush my skin, wrapping around my waist and then cupping my ass, I groan.

"Off," I plead. "Just take them off, please."

I want to, God I want to, but right now, I can't even think straight. Bo smirks, stepping back and yanking his shirt over his head. His pants are easily pulled down to his feet.

"Commando?" I ask, eyeing his already erect cock standing at attention.

The laugh that comes out of him goes straight to my core. "Thought you might like that."

What a fucking cocky bastard.

"When did you get so cocky?" I ask, his hands resuming their position on my ass and my arms going up to wrap around his neck, our bare bodies feeling amazing as they press together.

He tilts his head, like he's really giving it some thought. "Oh, I don't know...maybe three...four months ago." My lips curve into a smile as I lean in and place them on his jaw, which is still scruffy and feels amazing. Apparently, it's hanging around until their winning streak ends. I'm hoping for it lasting the rest of the season.

After the shower sex, we opt for some indoor floor sex, and then some bed sex...and then sleep. We only have forty-eight hours in this secluded bungalow and by golly, we're getting our money's worth.

The next morning, before I can even get my body moving, my muscles feeling like Jell-O, my phone rings from the nightstand. Rolling over, I stretch, Bo's arms tightening around me to keep me next to him. When my fingertips find the phone, I put it to my ear.

"Hello?"

"Charlotte," Janice Hopper, my new manager, says. "This is Janice. Did I wake you?" Her tone is full of regret, something I never got from Terry.

Firing him two weeks ago was the third best day of my life.

The first was the day I became a mom, because even though I don't get to raise my son, he's out there in the world and I get the privilege of knowing I gave someone life.

The second day was the day I met Bo Bennett.

"No, Janice. I was already awake," I tell her, pushing up to lean against the padded headboard...and can I just say, thank God it's padded? My head is grateful. Smirking at the memory, I ask, "What's up?"

"Well," she says, drawing out the word. "I have some great news and it just couldn't wait until you were back."

Glancing down at Bo, I see him squinting up at me, a lazy smile on his face. Unable to stop, I lean down and kiss him...his cheek, his nose, the side of his lips. "Good news?" I ask between kisses. "What kind of good news?"

"Three words," she says, excitement evident in her tone. "MTV Music Awards."

I sit back up, my eyes going wide. "What?"

"You've been nominated for best album and best song."

Me?

Nominated?

"Are you fucking kidding me?" I ask, that adrenaline I feel from time to time rushing through my body.

Janice laughs, "No, I'm not kidding you. The nominations were just announced. Looks like I'll need to make you some travel plans."

"What?" Bo asks, sitting up beside me and letting the sheet fall to his waist, almost giving me the full show.

"I've been nominated for best album and best song...at the MTV Music Awards," I whisper, my smile growing with each word. "Can you believe it?"

Bo's smile matches mine when he grabs me and manhandles me into his lap, kissing the side of my head and squeezing me to him. "So proud of you, baby," he says against my hair.

Remembering I'm still on the phone with Janice, I confirm what she'd asked. "Yes, please make travel plans," I tell her. "Casey will definitely accompany me. I'll let you know if my parents can make it, but I'm assuming they will—"

"And me," Bo interjects, causing me to turn in his lap to face him.

His pointed stare makes me pause. "You have games," I tell him, not even bothering covering the receiver.

"We'll work something out...I'll check my schedule and see if it's an off day. If not, maybe it'll be a day game and I can fly out afterward," he tells me, his expression leaving no room for argument.

"Bo will be my plus one," I tell Janice, looking back at him once more. Just in case he can swing it, because I'd give anything for him to be there.

When I get off the phone with Janice, Bo gives me a congratulatory orgasm.

Returning the favor, I give him a thank you blow job.

And then we have nomination sex.

I can only assume award sex will be out of the park.

AUGUST

Bo

Stepping out of the limo behind Charlotte, I know I should be nervous. All of the cameras. All the people. And not a baseball diamond in sight. But I'm not, because holding my hand is the most beautiful woman in the world, and she's mine.

Fortunately, the Revelers were playing a four-game series in Seattle that ended today. I was able to get a flight to L.A. instead of New Orleans, and I'll have to fly back out at the ass crack of dawn tomorrow for a home game, but it's worth it. Being here, with Charlotte, is worth all the lost sleep and fucking airport bullshit. Anything to be by her side.

"Lola," reporters and interviewers call out when they spot her in the long line of celebrities, everyone from the hottest box office star to the latest boy band is here.

"Lola, over here!"

"Bo!"

Hearing my name makes me turn around, a flash nearly blinding me, Charlotte's grip tightening. "Stay with me," she whispers, but she doesn't need to tell me that. I'm not going anywhere without her. Ever.

"Lola, are you and Bo engaged?" one reporter yells, more flashes.

"Lola, what's next?"

"Will you be touring next year?"

"Lola, will there be another album in your future?"

All of the questions they're asking are things we've talked about, but I know she won't be giving them answers tonight. Charlotte wants to finish out the season on the road with me, which makes me the happiest person on the planet. She's ready to take a step back for a while. That's not to say she won't consider doing a tour at some point or another album, but she's keeping her schedule clear for the foreseeable future.

After posing for a few photos, Charlotte takes a couple scheduled interviews, talking briefly about her album. Janice, Charlotte's new manager, giving every reporter strict instruction on what they can and can't ask.

This woman is amazing. I don't know her very well yet, but right off the bat, she came across honest and like she has Charlotte's best interest at heart and that's enough for me.

Once we make it to the auditorium, we're guided to our seats, and not long after, the show begins. Having watched things like this from my living room hundreds of times, it feels a bit surreal seeing it in person. Charlotte's parents are here with Casey, but they're sitting behind us somewhere. We have plans to meet up after the show.

I find myself amazed at the production, my eyes constantly jumping from one thing to the next, but every time I look at Charlotte, she's looking at me. Every person in this place is looking at her, but she's spent the whole night looking at me

"You okay?" I ask.

She offers me a soft smile, her eyes roaming my face. "Never better."

"Nervous?"

Shaking her head, she leans over and places her lips on my cheek. I wouldn't doubt that a camera somewhere is getting all of this, but I don't care.

"And the award for best song goes to…" The girl announcing is someone I've never heard of, but she's wearing a ridiculous dress, the sequined skirt barely covering her ass. Charlotte's hand squeezes mine and I stroke the top of hers with my thumb, letting her know it's okay. I know she wants this, but if she doesn't win, it won't change anything…definitely not the way I feel about her.

"Lola Carradine for Hard Hitter!" The squeal the girl lets out and the way she bounces on stage makes me like her a little more. If she's a fan of my girl, then I guess I can let her poor choice in clothing slide.

Charlotte's gasp, followed by a loud exhale brings me out of my stupor and into the moment. We stand in unison and I wrap her in a hug, kissing her passionately. "Congratulations."

There are unshed tears in her eyes when she leans back. I know those are for a lot of things—the years, the hours, the struggle, the heartache, as well as the triumphs and gains.

Stepping back, I make room for her to slip past me and I fight the urge to follow her to the stage, wanting to make sure she's okay, protect her from any bad that could possibly come her way. But I know that I can't... she doesn't want a bodyguard. She has one of those. She wants someone who will be there for her, stand beside her, support her, and cheer her on.

I'll gladly do that. Every day for the rest of my life.

Whistling like only a true baseball player can, I watch as Charlotte takes the stage, her eyes coming back to me. *I love you*, she mouths, blowing a kiss in my direction.

I say it right back.

"Wow," she says, holding the award out to get a good look at it. "I... uh...wow." She laughs, her bright eyes and wide smile winning over the crowd. When they cheer, she holds the award up in the air. When the room quiets again, she unfolds a small piece of paper. "This is crazy," she continues, glancing back up, so calm and collected, even in the face of all of these people. "After all these years, being on television and writing music... performing...I've never won an award, but it's fitting that this would be my first."

She pauses, her gaze scanning the crowd and then settling back on me.

"This song was inspired by someone who inspires me. Thank you, Bo, for everything." Taking a deep breath and turning back to her piece of paper, she continues. "I'd also like to thank my parents and my sister. Without your support, I wouldn't be here today. I love y'all so much. To my label, thank you for believing in me and giving me the freedom to write my own songs. To my new manager, Janice, thank you for agreeing to go on this journey with me. And to my fans, thank y'all so much for loving this song as much as I do." Her smile so wide, it lights up the stage. "This is for you!"

Pete Rose once said he'd walk through hell in a gasoline suit to play baseball.

I used to feel that way too, but now I feel that way about Charlotte Carradine.

I'd do that for her, whatever it takes to be with her. Baseball will always be here, it's in my blood, I was born to play, but I was also born to be with her.

She's my true home plate, where I want to be when everything is said and done.

Acknowledgements

And now for the part where we say thank you, which seems entirely insignificant because everyone we mention plays such a big part in this process.

To the VIPs in our lives—our kiddos, family, friends, and readers. What is life without amazing people to share it with? We think this is a valuable lesson Bo Bennett and Charlotte Carradine learn throughout TRATR. We all need people...and we're so thankful for ours.

First, we'd like to thank Pamela Stephenson for being our beta reader! She's always there from the beginning, watching and reading as the story takes shape. Thanks for being you, Pamela!!

We'd also like to thank Nikki, our editor. Thank you for always approaching every new story we throw at you with an insightful eye. We knew this book would need your expertise and you came through for us. Also, to Mr. Strauss, thank you for the baseball insight.

Our proofreader, friend, and drinking buddy, Mrs. Karin Enders. Thank you for everything! We appreciate your time, effort, and most of all, your friendship!

We'd also like to thank our cover designer and formatter, Juliana. Thank you for the creativity and time you put into this one...making it something different that stands out. We love your attention to detail!

Also, a huge shout-out to our pimp team—Pamela, Lynette, Megan, Shannon, Candace, Stefanie, Laura, Kat, Debbie, Polly, Letica. Thank you for always putting your two-cents worth in and giving us a safe place to bounce ideas! We love y'all!

Thank you to all of our readers and everyone in Jiffy Kate's Southern Belles. All of you make our days better. BTW, if you are a reader and you're not in our group, you should join! We have a lot of fun and have frequent giveaways. You don't want to miss out.

About the Authors

Jiffy Kate is the joint pen name for Jiff Simpson and Jenny Kate Altman.

Jiff was born and raised in Louisiana, but she now lives in Texas with her two teenagers and her two English Bulldogs, Georgia Rose and Jake. She loves Project Runway, Queen, 80's music and movies, and the color purple. When she's not shaping the lives of our future generation, you can find her planning her next vacation to Disney.

Jenny Kate is a small-town girl from Oklahoma. She's a self-proclaimed coffee junkie/connoisseur. Her husband stays annoyed at her taste in music and her teenager thinks she's weird, so basically, she's winning at life. Between a full-time job as an accounting assistant and her three rambunctious fur babies, she's often dreaming about maid services and vacation days.

Together, they spend their evenings and weekends spinning tails and hoping one day they hit a best-sellers list.

You can connect with them and follow along with their shenanigans on social media.

CPSIA information can be obtained
at www.ICGtesting.com
Printed in the USA
LVHW050945140419
614125LV00042B/3404